The Chinese Dam

Secret of the Three Gorges

A Pure Life Thriller by
Benjamin Cullen Yablon

Copyright © 2013 BENJAMIN C. YABLON
All rights reserved.

ISBN-13: 978-0-9856057-7-3

DEDICATION

Without the love, support and understanding of my wife, Kara, my writing career would have stalled out long ago. Thank you for helping me stay the course through the many years it has taken to arrive here.

ACKNOWLEDGMENTS

This project would not have been possible without the hard work of many talented people. A very special thank you to Nicholas Heckman for his graphic design work, Nancy Hutchins and Seth Fullerton for their editorial guidance, and Marshall Yablon for his continued support of the Pure Life series.

The Chinese Dam

Prologue

Yangtze River Valley, China

Dr. Emanuel Founder knew he'd been poisoned, but there was no time to worry about it now. He focused instead on stumbling back to his tent. He hazarded another look at the hieroglyphs on the cliff wall and was sickened by what he saw. The water was already lapping greedily at the lowest of the four carvings. He didn't need anyone to confirm his conclusion. The Yangtze River was minutes from overwhelming the sandbag barrier his excavation team had built only the day before.

With one eye on the sandbags, he snatched his journal, the hand-drawn maps of the Wu Gorge, and his latest mercury test results from his faded canvas cot. One map tore slightly as he folded it and stuffed it into the journal. He forced himself to slow down, but wondered if he would ever see his research again.

Emanuel accidentally leaned against an unlit oil lamp and knocked it over, spilling thick kerosene over the table and soaking his precious journal. He grabbed the journal and frantically wiped the oil off with his shirt. The damage was done, though; the leather was stained and some of the pages were soaked and translucent. Fortunately, however, his research notes were still legible.

He couldn't seem to get warm despite the pleasant morning temperature. He realized with an involuntary shiver that the river water had seeped into his boots. His hands felt stiff and cold despite the heat of the day. The water wasn't supposed to hit this level for another month. He needed to get his journal and the maps out of China and into Vivian's, and his daughter, Danielle's, hands. Just in case . . .

He didn't want to think about it, but he had no choice. He turned away from the entrance to the tent, sloshed to the portable desk at the far end, and searched for the strong mailing envelopes he always carried in his satchel.

If he was right about his assistant, he needed to do something to save his research. As he struggled to address two of the envelopes, he realized the water in his tent had already risen to his knees, filling his well-worn boots. Shivering again, he tried to ignore the cold dampness enveloping his lower body. He picked up his journal and opened it to the place where his hand drawn maps had once been. All that remained were the rough edges of the pages someone had torn out. He removed the mercury test results from the journal and folded them carefully inside the letter he had sat up all night writing. He stuffed them into one of the envelopes. The letter and test results would go to Danielle; then he pushed the journal into the second envelope addressed to Vivian.

She would do the right thing.

He hoped.

Ten Years Later

1

Shell Cove Way, Florida

Vivian Goldfarb stood on the veranda of her exclusive Florida home. She replaced the receiver and stared at the phone on the table beside her. She fingered the journal lying on her lap that her ex-husband, Emanuel Founder, had sent her only a few days before he'd fallen ill in China and had been expelled from the country.

She focused again on the stained leather book that contained Emanuel's notes on what was supposed to be the most ambitious research project of his career.

She flipped to a passage written ten years earlier, just before he was thrown out of China. He said he was in a tent on the banks of the Yangtze River in central China. For the first time, she did more than just scan his writing. Perhaps there was something to his theory after all.

January 12th, 2002

The Yangtze River cuts an east-to-west swath through central China. In the middle are the Three Little Gorges, soon to be under 200 feet of water forever. China is making a huge mistake with the Three Gorges Dam Project on the Yangtze. Sun Yat-sen first envisioned the dam in 1919 but the political will to construct it has only just been realized.

"He always was a bit dramatic," Vivian thought, turning the page.

The water is not a new problem. The Chinese government is flooding the river valley and constructing the Three Gorges Dam to control flooding and generate a massive amount of power. It will be the largest dam in the world. It will use more concrete than any structure ever built, roughly enough to construct 60 Eiffel Towers. It's supposed to provide enough hydroelectric power to run a city four times the size of Los Angeles. Low-end estimates predict 1.3 million people will be displaced.

Vivian shifted in her seat.

January 15th, 2002
Only under a regime like that of communist China could this cruel project go forward under the heading of "progress."

It is progress, in its own way. Water power to run an entire city. But at what cost? The Yangtze River Valley has been a cradle of human life for tens of thousands of years. In a single decade, eons of human history will drown.

My colleagues from around the world are up in arms—at least what passes for "up in arms" in academic circles. It's taken fierce lobbying to get enough pressure on the Chinese to let us in here for however short a time we will have. That smug general made my skin crawl. He seemed perfectly content to allow their history to be washed away. Well, not all of those in charge were. But those with the most control have allowed less than one percent of the dam's budget to save the treasures hidden in the gorges. I can hardly imagine how many treasures will be lost. All I have been allowed to see are the towns they've evacuated.

These valleys are so old I can almost feel the ghosts around me screaming for solace. It is my job—and the job of others like me—to save as much evidence of their passing as we can. The Chinese government has allowed several teams unfettered access to the river valley, a last-ditch attempt to save some of the treasures. But the river has risen almost 60 feet a year since 1998.

There has been impressive progress made on several of the other dig sites since 1999. Most teams felt they were close to finding treasures, but we've all lost ground every day as the water slowly rises. It has been both an exciting and miserable time to be in the field. Those of us who have worked our entire careers dreaming of being allowed into China are finally here for a taste of what we have been missing, but a taste is all we will get. The water is rising so fast it's frightening.

We started our work on a site as close to the water as we dared, but we abandoned that plan. We were only getting fragments out before the water took the rest, only whetting our appetites for what might be found before it was gone. To properly research and catalogue finds like these takes months, sometimes years. We have pleaded with the Chinese to slow the rate of fill but have been roundly ignored. I am lucky. My site is fairly high up, so at least the landmarks I've used to locate it will survive a little longer.

My grad student, Lin Huan, has been invaluable. He was nervous about facing his family. He said they are very conservative and didn't approve of his dream to study in America. He visited his parents for the first time last week and didn't talk much when he returned.

January 16th 2002

We are out of time. The water has almost taken the site from us, but we have gotten farther than anyone thought we could. The discoveries I'm making are turning heads in important places, here and at home. But nothing is going to stop the flooding now. The dam project is worth $30 billion. No archeological dig is going to justify a work stoppage.

My project is close to proving the Sino-Egyptian link. I am convinced, from evidence catalogued at our site, that there must be another and bigger site. I have recorded as much as I can in this journal of the maps and landmarks used to hide the main temple.

I'm headed to the Fengdu Temple again. There is more to that place than is written in historical documents. The Water of Life is nearby. I'm sure of it, but I don't dare mention it to anyone else. I'm worried that Huan has attracted attention from some dangerous elements within the Chinese military. He tells me the only way to get the access we need is through them, but I shudder at the thought of involving anyone capable of dislocating millions of their own people the way they have.

January 18th 2002

My God! Think of it. Seven thousand years of history and two million people in this valley and the bastards are flooding it! The ruins I've found are perfectly preserved and represent, at most, a hundredth of what is still out there! Nothing has been pillaged like the sites in Egypt, because these are still holy places to the residents of the valley.

Down river, it's as developed as any waterway in the

world . . . and as polluted. But here it's all preserved. Until now, water has never touched it.

I can only hope that the main temple will survive this flood. The river floods every few years, but the water always recedes. This time, it's going higher than ever and never going back down. The thought makes me madder than hell, then sick.

I'm making notes of the landmarks that surround the area. I've started at the highest points and clearly referenced the ancient wall carvings that will help me find the spot again . . . if I ever get back here. That is in Huan's hands now. He is my last hope. God! The members of every team are utterly miserable, as discovery after discovery is hastily located, mapped, and then washed away. The only record is what these international teams can scrawl in notebooks. I am no exception.

January 20th 2002

Huan had to drag me out of the dig site as the water came in today. It's the worst day of my life. We were there. I may never be able to prove what I know in my heart to be one of the most profound historical connections of our time. I feel hollow. But if Danielle reads this journal, maybe there is still a shot. Maybe all is not lost.

"The damn fool was right," Vivian said. She glanced up from

the journal pages for the first time in several minutes and stared into space. "After all this time . . . he was right."

She took out a folded newspaper article from the journal that was written about Emanuel and his best friend, William McCrystal. They had worked in different departments at Boston University but had been interviewed together for the article, because the subject matter drew on both of their fields of expertise—archeology and neurochemistry. The article was published just before Emanuel and his BU team left for China.

It had nearly cost them both their careers.

BU Scientists Stake Careers on Dubious Theory

Boston Examiner, May 20th 2001

According to Boston University research scientists, Dr. Emanuel Founder and Dr. William McCrystal, the *Vin De Vie*, a supposedly life-prolonging wine, long believed to have been lost in the Nile Delta nearly three-thousand years ago, is likely hidden in China. Known in Egyptology by the name given it by the French archeologist Jean-François after his discovery of the tablets at Tell el-Dab'a describing it in the early 1800s, *Vin De Vie* translates to "Water of Life." The wine has disappeared from the recorded history of Egypt as if it never existed.

The two scientists have staked their careers on an unproven theory of ancient cultural contact between the Egyptians and Chinese and claim that history has overlooked one of the great treasures of the ancient world.

So far, only Drs. Founder and McCrystal have signed

onto the theory. They posit that the *Vin De Vie* was removed from the imperial vaults of the Egyptian pharaohs by the usurper Hyksos dynasty, a culturally distinct people who ruled Egypt during the Second Intermediate Period of Egypt's ancient history. The Hyksos had to be driven out of the land by the last ruler of the 17th Dynasty and the earliest ruler of Egypt's New Kingdom, known as the Theban pharaohs.

Recent discoveries from the time of the Hyksos rulers reference the Water of Life and add credence to its existence and disappearance during that time period. The newly translated obelisks from the Tel El Dab'a site explain why the Water of Life may have been taken: namely, to spite the conquering Egyptian monarchy that set up the New Kingdom dynasty that ruled for thousands of years after expelling the Hyksos.

The Tell el-Dab'a obelisk speaks of a wine reserved only for the pharaoh. Dr. Founder's interpretation of the ceremony is highly controversial. He claims that the wine was extending the pharaoh's life. Dr. McCrystal claims that a substance which interferes with programmed cell death could in theory prolong life. Of course, only a test on the chemical properties of the actual substance would allow Dr. Founder's controversial theory to be confirmed.

Dr. Founder hypothesizes that as the Hyksos were driven from their land, they managed to remove the wine, as well as the secret for its production. Dr. Founder explains, "The Tel El Dab'a obelisk tells of the great sorrow of the Egyptian priests who returned to find their greatest treasure gone. They had planned to open the first cask and begin the process of serving the pharaoh in small amounts. He was to remain a living god for all ages. The process was never replicated by the Egyptians."

Evidently, the Hyksos tribes then began their long

migration across the Silk Road to meet up with their cousins, the Shang, in China. It should be noted that this cultural contact is itself disputed by historians. Dr. Founder is a renowned scientist, but his colleagues in Egyptology find this theory dubious at best. However, Dr. Founder claims that the Chinese town of Fengdu tells a story of outsiders coming to the riverbank with an elixir that could have been the *Vin de Vie*.

Dr. McCrystal has hypothesized about the promise such a wine could hold. By interfering with cell deterioration, aging, as we know it now, would stop. "The process the wine starts cannot be replicated exactly in the laboratory," he avers, "because we have no way to age wine thousands of years. We do, however, have a theoretical computer model that shows how the wine might have worked, and its conclusions are not beyond the realm of possibility."

The Egyptian site claims that the wine is aged in papyrus-lined casks topped with mercury plugs to keep the air from reaching it. The pharaohs wanted to live forever, and the well-aged wine is tangled in their lore of eternal life.

Dr. Founder's radical theory suggests that the Egyptian idea of eternal life became confused when they no longer had the wine. The priests resorted to the next best thing, mummification. Without the ancient wine, the dream of eternal life eluded them. If this theory is to be believed, the Hyksos took the most powerful tool of Egypt with them, as they fled east across Tibet toward the lower Yangtze.

Dr. McCrystal explained his research. "Our model predicts that the effect of a glass of the wine would last a few days. A person would need a massive amount to keep living indefinitely."

Vivian refolded the faded newspaper article and thought about the last time she had seen Emanuel, a year ago. He had been a patient in a Cape Cod hospital, his pale body coiled like a spring. The advanced paralysis was ruining him. Their daughter, Danielle, would probably be with him right now. Such a disappointment. If she'd stuck with her swimming career she could have had the gold. William would be with them right now, as well.

William. She lowered her gaze to the journal again and couldn't help smiling when she thought of him. On impulse, she picked up her cell phone and pressed a speed dial key with one of her perfectly manicured fingers.

2

Cape Cod, Massachusetts

William McCrystal glanced at the number on his caller ID and silenced the soft ring with a flick of his thumb. He returned the phone to an inside pocket of his sport coat, next to his pistol, without answering the call. Then, taking a few more steps, he knocked on Emanuel's hospital room door and pushed it open without waiting for an invitation.

"William," Danielle said, smiling. "I didn't know you were on the Cape this weekend."

He smiled at her and strode directly to Emanuel's wheelchair, patting the immobile man on his blanket-covered leg. "How are we today, old man?" he asked, in his polished New England accent. William removed his faded captain's hat and smoothed his white hair.

Emanuel couldn't respond to him. He stared out the window at the cold grayness that represented a typical Cape Cod winter day. He couldn't move, yet the muscles in his neck were tense, the sinews greatly accentuated like bass-sized guitar strings. Tears fell every so often from the green eyes that had dulled considerably over the last decade.

Danielle moved to her father's side and dabbed at the tears. She held his clawed hand and stroked it with gentle movements as he worked his jaw muscles furiously, trying to open his mouth. His lips parted and he squeezed out the only two words he had spoken aloud in weeks.

"Huan." He stared into Danielle's eyes as sweat beaded on his brow. "Jour . . . nal." He gasped for air and slumped in his chair.

Danielle hushed him with a knowing nod, fighting back tears of her own. "I know, Daddy," she said, fighting her grief. She hugged him and turned to William. "He's doing well today." She reached up to hug William too.

William embraced her tightly, enjoying the smell of her hair. He was able to ignore the arthritic stab of pain in his back for a moment. "You look more like your lovely mother all the time, do you know that?" He said.

Danielle said nothing, but she smiled broadly up at him. William released her after a moment and turned back toward Emanuel. "You know that student of his had some hand in all this," he said. Danielle remained silent. "I only wonder how close they were to finding the *Vin de Vie*," he said. "If I just knew what the toxin was that Huan gave him, I—"

William didn't finish the sentence. Danielle was crying softly and he pulled her back into his embrace and held her. "We'll have the support we need soon to go back into China. My nephews have a great candidate picked out. He's ready to explore life outside the military and he is deeply fascinated by alternative lifestyles." He regretted the choice of words but she didn't seem to pick up on them. He nodded at Emanuel. "Are we ready to sail a bit, old man?"

Danielle turned to her father. "What do you think, Pop? Want to go out on William's boat today?" She examined her father's face, searching for a reaction, before answering for him. "I think it would be good for him. Are you sure you have time for it, William?"

"It would be my pleasure, as always. Will you be joining us today, my dear?" William stroked his cheek. "Or are you going to leave your father to the care of your old Uncle Willy and his nephews, as usual?"

"I think I'll stay here. Thanks for getting him away from this room." Danielle took a deep breath. "It…it means the world to me. To both of us." She slid onto the edge of a chair next to her father's wheelchair. "How is it that you stay single? I'm sure there are armies of available women for a guy like you."

"Just lucky I guess," William said as he ran a hand over his jacket pocket. He smiled and said, "I'd kill to be young enough to have a shot with you, though."

A few tears slid down Emanuel's cheek as Danielle wheeled him outside the hospital to William's large BMW sedan. He made another feeble attempt to communicate with her and then slumped into his chair.

"I love you, too," she said, stroking her father's hair.

William smirked at the gesture and pulled her in for a final embrace. She seemed to be holding him tighter than she ever had before and he felt the beginning of an erection, the first natural one he could remember. It wasn't every day that he got to squeeze an Olympic athlete. They stood like that for several moments, neither wanting to release. He savored the feel of her pert breasts against his chest, remembering her silver medal winning performance as a sixteen-year old.

His thoughts turned to his nephews, who were too stupid to do anything in China other than make a bigger mess. They needed Danielle. She had given up her athletic career to follow in her father's footsteps. Her masters at Hopkins was complete and she would have her Ph.D. before it was all over. She knew as much about Emanuel's work as anyone else and she could really open doors for them. Huan still trusted her, and he was the key to everything William had worked for.

He'd finally have something to offer Horst Mendelbaum in exchange for a stay aboard the *Pura Vida* and the chance to live forever. The research potential of the *Vin De Vie* was astounding. A doctor like Horst Mendelbaum would see that immediately. From the stories William had heard from Owen Tiberius, the man was making shocking strides into longevity research. William had been denied the chance to meet with Mendelbaum personally, another slight that had helped forge his heart into a knife-point of hatred at the world that had denied him so much. But *Vin de Vie* would change everything.

3

Pyongyang, North Korea

"Water?" Axelsen repeated.

His guard ignored the request, choosing instead to swing the leather strap onto the sole of his exposed foot again. This time Jonathan Axelsen couldn't repress the scream. It came to his lips shrilly and echoed off the walls of the small room in which his torture was being dispensed. He had been here for ten hours according to the clock on the wall. Somehow his cover had been blown before he'd even had the chance to set up. His father had pulled strings to get him the assignment, a fact that made its failure even worse.

Axelsen bit down on the false tooth the CIA had implanted before he was dispatched, but not hard enough to crack the small canister of poison inside. Not yet. Perhaps there were still options. He didn't want to die. He wanted to live stateside in his father's estate and never travel again. This was not the adventure he had been promised. Even as the thought occurred to him, he realized it was a lie. He couldn't stand the life his father led. He needed action. That was the whole point of this, his first truly high risk mission. Yet here he was, strapped to a chair in what was supposed to have been his safe house.

The week of training probably should have been taken a bit more seriously. He wondered what had given him away. The rest of the team knew nothing of who he was; they were in fact, employees of the Dutch-Chinese company, Xinjing-Netherlands, Ltd. They believed that his father was an influential member of the board of directors and had massaged his appointment to the important sales trip into the North. The truth was that his father *was* an influential man, but not at all in the way that they believed. The elder Axelsen served as the assistant to the Under Secretary of the Navy giving him the ear of one of the most influential military men in the world. Axelsen thought about asking his tormentor the question of how he'd been discovered, but another lash from the leather strap across the sole of his bloody foot melted the urge into a pitiful howl.

When the pain subsided he wondered why they were limiting the abuse to his feet. Not a single blow had landed above his sock line. And the damage, while horrific, was not permanent. It would heal within weeks if they stopped hitting him. He had been part of a Chinese-Dutch dam building team sent to aid in the North Koreans' plan to dam the Geumgang River. His mission was to covertly assess the North's progress on the acquisition of weapons of mass destruction, including the use of the dam itself to send a massive flood into South Korea. The seismic equipment his team was delivering was also scanning for signs of radiation in the deep underground cave systems that crisscrossed North Korea. In reality, *any* intel he brought back was welcome, a fact that his father had been sure to impress upon him. He remembered the last conversation they had had before the levers of power available to his father had been pulled, one more time, to make the next step in his career possible.

The scene in his father's massive home played before him for the hundredth time. His father had been livid about the latest domestic violence charge. He been arrested for hitting a stripper in a seedy Florida club, but his father had been able to talk the DA out of moving ahead with charges.

"You are a bigger disappointment than you can imagine," he'd said. Axelsen had just shrugged. His father continued, "What is it you want? I got you a great job as a CIA analyst and you're determined to throw it away."

"I want action. I've been working-out twice a day. I'm ready for the field. Make that happen, and you'll never have to help me again," Jonathan had said. The words haunted him.

His jailor received a phone call and left the safe house. When he returned he was not alone. A man in the uniform of a North Korean officer was with him. Their faces were unreadable but the officer held out a glass of water. The guard untied his hands and

Jonathan took the glass, greedily sucking it down until he coughed. The officer held out a piece of paper in his hands as well. Jonathan recognized it and knew he was screwed. It was a letter from his father and it was supposed to have stayed with his other personal effects back in the States. He must have overlooked it. He had his answer.

"I can explain about that," Jonathan said, his mind reeling. The two men stood impassively, the guard touching the butt of his gun. Jonathan had nothing. He was a large man, a starting lineman at a division three football program, but there was nothing he could do against these men. He made a decision.

"I'm a spy, I admit it. But I have no love for America. I'll give you the names of other agents that I know are in your country already. I'll tell you anything you want to know."

This drew a thin smile. "Please do," the officer said in perfect English.

Jonathan Axelsen started at the beginning.

When he had finished, the officer smiled at him warmly and sent his guard away. "You have done well today. You may well have done far more than save your own life. What if I could offer you unimaginable pleasures and a chance at a life in which your every desire will be met?"

"I'm listening," Jonathan said.

"No one knows you are ours now. You may return to America, gather information that will be of use to us, and come back."

"Come back?"

"Yes. If I send you home with something for your superiors, they will put you in an even more important position. You will continue as you were, building up the information we need. The data on the CIA servers is incalculably valuable to us. But first, you will be my guest at our Great Leader's Pleasure Palace. There you will learn what true power is about."

4

Cape Cod, Massachusetts

Jonathan walked carefully, trying not to put any real pressure on his feet. He didn't want to be seen limping, that would require a large round of lying. He was too tired to lie. It was OK being back in the States. For the first time he felt a true purpose. He was going to sell American secrets to North Koreans; that was fine. No big deal really. The money he would receive was tremendous, but it was nothing compared to the joy waiting for him back in Pyongyang. Young girls, boys even, ready to service his every desire night and day. The North Korean officer was not kidding when he said that there were certain things money could not buy, certain joys in this life that were available to only a select few.

That was true power. Power to kill, rape, own another human being. Total dominance.

It was the most liberating thing Jonathan had ever experienced. His tour of the Pleasure Palace was far too brief, but he was granted an hour with a girl of his choosing. He was told point blank that he was allowed to beat her if he wanted; kill her even, if it served his needs. The only catch was that they had made a video recording of him doing it, for insurance purposes, should he have a change of mind once he was stateside. There was nothing he couldn't do to the girl, and no possibility he was going to have a change of mind. He felt a strong stirring between his legs at the memory of what he *had* done. God that had been sweet. The hour had been over in a blink and he still hadn't cum, he'd had to beg the officer to let him finish. He'd been obliged to humor him. Jonathan was a highly valuable asset after all.

Jonathan's daydreaming was interrupted by the approach of his father's sailing buddy, William. He was one of the few men his father kept around that Jonathan didn't despise.

He certainly didn't *like* the grey-haired bastard, but he did have fairly decent jokes.

"Jonathan, my boy," William said in his annoying New England accent. "Heard the one about the dishwasher?"

Jonathan shrugged at him, fighting the urge to tell him to fuck-off. He was in no mood.

William leaned in close and asked, "What do you do when the dishwasher breaks down?"

"You tell me," Jonathan said.

"Kick her fat ass."

Jonathan couldn't repress the guffaw, heads snapped around to stare at them. It was hard to hate William.

His father was among those staring at them. He was talking with two men Jonathan recognized, Admiral Lantana and Owen Tiberius. William recognized them, as well, and gave a brief but utterly ignored wave.

"Smoke?" William asked motioning to the patio.

Jonathan pulled a silver lighter out of a pants pocket and nearly lit up inside the stuffy yacht club. He stopped the flame just short of his cigarette; he needed to be smart, this was not the place to show off his new attitude. He took a deep breath, tucked the unlit smoke behind his ear and led the way onto the patio. The two men stood alone, silently smoking one cigarette, then another.

William cleared his throat and said, "You ever have any guns to sell anonymously, you let me know."

Jonathan's head snapped up, his cigarette nearly falling out of his mouth. "What kind of a question is that, Willy?"

William hated being called Willy, but he deserved it for that question. Both men fell silent again. Jonathan was desperately in need of cash if he was going to have any chance of satisfying himself with a hooker, because no ordinary hooker was going to do. William wasn't a cop; he probably just had a *female* problem that he needed to take care of with a silenced bullet. He could relate to that. And god, he *needed* cash. He wasn't going to be back in the Pleasure Palace for months. He would need a pimp that was OK with him beating on the girls a bit. He had always liked it rough, but it wasn't until North Korea that he'd realized *how* rough. William was staring at him. He seemed to know what he was thinking, but he didn't mind. He was smiling in fact, like a kindred spirit. Perhaps he didn't hate William. "How much cash you got?" he asked.

"I can get you fifty-grand tonight. Do you have access to these?" He asked as he passed over a neatly printed list of weapons and hardware.

Jonathan smiled. "I'm the fucking CIA liaison to a SEAL team, of course I have access. I was just assigned to the Special Ops Group, I'm no bullshit now."

"Your dad told me. Congratulations."

There was something about the tone with which William said congratulations that made Jonathan suspect he didn't mean it, like he *knew* his father had pulled the strings that made the promotion happen. His distaste was probably apparent because William sputtered for a moment and then said, "I also know a great pimp in South Florida, very discreet. As long as you've got the cash, he'll let you go pretty far with his produce. Be sure to ask him for the full salad bar. Call this number."

"How do you know you can trust him?" he asked.

"I got it from the son of that fat bastard your father was talking to, Owen Tiberius. His son's a big deal in the Paris hooker business."

"Jean-Pierre Tiberius? No shit. I knew him growing up."

"Yeah, his father won't talk about it, but the kid is really the one to know for such leisure pursuits."

Axelson pocketed the number and turned to leave. "One other thing," William said before he reached the door. "Have you given any other thought to the little side project I told you about? If the CIA isn't giving you what you want, there's always money in private contracting. This thing I have going is gonna pay off big, but I need someone that can manage my nephews."

"I'm happy where I am," he spat.

William recoiled but stayed silent.

Jonathan did his best to soften his tone as he said, "I'll get you the supplies you need, though."

5

Naval Air Station, Jacksonville, Florida

Sam Drake bit the inside of his cheek until he tasted blood. It was all he could do to keep from screaming at the man leering at him. Sam kept his arms pinned to his side but didn't back away from the taller man whose nose nearly touched his. He knew that Commander Axelsen was out of his mind. But it was more than hatred he felt for the man; it was a seething resentment. He had lodged a formal complaint against Axelsen and it had only made things worse.

"Hey, there, Sammie, you gonna file another grievance?" Axelsen repeated.

Sam released his cheek and bit at his bottom lip instead. There was nothing he could do about Axelsen now. He had done what he could through official channels, now he had to let things play out. Sam released his clamped jaws, and said, "Sir, I stand by my report. I find your tactics reprehensible and I will not serve under you a day longer than I have to."

Axelsen laughed. "You'll fucking serve under whoever we tell you you're serving under, got that? Now, the mission into North Korea is a go. You best stow your bullshit attitude and get back on the team. Are we clear?"

"Completely, sir." Sam said. This was insane. They were scheduled to be wheels up in less than forty-eight hours. That meant his window to document his fears about Axelsen's little side business was nearly closed. He needed something irrefutable and there was only one place left to check.

Three hours later, Sam sat at the Celtic Pub with his best friend, James Jones. To Sam and the rest of the unit, he was just Jonesy. They had been friends at Annapolis and had earned their SEAL credentials together. Jonesy was as likeable a person as Sam had ever known, everyone thought so. He knew all the right people on base to get information pulled from confidential personnel files. "The guy's a traitor," Sam said.

"What are you gonna do? Nothing in the guy's file; I've been over it ten times. He's a crazy, but nothing points to traitor. CIA goons are always like this. Besides, you can't screw with a blueblood like that. His whole family's been in the service. His father is the assistant to the Under Secretary of the Navy."

Sam knew he needed more evidence and that he would have to do the unthinkable: risk a dishonorable discharge by breaking into Axelsen's office and searching it. Sam's career didn't matter; it was his team that he cared about. They knew that he would sacrifice his life to protect them, as each of them would do in turn had they harbored the suspicion he did. The other four men in his unit being sent into a hot zone on Axelsen's bullshit intel, they were the priority.

"Jonesy, I just know this intel of his stinks. He claims he found documents during his last mission into North Korea that confirm the Chinese weather modification technology is in play again, but that the documents were somehow destroyed in the firefight *after* he read them. What he brought back is too convenient for me. It's all his conjecture and a few notes he managed to save. We're basing this mission on his word and I can't shake the feeling that he's made the whole thing up."

"Now why would he do that?" Jonesy asked as he finished his beer.

"I don't know yet. But I can't put stock in coincidences like this. You've seen the way he operates, he's bad news. And I'm betting he's the one that stole the gear. He's probably got a side business selling guns, or secrets. I mean, as soon as he's appointed CIA liaison to the unit, weapons go missing and intel materializes out of thin air." Sam laughed without humor and took a swig off his beer. "The brass thinks I've got it in for the guy, but this is for real. You believe me, right?"

"Course I do, Sammie. But orders are orders. We're going wheels up with this thing at o-eight hundred. You gonna be with us?"

"I'm not letting you follow that bastard by yourselves. I'll be there. I just have to check something first."

"Tell me you're not planning to break into Axelsen's office," he said, staring at Sam. He took a deep breath and exhaled as he said, "You are. He's a decorated CIA spook, you're not going to find anything. He'd be more careful than that. If you're right, and it's a very big *if* . . . we're all toast anyway. If we refuse to go wheels up with him tomorrow, our careers are finished. If he's lying, we're dead."

"I hear you, but maybe he was sloppy. He's careless with everything else he does; maybe he left me something I can take to the brass before we're off the ground, save all our asses."

"What about Admiral Lantana?" Jonesy said. "You can get access to him, right?"

Sam looked back at his friend. True to his reputation, nothing was a secret to Jonesy. "Yeah, my sister was married to his son,"

"Sharon? The one that, ah, you lost?"

Sam nodded but stayed silent for a moment. "Our fathers served in Nam. Lantana was with him when he died. The admiral's my godfather. His son Jim and I were close growing up. I haven't spoken to either of them since Sharon passed, though."

"It's breaking the chain of command to go directly to him, but if you're right it's worth a shot."

"I know," Sam said shaking his head. He'd thought about contacting the admiral about Axelsen on more than one occasion. But the move would look incredibly desperate. He needed some proof first. "I'll send a message to him before we go wheels up," Sam said. Contacting Admiral Lantana had been his back-up plan, a move he wanted to steer clear of for reasons that went far deeper than simply avoiding breaking the chain of command. His resolve hardened; he'd break into the office of his CIA liaison regardless of the consequences.

Sam picked the lock on Axelsen's office door easily. Once inside, he switched on his penlight and played the beam back and forth. He knew what he was looking for. It was a small lacquered box he had seen in Axelsen's office before their last mission briefing. The wooden box was painted black and was adorned with a flowing Asian script he couldn't read. Axelsen had seen him looking at it in the filthy office and had intentionally distracted him from it by pointing out a set of dried ears his father had taken as a war trophy in Vietnam. When Sam had turned back to the desk, the black box was gone. Axelsen had acted like nothing had happened. Sam hoped it held clues to the missing weapons; if he could link Axelsen to that, there was no way the mission could be cleared.

Sam shined his light onto the cluttered desk. Other than a half-eaten tuna sandwich, there was nothing but stacks of papers that detailed the mission they were slated to undertake in less than six hours. Sam walked around the desk and pulled out the worn office chair. He sat down, stuck the light into this mouth, and began trying the drawers. Each slid open and reveled innocuous contents except for the bottom drawer, which was locked.

Sam removed his lock-pick kit from his pocket and had the drawer open in less than ten seconds. The polished black box was the only thing in the drawer. Sam took it out and set it on the desk. His palms were slick as he opened the lid and shined the light inside. The light played over several images and his jaw went slack. The penlight dropped from his teeth and clanked on the chipped linoleum floor. It rolled under the desk out of reach. He clutched at the box in the dark and only managed to knock it to the floor.

He couldn't believe what he had just seen. It was a North Korean passport with Axelsen's picture on it. Stuffed into the passport were three photos: one of a bridge with a small name clearly visible on it and two jailhouse mug shots. Sam felt his stomach relax and was met with a deep sense of embarrassment. He had been in intense combat and never batted an eye, but the passport had rattled him like a recruit. Was it proof that he was going to defect to North Korea? No one in the unit needed a passport, so why did Axelsen have one?

A light from under the door caught his eye. There was a military police sentry on patrol. Sam scrambled under the desk for his penlight and doused its beam. The passport was under the desk and he had to lie on his stomach to reach it.

He had found the proof that could at least sideline Axelsen, if not end his career completely. Now he just needed someone else to find it. Sam's mind reeled as he grasped the stupidity of what he had just done. There was no way to pin the passport on Axelsen now. His fingerprints were all over the box. Axelsen would allege that he planted it, and there was nothing he could do or say to refute that. He had lodged a complaint against Axelsen that had been found to lack merit. He would seem desperate, and in fact, he was desperate. And another thought was creeping in. Axelsen was CIA. Maybe he did need a passport. Sam looked at the document carefully, picking at the edges with his thumb nail. It appeared to be brand new; the glue was still tacky on the lamination.

The sentry's light faded away and Sam considered his options. None were very good. His unit was wheels-up on a mission he couldn't stop in less than six hours. He would send an email to Admiral Lantana even it would mean breaking the chain of command. It was his only play. Sam thought about what his life meant. It meant nothing without honor. He would be on the plane with Axelsen and the rest of the team, and he would kill Jonathan Axelsen at the first sign of trouble.

Two Months Later

6

Key West, Florida

Sam was out of patience with everyone, especially himself. He refused to skip his daily bike ride, even with a splitting headache. He deserved it. Riding was supposed to be his stress-reliever. Hard as he tried, however, he couldn't keep the pictures of his last mission out of his mind.

He had nothing, not even a home; he lived on his diving boat now. He'd been prepared to throw away his military career to stop Axelsen, but he hadn't. He'd let the mission proceed. He felt like riding off a bridge. He switched to a higher gear, and pedaled harder to outrun his memories. Riding was usually his favorite time of the day, but the headache allowed thoughts of his wrecked life to creep in, a bad sign.

Sam forced his focus back onto the bike trail. It seemed particularly quiet, for some reason. Normally, there were several locals or tourists around. The South Florida sun beating down on his bare back felt oppressive. Even cruising at an even twenty-five miles an hour, there was not enough breeze to evaporate the sweat he worked up.

He glanced over his right shoulder to see if anyone was coming behind him, and his eyes fell on the Navy SEAL tattoo on his upper arm. It was beginning to fade from the intensity of the sun. Good. That would make it a less painful reminder of what his life used to be. He couldn't go back to the SEALs. There was no unit for him to rejoin, and his refusal to take the psych eval wasn't helping. He had to figure out what had gone wrong in North Korea first. If he passed the evaluation, he'd be back on active duty and deployed within weeks. Then he'd have a new unit to worry about, a fresh group of brothers in arms that deserved his full attention. He owed a debt to the men he'd lost. That had to be paid first.

Anticipating a small hill, Sam clicked his bike into a lower gear. The trail wound around Key West, taking him close to his dive-boat home. Sam pushed his hand under his aerodynamic glasses and rubbed his eyes. He hated his life. Biking wasn't working today. His head pounded and he felt like throwing things or punching something . . . or perhaps some*one*.

Sam pushed his glasses up the bridge of his nose and sped up. Sometimes, after a few hours on the bike, the fog hiding the details of what happened on the last mission cleared a bit and the answers locked in his head seemed accessible. So far the pieces he had just didn't make sense. Maybe today he'd be able to ride it all out, remember those last few minutes before he'd been shot. It had been two months since the mission and his memories were no closer to him now than when he had awakened in the hospital.

Once he had the memories back, maybe he could start over, move back into active duty and get on with his life. But that really depended on what the memories were. If the official version of events was accurate, he'd accept the failure and move on. But he knew in his heart that they were not. There was much more to what had gone wrong.

He rode across the first of two pedestrian bridges that he crossed on every ride. The second bridge was just ahead of him at the top of a rise. He stood up in the pedals, and worked his legs frantically, feeling the sweat pour down his back and arms, and allowed the events of the last two months to wash over him.

This particular bridge was where the arms sale meeting was supposed to have taken place—according to the photos he'd recovered from Jonathan Axelsen's office. He had awakened in the hospital after the mission was over with a sick feeling in his stomach, like the moment before a roller coaster begins a free fall.

The officer who briefed him was not a man he had ever met. His name was Richardson and he stank of too many hours on duty in a hospital. He explained that Axelsen's intel had been good. The mission had progressed exactly as it was supposed to. The North Koreans did have weather modification technology acquired from the Chinese, as Axelsen had asserted. Sam had asked to speak to Admiral Lantana and the officer's mood had darkened. He fought for words, unsure of how to break the news. So Sam made it easy on him. He grabbed him by the shirt and pulled him in close, only letting go after Richardson had told him the truth about what had happened. The admiral was in the same hospital as Sam. He'd tried to end his own life.

Nothing made sense anymore. His team had been the best. In six years together they'd lost only two team members. But in their last mission everyone had died but Sam. Richardson told him that the video feed on Sam's helmet captured the scenes after the ambush. It had started with a stun grenade that came out of nowhere. Sam peddled harder, thinking about the stun grenade, as if he could outrun it. But today he couldn't pedal hard enough and he was dragged back into his last odd day on the base.

Sam had sat quietly in the small assembly room. He had been cleared to leave the hospital to attend the private ceremony for a member of his team receiving the Congressional Medal of Honor, which should have brought joy to his heart. But not that day, not for this team member.

Looking around the gathering of high-ranking officers, Sam couldn't help but wonder if maybe he was wrong about Axelsen. Maybe Axelsen did save his life and lose his own in the process. But something more than the gunshot wound had made his guts twist as he sat in the air-conditioning back in Jacksonville. It was the images that he found in Axelsen's office before the mission.

There had to be more to this. And none of the other SEALs' bodies had been recovered. Their helmet videos were all disabled by the North Koreans shortly after they were killed, so there was nothing to dispute the version of events that was being forced on him.

The mission details were classified and this ceremony was being conducted behind closed doors. A public acknowledgment of a mission into North Korea was out of the question, but Axelsen's family was wealthy and influential and the death of their son as a hero was not an event his commanders would pass up. There were just too many political points to be scored.

So Sam had sat in his seat and did not stand up when the others did, presumably because of his gunshot wound, but really because he was nervous that he would not be able to keep up the charade if he'd pushed it too far. It had all been bullshit and he knew it. The details of the mission were still so foggy. There was a five-minute window that he couldn't penetrate, no matter how hard he tried. And he knew that in that five minutes he had failed his team. Somehow, someway, he should have seen it coming and reacted sooner. He was on point. Axelsen had been behind him. How could he have let Axelsen get behind him? Had Axelsen thrown the stun grenade at Sam? There was no video evidence of that.

The video that they recovered from Sam's helmet showed exactly what the brass said it did, an ambush and then a flash-bang grenade that knocked Sam out of the fight. In the melee that followed, Sam had been shot, but he had not returned fire. Instead, his helmet video showed him crawling for cover while the rest of his team was taken apart by an overwhelming force. Then Axelsen's face was in the frame, standing over Sam, and the family members at the ceremony cried as Axelsen hauled him up and over his shoulder and carried him out of the complex and back to the beach. He'd thrown Sam into the Zodiac that was to be their escape, placed Sam's hand on the outboard motor and run back toward the battle. It was presumed that he died trying to recover other men, hence this ceremony. That was it.

But even after the medal ceremony, he kept thinking the same thing: *There is something wrong with Jonathan Axelsen.* His memory of the office search from before the mission was crystal clear, so he started there.

Sam focused his thoughts back on the photos he had seen in Axelsen's office. He wanted them for no other reason than to prove that the man was a scumbag. There was a computer printout of their last mission target—a Major-General Tsang from China—that stuck out to Sam. Axelsen had highlighted a paragraph about the general's obsession . . . a project called the Three Gorges Dam. Sam knew that Tsang was the general who was supplying the North Koreans with weather modification technology to aid in a possible invasion of the South. Locating the intel, assessing it's credibility and destroying any prototypes, had been the purpose of their last mission.

Among the scattered documents in Axelsen's filthy office was an article about someone named Emanuel Founder, but Sam had never been briefed on the role he played in the project. The article talked about the archeological digs along the banks of the Yangtze and how it had been affected by the flooding. It was believed that the area had been a test site for Chinese Weather Modification.

Sam left the office feeling sick in a way that he knew drugs could not treat. The only names that looked like viable targets for arms sales were "M. and C. McCrystal." They both had rap sheets and no current employment info. It wouldn't make sense for Axelsen to try to sell weapons to a stodgy archeologist, but his name had been in the same file, so Sam would follow up on him. The photos and scraps of information about meetings between Axelsen and "M. and C." near a bridge in Key West, Florida, were the straws Sam had to grasp. He'd searched the area for a month, thinking perhaps the weapons themselves were hidden nearby and found nothing. He'd held his own surveillance duty for a few hours now and then, but nothing had turned up. He knew his search was a long shot, but his pride kept him coming back. At least he was getting some decent exercise.

His memories of the mission were distorted and hazy, presumably a byproduct of a nerve agent the North Koreans had used against them. He was more upset by a feeling than a specific memory; it was out of reach, shimmering just beyond his consciousness. It teased him, refusing to let him understand or move on. What he could remember left him feeling betrayed.

In a flash, he remembered jumping out of the plane with the rest of the unit and feeling very angry, as if something Axelsen had done was wrong. He had it then: Axelsen had nearly blown the mission by standing near the open hatch without his safety tether. A single errant bump and he could have been sucked out before the rest of the team, dooming the mission before it started. Sam smiled at the tiny victory; he'd pulled a thread of the mission out of his mind that had eluded him. He pedaled harder, recalling that the mission progressed as it was supposed to from there. They completed their High Altitude Low Opening jump, known as a HALO, without incident. They made it into North Korea and into the Pleasure Palace that was their target. Axelsen was in a strange mood. He seemed oddly calm, as if they were on a training mission and not a live action insertion. That was what was still nagging at Sam. The way Axelsen moved in without cover, almost inviting an attack. It was more than sloppy, it was reckless. Then all hell broke loose. Shots from multiple directions, Jonesy taking a round through the face. Then the flash-bang grenade. And nothing until he was being hoisted into the Zodiac.

He had been briefed on the mission into Pyongyang after he woke up, but he still didn't understand why Axelsen wanted to be part of the mission in the first place. It was an assignment that Axelsen had requested after being demoted. Jonesy had learned that Axelsen had been out of regular combat for three years before he had chosen to get back in. He had been on an undercover mission into North Korea that had mostly failed, but he had brought back intel on the weather modification technology that convinced the brass to authorize the tactical mission with the SEAL team.

Now, as he pedaled closer to the bridge, he wondered about the meetings that had supposedly taken place. He wasn't sure what he was hoping to find by riding this path every day. He forced himself to mentally catalogue other details of the search, reciting the contents of the financial records of offshore accounts that appeared to be research for an upcoming mission. The name on the accounts was "Caligula's Toenail," Axelsen's favorite Roman emperor—a point he loved to share with the unit—which had raised his antennae and still troubled him.

Jonathan Axelsen had made Sam uncomfortable from the first moment they'd met. According to Jonesy, he was part of the CIA's Special Operations Group, or SOG. He'd only been given the position as a result of his father's influence as the assistant to the Under Secretary of the Navy. The CIA and the SEALs worked hand-in-glove on covert operations, a relationship that went back to Vietnam. Axelsen hadn't shared much about himself with the others. He had no friends in the unit and never seemed to do anything during his off-duty hours but practice on the shooting range.

Axelsen always earned top grades for marksmanship and physical fitness. It was his proclivity for taking risks that SEALs were trained to avoid that made Sam and the rest of the team nervous. Their CIA operator wasn't there to shoot; he was there to collect intel. But Axelsen insisted on being engaged with enemy targets just like the rest of the SEAL team. It was an unnecessary risk and meant only one thing: He got off on violence. He'd wait to pull the trigger until the last second, risking death. Sometimes, he'd miss his targets, pumping round after round into the non-deadly areas of an enemy's body before finishing with a kill shot to the heart or brain. His marksmanship was matched only by Sam's, a fact that clearly infuriated Axelsen.

What bothered Sam the most was Axelsen's total lack of emotion when anyone went down. Before their final mission, Sam had huddled with the rest of their team and they'd all agreed that Axelsen was sick. Sick, and maybe a threat to the team. And Sam had pledged silently to take him out at the first sign of real trouble. But that chance had passed him up and now he was stuck riding a bike day after day with no real leads, and—

Sam shook his head and kept pedaling. It was awkward to hate a man who had saved your life.

It was late in the afternoon and his hangover hadn't budged. The troubling memories kept pace with him even though he was peddling faster than the path warranted. He began the quick descent down the hill toward the second pedestrian bridge. Peering through the dim light of approaching dusk, he thought he saw two large figures hunched over a smaller, struggling form. As he passed them, he heard a snippet of their argument. What was it about them? *Wait. Was it possible?* He blinked rapidly. Then, in a flash, pieces clicked into place and he was sure these were the men from Axelsen's file.

Pumping hard, Sam flew under the bridge and passed the group, and up the other side of the hill. Once out of sight, he slowed and turned around. He balanced himself on the bike pedals and faced down the hill, processing what he'd just seen. The person on the ground was female. The two men he'd been looking for were arguing with her. She had said that she didn't want guns; she wanted seismic testing gear. That was when the larger man took his hand off her arm and struck her. The argument didn't make sense to him, but it didn't matter. He had no choice. Without stopping to consider other options, he jumped on the pedals and shot forward.

The smaller of the two men had moved onto the trail. The bigger one was again shaking the woman by her shoulders. As Sam neared the group, the one on the trail turned. He reached into his jacket. *Does he have a gun?* If so, he was a second too late. Sam was still ten feet away, but he instinctively locked his front brake. The bicycle tire came to a dead stop and Sam's forward motion catapulted him over the handlebars head first, his bike following. A second before impact, Sam lowered his head and felt his helmet connect with the man's face.

Landing in a tangled pile of bike and man, Sam struggled to free himself. Dazed, but unhurt, he heard the spinning sound of his back wheel. His helmet dangled behind his head by its straps, choking him. He yanked it free and saw that the other man was unconscious. Good. That would give him time to—

A hard kick to the ribs spun him to the ground. He groaned. He'd been kicked before—kicked, shot at, thrown out of helicopters; he knew his best chance was to pretend he was unconscious. A second, harder kick to his stomach took this option away.

"You all right, Chris?" the kicker yelled, his third kick poised to strike at Sam.

So he was right: These men *were* Axelsen's contacts; the guy on the ground was "C." Lying face up, Sam tensed against the next blow. As "M's" foot began its powerful down stroke, Sam noticed a form moving quickly behind him. Then, a split second later, the third boot blow connected.

Sam's partially healed gunshot wound tore open and he felt warm blood on his hands. He realized how stupid it was to confront two men when he was only wearing spandex and riding shoes. He focused long enough to see that he was about to be kicked again, when a blond-haired woman with a smear of mud on her cheek swung a rock at his attacker's head.

Sam passed out when the big man crumpled to the ground next to him.

7

Key West Medical Center

Dr. Carl Genoisa lifted his eyebrows and crossed his arms over his chest with a look that said he didn't believe what he was hearing. "It's a good sign that he woke up, but he should be in a hospital, not an urgent care clinic. We need the results of his MRI before I'd sign off on releasing him," he said. He turned to Danielle. "I'm concerned about his abdominal surgery scars. They can't be more than a month old and it appears that the altercation opened the internal stitches. He could need surgery to close them. That's a Navy SEAL tattoo on his shoulder." He pulled down the sheet covering Sam and pointed to it. "I'm betting he was hunting Al-Qaida or the like."

"But . . . he'll be able to dive soon. Right?" Danielle asked, reaching into her purse and handing the doctor a check. "I want to take care of all his medical expenses and your trouble."

Carl Genoisa peered at the check and smiled. "Don't worry. I'll make sure he can dive."

Sam struggled to open his eyes. Was he back in North Korea? No, he had been injured. Was he in a military hospital? He lifted his eyelids far enough to focus on the shape of a man standing over him. He was wearing a white coat. A doctor. But he didn't look familiar. "W-who are you?" he asked, barely moving his lips.

"I'm Dr. Carl Genoisa," the man said, lifting his eyelids wider and shining a light straight into his eyes. "You've been unconscious. You may have a slight concussion."

Sam fought to clear his head. His abdomen burned like white fire. Something had happened. He needed to remember. Had he been on another mission? Had he been injured again? Then he remembered. "Is she . . . okay?" Sam tried to say more, but his voice sounded like a frog's croak.

"She's fine," Dr. Genoisa said. "Can't say the same for you and your attackers. You're bleeding internally so you need more surgery to repair these fresh wounds. By the way, the fellow you knocked out with your helmet is still unconscious. The other guy can't remember his name yet."

"Good. Sonofabitch kicked me . . . while I was . . . down." Sam winced and peered up at the doctor through half-closed eyes. "Who is . . . the blonde—"

"I'm Danielle Founder," a voice said, interrupting him. She approached Sam's bed. "Thanks for your help." She placed a hand on his and smiled. "Sorry I didn't find that rock sooner."

"Better late than never at all," Sam said, pulling his hand away. "I'm . . . Sam."

"I know. I was hoping to rent you today. I mean . . . your boat. The doctor told me you have a boat I can charter."

"No problem," Sam said, shifting his weight and attempting to sit up. "Did you know those apes that attacked you, by the way?"

"Hold it, pal," Dr. Genoisa said, pushing him back. "Let's wait a bit, before you go sitting up. You're going to need surgery to repair that wound, remember?"

"You were pretty impressive, for a guy in spandex." Danielle smiled at him.

"I do what I can," Sam said. "But don't change the subject . . . ." Sam felt his forehead grow hot and then cold as he lapsed back into a state of near unconsciousness.

8

Key West, Florida

Danielle stared at the red circles of refracted light on the starched tablecloth and carefully swirled her glass of wine to make them dance. Bringing the glass to her lips, she noticed the lipstick mark on the rim and wondered if it were really as unique as a fingerprint, as her father had once told her. She glanced around the nearly empty restaurant. Pagliacci's Italian Bistro was popular with the locals. The plastic grape clusters on the dark walls annoyed her, but the place was perfect for a quiet meeting.

It was the middle of the afternoon and the lunch crowd had eaten and left, and it was too soon for the dinner crowd. An untouched zucchini appetizer sat before her. She was too excited to eat. She swirled her wine again, forced her eyes away from the décor, and checked her watch one more time. She had been waiting for an hour. Sam had been out of urgent care for one week. He claimed that he was ready to meet with her to discuss her proposition, but he was late.

Ten minutes passed before she finally waved for the waiter to bring her the bill. Sam chose that moment to stride in as if he were on time. She rose from the booth to catch his attention.

"Sorry I'm late," he said, shaking her hand and sliding onto the bench opposite hers. "I had to check on something that I thought was done in error."

"That's all right," she said. "I took the liberty of ordering us a bottle of Chianti. Hope you like it." She lifted the bottle and held it over the empty glass in front of him.

"Thanks."

Danielle watched him sip the wine. "Have you thought any more about my offer?"

"I have."

"And?"

"Well, it looks like I'm done in Key West. My license to run the dive operation was revoked; that's what I was checking on."

"Oh?"

"Last month some tourists on my boat came up from forty feet of water too fast. The change in pressure could've killed them. They usually put instructors on probation for this kind of thing, but not this time. They pulled my license without further comment. I'm kind of getting used to that treatment these days."

Danielle's heart leapt to her throat. This was a big piece of her gamble. "I'm so sorry, Sam. You must be devastated. But . . . you'll do it then? You'll help me out?"

Sam glanced at her and then across the restaurant, lost in thought.

"An all-expenses-paid trip and ten grand a week to go to China with me," she said. "And a nice bonus if we find what we're looking for—"

"*If* we find whatever you think is there? I want the bonus at the end of the trip either way. I've got legal bills." Sam swallowed the last of his wine in two gulps and planted the goblet on the table.

"Paid your mooring rental this week?" Danielle asked, shoving the plate of fried zucchini toward him.

"You know I haven't." Sam fingered the goblet stem and ignored the zucchini. "My dive operation is done and my savings are going faster than I'd like."

"Again, Sam, I'm sorry. Let me give you a couple hundred bucks, as an advance, while you think about my offer." Danielle reached into her purse and found her billfold. "Here," she said, pulling out three bills and placing them on the table in front of him. "Three hundred. To help you out while you decide."

He stared at the money without taking it. "You really think we can get into China?"

"I know we can. I have a valuable connection there. He was one of my father's students."

"All right, I'll trust you." He reached for the cash and stood up at the same time.

"So . . . you're in?" Danielle tried to hide her elation.

Sam nodded. "I've got nothing better to do. When do you plan to get underway?"

"Tomorrow," She said sliding a folded piece of paper across the table to him.

Sam glanced at the equipment list, nodded and walked out.

Danielle fought another wave of guilt. She'd never done anything as underhanded as bribe a state official. It had been William's idea, and it had worked easily. Sam hadn't been given a hearing to plead his side of the accident. They had told him that the revocation was in place until a hearing could be set, but that they were booked out for six months. She did her best to swallow the guilt; the trip to China was too important to allow feelings of doubt to cloud her resolve. She had come too far for that.

She reached into her purse again after Sam left and pulled out a small cell phone and pressed a speed dial key. "William? It's me. Sam Drake just left. He's taking the job." She glanced over her shoulder to ensure privacy. "Uh-huh, the board revoked his license. I didn't think I'd feel so guilty about it," she said, looking around.

She paused to hand the waiter her credit card and then turned away from him. "Yes, William, he's definitely onboard. His record was spotless, until his screw-up with the tourists last month." She said a bit too loudly. "The doctor says he was wounded in combat but he should be able to dive. Only thing he seems to care about is his unit." She paused to listen for a moment. "I didn't choose that last CIA goon, your nephews did. Why don't you believe that he was killed in combat?" The waiter placed a tray containing her bill and credit card in front of her. She shifted the cell phone to her left hand and signed the charge slip. "It'll work this time, I'm sure. I told you that your nephews shouldn't be the ones handling personnel," Danielle said. She regretted her tone immediately. He did not raise his voice, but she could tell he was upset with her. "I know that you want them there to protect me. There's just no time, William. The water may have destroyed the site already. I have to go now; there's a lot to do. Sam Drake will have to work. Give my love to Dad."

She hoped she was right. Sam had reeked of alcohol under the bridge. Even so, Williams' thuggish nephews hadn't bested him. Her fist clenched involuntarily. Those two. William *insisted* that they come along. She relaxed her hand; he always knew best.

On her way out of the bistro, Danielle caught a glimpse of her reflection in the bar mirror. Her forehead was creased with worry lines. She took a deep breath to relax and looked in the mirror again. Her face was not at all unattractive and her well-defined features were compliments of her father, more than her mother. She frowned and turned away from the mirror.

She tried to think about her mother, now "Mrs. Goldfarb," as little as possible. Her mother had abandoned her father two years earlier, not long after his return from China and after he'd been diagnosed with an unknown health problem that ultimately caused his worsening paralysis. All Danielle knew was that her mother now lived in Florida, a short drive up the Intercoastal Highway toward Miami, and that "Mrs. Goldfarb" sent her large checks every month, despite not being thanked for them.

Danielle reached into her shirt pocket and fingered a neatly folded piece of paper. She repressed a shudder and said aloud, "See you soon, Mom."

Danielle had no time or interest in sightseeing. Time was running out. Not even the view over the bridge connecting the Keys to the mainland interested her. She kept her eyes fixed on the road and drove only slightly above the speed limit. Her nerves couldn't afford a ticket right now.

Her lips moved unconsciously, as she worked through what she would say to her mother. She had made no attempt to see her since her mother left the family and filed for divorce. She knew her address only because it was printed on the envelope holding her monthly check—1010 Shell Cove Way. She'd looked it up on online, and as she'd guessed, her mother now lived in an exclusive area outside Miami.

That first month the check had arrived, Danielle had torn it up. But to her chagrin, she realized that without the extra cash, she couldn't afford her father's ongoing treatment. His savings had run out within a few months, and his health insurance didn't cover the experimental therapy his physician was using to try to stem the advance of the mysterious paralysis. Although William was, of course, working for free on further treatment options, even he had to eat, so a sizable portion of the money from her mother's checks went into his research budget.

Danielle jammed her car into a lower gear and accelerated to 100 miles per hour before she took a calming breath and slowed back to 80.

Her mother hadn't tried to communicate with her over the phone, thankfully. She simply sent the checks month after month. This month had been different, though. She had included a note. Danielle reached into her purse for the note. She read it for the hundredth time.

> Dear Danielle,
> I have your father's journal. I found it while cleaning out some of his old things. I remember you telling me once that you wanted it, so call me and let me know if I should drop it in the mail for you. Love, Mom.

She's had the journal the whole time, Danielle thought. Her mother knew she wanted the journal. She had always wanted it. It was the final testament to his life's work. There was no way she would allow her mother to "drop it in the mail," as she had so flippantly suggested in the note.

No doubt her mother knew that, and the note was a ploy to get her to come get it. She had to gamble that her mother would be home alone. She needed to catch her off guard if her request had any hope of being successful. Calling her and giving advance notice of the brief visit would be far too considerate. It was immature and spiteful of her, but she didn't feel like offering any amount of thoughtfulness. Not after what she'd done.

A lump stuck in her throat just thinking about her father. She hadn't told him about her plan to take a trip to Florida. William was going to cover for her. Realizing that she was within forty miles of her destination, she decided to grab a bite to eat. She needed to freshen up and she didn't want to confront her mother on an empty stomach. Who knew what the conversation would hold? This was her only opportunity.

An hour later, she passed massive homes perfectly placed behind their palm-tree screens. She had noticed that mile after mile of guarded coastline was completely hidden from all but the fortunate few who could afford the adjacent land. Five- to fifteen-thousand square-foot homes seemed to be the norm.

Danielle pulled into a U-shaped driveway, parked under an enormous Mediterranean-style portico, and switched off the ignition. She leaned forward far enough to peer through the windshield at the house her mother called home. As expected, her mother had married into considerable wealth.

"Hello, Danielle," a familiar female voice greeted her from behind the car. "I wondered how long it would take you to get here."

Danielle jumped out of her car and stared at the woman who was not at all like the mother she had known. She had acquired the services of a skilled plastic surgeon. There were no easily discernable wrinkles on her face and her figure was well-shaped and dressed in an expensive-looking white linen pantsuit. This woman looked half her mother's age, but she managed to pull it off. "Not long, obviously."

"Care for a drink? You must be feeling the heat," Vivian said, walking toward the massive home. "It's not at all like the Cape down here."

"Thank you, I'm fine. I stopped for a little lunch on the way." Danielle found her mother's demeanor difficult to understand. She should be shocked to find her estranged daughter on her doorstep, but she wasn't missing a beat. Someone had obviously informed her of the visit. But who? "You're looking . . . different. Different, but healthy. Your new life must suit you."

"Thank you, dear. Actually, life is quite boring here. Everyone in Florida is so old."

"Like the man you married. You look young enough to be my sister."

Her mother laughed. "You always had a wonderful sense of humor, Danielle. Saul treats me very well. I'm grateful to him for so many things. He saved me from myself."

"He was your therapist's *father*."

"Why don't we go inside and have a nice sit-down talk?" Vivian Goldfarb headed for the impressive front door and then turned. "I don't suppose you brought any luggage."

"No. I don't plan to stay. I came for the journal."

"Of course you did. Well, come inside while I get it for you. You might like to see my home. Perhaps you'll take a minute or two to tell me something about yourself . . . what you've been doing since I saw you last, besides taking care of your father."

Danielle followed her mother into the house and fought the urge to stare. "Wow. This is really something. Not quite the three-bedroom you and Dad shared, is it?" She followed her mother down a long hallway before saying, "Anyway, thanks for your financial support." She said the words with obvious distaste. "It's the only way I've been able to take care of Dad." Her mouth twisted around the words.

"Saul and I feel it's the least we can do. Your father is lucky to have you. Many children don't care about the well being of their parents."

"Look," Danielle said. "Drop the act. We both know why I'm here."

Her mother stopped smiling. "Yes, of course. We haven't spoken in years, but I hoped you'd drop by to see us." Vivian sighed. "We . . . Saul and I didn't want to force you to visit. I've tried to be patient."

"Why did you leave Dad?" The question was out before Danielle could think about it.

For a moment, Vivian looked her age. "Please, Danielle, let's not spend our brief time together arguing. You know, whenever I think of your name, I remember the day your father chose it for you. It means 'God is my judge.' Your father always liked that."

"I know. You've both told me that a thousand times." Danielle swallowed, fighting for calm. Her mother was trying to provoke her. She strode across the expansive living room to the glass wall facing the Atlantic, allowing the view of the water to dominate her senses. Her mother must revel in it. For some reason, it reminded her of the way her Dad had liked to call her 'Yelle.' Her parents had always loved the water. "I came here to get the journal," she said. "I'm going right back to Dad. He needs me."

"I ceased to exist for him, Danielle. He only tried to talk to you. His babbling about some connection between the ancient Egyptians and the Chinese was driving me crazy. He turned on me. I saw a therapist because I needed someone to talk to about it."

"A lot of good he did," Danielle said, hearing the bitterness in her voice. "He fixed you up with his father. What kind of therapy is that?" The last time she'd seen her mother was when she pulled away from the curb in front of their home in Saul Goldfarb's car.

"Yes, Harold did arrange for us to have dinner together. We don't plan these things. They just happen. Can't you see how much better off I am now? I was a physical and psychological mess before I met Saul. I spent so much time alone. Your father's work meant more to him than I did. Saul enjoys my company."

Danielle was silent. *Her mother had said "I" one too many times*, and she was close to screaming.

"Don't *I* deserve to be happy?" Vivian asked.

That was it. "Forget that I asked why you left Dad. I don't want to talk about it." Danielle whirled from the window and faced her mother. She had seated herself on the white brocade couch. "Just give me what I came for."

"Yes, dear, I will." Vivian patted the cushion next to her. "Won't you sit for a few minutes? How is William? Still single?"

Danielle remained silent. *How dare she ask about him!*

"Why don't you tell me about this vacation you have planned?" Vivian said finally.

"It's not a vacation," Danielle said, through clamped jaws. "I'm finishing Dad's work. I'm going to China."

"China!" Vivian said. "It's not safe."

"The answers are in China. I'm going, whether or not it's safe."

"I wish you'd think about this a while longer. I don't want the same thing to happen to you that happened to your father. He never found anything useful there. He drove himself mad over it. You know all of this, honey. He left China because his work was destroyed. The Chinese government built that dam—"

"And flooded his dig. I know that. But Dad knew he was the closest he had ever been to proving his theory. I need to find out if he was right." Danielle moved to the couch and perched on the edge of the cushion. "I know his work was destroyed, but I've been in touch with someone on the inside. He's the man who helped Dad in China . . . his student, Lin Huan."

"Lin Huan?" Vivian sat up straighter and stared at Danielle. "Him? How . . . how did you manage to get in touch with Huan?"

"That isn't important. I told him I had the piece that led Dad to China in the first place. He seemed to know that Dad had sent something out before his arrest, but he didn't know what it was. Whenever I mention it to Dad, his eyes light up. He knows what

I'm talking about. He can hear me. He mentions Huan's name over and over again." Danielle peered across the room and at the ocean just beyond the floor-to-ceiling windows. "Anyway, Lin Huan can get me into China." She turned again and peered directly into her mother's eyes. "I-I need some money, Mom. Enough money to finance my trip." She took a deep breath. "You know it kills me to ask you, but I have no choice. Somehow, I'll pay you back."

"You know I want to help you, dear, but I'll say it again. China is not a place for Americans to be poking around these days. Not for anyone . . . even the daughter of a well-known archeologist. Your father's team was one of the last allowed in, and look at what happened to them." She turned and reached for a small but very thick, leather-bound book on the table next to her. "By the way, here's your father's journal."

A tingle shot up Danielle's spine as the book touched her hands for the first time. At last, she was holding her father's notes. Finally, she'd be able to share his thoughts and impressions before things went totally wrong for him. It had been worth having to talk to her. Slowly, she became aware of her mother's voice again.

"I'm only agreeing to help you with this trip of yours because I know you'll find some way to get to China, even if I don't help. You're as stubborn as your father when you get something into your head. Wait here while I get my purse. I'll write you a check."

Vivian walked back into the grand room holding a folded check.

Danielle took it and couldn't find words for several seconds.

"Mom, this is a check for a million dollars," Danielle said when she'd got her breath back.

"It's the least I can do, Yelle, after what happened."

Danielle wanted to scream that she couldn't be bought, but she realized how much her chances of success had just changed. "Thanks for this. I won't stay in your debt a minute longer than I have to," she said, looking at her shoes. "I have to get moving. There are a hundred details to arrange in China before I arrive."

9

Shell Cove Way, Florida

As they said an awkward good-bye, Vivian realized how much her daughter was like her ex-husband, especially the way she had hunched over his journal with the same intensity. That, and her desire to plan out as much of a trip in advance as she could. Emanuel was always one for details and back-up plans.

She and Emanuel had both taken the same anthropology class back in college.

"Are you going to major in Chinese History?" Emanuel had asked her.

"I'm not sure yet. But I got a wink and a pat on the ass from the professor, so this is an easy A."

Emanuel had been shocked by her candor. They had paired up as lab partners and Vivian had quickly switched gears when she discovered her lab partner was a brilliant student.

"So, how does a physics nerd like you end up in a Chinese history course?" she had asked him. She could still remember his answer because it had been so sweet.

"Well, I'm required to take something outside of physics to graduate. This one sounded as good as anything else."

Vivian had laughed in his face and then asked, "Are you sure it's not because you're trying to get a date with a Chinese girl from one of your physics classes?"

She'd felt bad for teasing him. She covered by asking him out on a date to make it up to him, and to copy his notes. His boldness on the date had surprised her and they had quickly become an item. Emanuel Founder may have been a nerd, but he was not a shy one.

Halfway through the term, Emanuel had decided to pick up a double major in physics and anthropology. The move stunned his physics professors and solidified his relationship with Vivian. She didn't care what her sorority sisters said, at least at first.

It wasn't until they were married that she came to appreciate how slow the wheels of academia turned. Emanuel was a gifted professor and on a tenure track within years of earning his Ph.D., but he was never going to be a rich man. The fact that this didn't bother him, bothered her as much as their middle-class lifestyle.

Vivian strolled back into her Florida mansion, deep in thought. She remembered a conversation she had overheard between

Emanuel and William years earlier, while they were working on their collaborative material. Both men had been drinking from a very nice bottle of Maker's Mark bourbon, a gift from William's father.

"Tell me about your father," Emanuel had said.

William had cleared his throat and shrugged. "He's quite a man. Until that English bitch corrupted him, he was the best man I ever knew. Fucking harpy that he hired as a secretary gave him head and then tried to blackmail him. He wouldn't give an inch and the bitch sent pictures to my mother. Mom's suicide was the talk of Providence. Couldn't believe it myself, at first. But Dad knew what he was doing. He never paid Irene a dime. She was deported to Britain after my father testified against her to the INS. Dad and I are still in touch every week. He lives on his old boat in Nantucket. Plays golf as much as possible, amazing handicap. He won't remarry. Likes playing the field too much, he says. Since his doctor put him on Viagra, he has been nailing sixty-year-olds like it's his job. Anyhow, I try to do my best to keep in shape, because he is such an inspiration."

Vivian had known William was different. They had first discovered their feelings on a ski tip to Vail in 1985. Vivian felt her pulse quicken as she recalled the weekend. It was blue-bird spring day and William had unzipped his tight one-piece ski suit, exposing his hairy chest. Sun glinted off his stylish aviator sunglasses as he carved perfect turns through Colorado's soft and forgiving late-season snow.

Emanuel was a lousy skier and as usual, only had a few runs in him before he wanted to retire to the lodge and a few hot toddies.

"I'm not ready yet," Vivian had said.

"Ski with William; god knows he has the energy," Emanuel said.

Vivian and William left him in the lodge and headed for Vail's Lionshead Gondola. The ride took fifteen minutes. William carried her skis over his right shoulder and his own over his left. She carried their poles and struggled to keep pace with his stride. They climbed aboard the gondola together and William put a hand out to stop a group of Mexican tourists from getting on with them. "This one's full," he announced confidently.

She loved his ability to take control. They rode in silence for a few moments, both staring out at the late-season snow. After a moment, she realized that William was looking openly at her tight ski pants, the black-and-neon-pink stretch material showing the curves of her legs. She shifted in her seat, turning all the way around to look out the window, giving William a better view of her body. William had taken the hint.

Wordlessly, he had pushed his sunglasses onto his forehead and unzipped his suit to below the waist. "I've thought about this for a while," he said.

Her heart pounding, Vivian moved awkwardly to her knees. The gondola was nearly at the top when he finished neatly in her mouth.

He quickly became the kind of lover Emanuel had never been. It didn't matter to her that William was one of Emanuel's co-workers and closest friends. His good looks and visible athleticism stood out all the brighter in the drab world of the university. She had been drawn in like a moth to a brilliant flame.

Although they worked in different departments at the university, the two men enjoyed co-authoring papers. Emanuel's ability to create cross-disciplinary synergy astounded the faculty. Most impressive was the work he had done on ancient Egyptian neuro-chemical processes. Emanuel was awarded a major grant for disbursement as he saw fit.

William tried to hide his embarrassment at having been left out of the award. She could tell he was upset by the aggression with which he had made love to her afterward. She was sore for days but still didn't turn him down when he came back for more. She couldn't resist him, once a day was never enough.

10

Key West, Florida

Sam walked past the t-shirt shops and bars on Duvall Street and was revolted by the smell of alcohol that permeated the air. His lunch with Danielle had been interesting. She had been very happy to see him, shocked even. This made Sam uneasy. Aside from the fact that he had never done contract work like this, it was unsettling to be headed to China under the thumb of an obvious amateur.

Then there was the matter of his dive license. Sam hadn't enjoyed the dive boat operation. He had done it because he was an elite diver and could make a subsistence living at it while he tried to put the pieces of his life back together. The revocation of his license had come much too quickly, and Danielle had been waiting to hand him a stack of cash the same day. Too much of a coincidence. There was clearly more to this.

Danielle was the closest thing he had to a lead to Axelsen, because Axelsen had known the thugs who attacked her and apparently her father. It was not crazy to assume he might also have known Danielle. Her father was none other than the Emanuel Founder he'd read about in the report. So he and Axelsen had had ties to a project called the Three Gorges Dam in central China.

And now Danielle wanted to go to China to finish her father's work. She was paying him well to assist in her private sleuthing. But she didn't have a believable excuse for why she had been attacked under the bridge. She claimed not to know the men, a fact Sam had already disproved in his mind. Her father's name had been in the file with them. He wouldn't push the issue now or she might have second thoughts about taking him to China at all. That had to be where the answers were.

Sam rounded the final corner to the famous Sunset Pier and saw Danielle standing alone, looking out to sea. She seemed too innocent to be mixed up in something illegal, so he was going to push his luck with her. He walked up next to her, purposely entering her peripheral vision so as not to startle her. She cast him a sideways glance and smiled, then focused her gaze back out to sea.

Neither said a word as the sun went down before them.

He had to admit she was pretty. Pretty and brave—but not telling him everything. He wondered why she'd sided with her father, rather than her mother after the divorce, but he decided not to get into that either. The reasons didn't matter now.

Danielle turned to meet his gaze. "When we get to the museum, I'll tell you about my father's research and the archeological expedition. You'll know everything before we go to China. I promise."

"That's not good enough," Sam said.

Danielle looked at him warily and then seemed to make a decision. "Okay. What do you want to know?"

"I need to know more about your father and why you think this theory is worth risking an illegal trip into China."

Danielle took a deep breath and looked back down at her half-empty drink. "My father believed that he was on the verge of the greatest archeological discovery since the Rosetta Stone."

"Rosetta Stone. The tablet that allowed us to translate Hieroglyphics into English?"

"Something like that. Dad believed that the Egyptians' preoccupation with the afterlife inspired a sort of cult of ancestor worship that included a belief in a resurrection, hence the mummies and the elaborate burial chambers. He and his friend, William McCrystal, believed the mummy ritual was a celebration of something long gone, that somehow an important piece of their culture was no longer available to them. They theorized that a group called the Hyksos dynasty stole the treasure of Egypt and fled with it to a place known as the 'Land of Long Water.'"

"You mean *a* treasure of Egypt, not *the* treasure. And wouldn't Egyptians referring to a 'Land of the Long Water' be talking about the Nile? What was your father doing in China? I don't get the connection."

"Most archeologists would agree with you, but my father was convinced they had it all wrong, and that the Long Water was really the Yangtze River, not the Nile. I think he was on the brink of proving his theory and turning the world of Egyptology on its head." Danielle fished for something in her bag. "And no, I didn't misspeak. I meant to say *the* treasure of Egypt."

"Your dad believed this so-called treasure was taken to China? That's thousands of miles from Egypt. Why would they do that?"

Danielle pulled out several items from inside her bag. The one that caught Sam's eye was a six-inch stone shaped like the Washington Monument. He realized with a smile that it was the other way around, the Washington Monument was shaped like this object: a perfectly proportioned obelisk. It was carved from a single piece of black stone. It seemed to absorb the light around it and it took several seconds for his eyes to begin to pick up the fine detail work carved onto nearly every inch of the surface. Only the tip of the obelisk was unadorned; its planes were polished and perfectly smooth.

He took the folded document and a worn leather journal she handed to him.

"My father started this journal twenty years ago, when he first hypothesized that the Yangtze was the Land of Long Water. He added to it every day while he was in China. The letter is a coded cry for help and the last thing he sent me. I think he was so cryptic because he knew this letter would be seen by many eyes other than mine before it left China. It appears that it worked because no one has completed his work. At least not publically." As he unfolded the first paper, she added, "The treasure is known as the *Vin de Vie*." She leaned closer and lowered her voice. "Its implications are immense, Sam. It will change how we think about the Egyptians forever. The fact that the *Vin de Vie* was never recovered has led modern scientists to dismiss it as a myth. My father is convinced it's real."

Sam lowered his eyes to the letter.

>Dear Yelle,
>
>Life doesn't always work out the way we plan; you know that better than anyone.
>
>Don't forget what I taught you about my work. If my suspicions are correct, I won't make it back to the States. Search the relics of what is commonly believed to be the Land of Long Water for the truth about the usurpers. The

> carved head of
> King Amenemhet III—the last
> pharaoh to die a natural death
> before the Hyksos took over—
> will lead you. Trust only an
> outsider.
>
> Love, Dad

After the waitress had taken their next round of drink orders, Sam folded the letter and reinserted it into the envelope. "What does it mean?" he asked, as he handed it back.

"It means that my father wants us to go to the British Museum in London."

"London," Sam said. "What do you think is there?"

"There must be something that helps make sense out of this journal passage," she said, opening the fat book with an almost reverent touch. "Start reading here."

> *Notes on Yangtze Cruse, Fall 2001*
> *We are headed toward the village of Fengdu, known as the "City of Ghosts." I've studied pictures of the demonic statutes meant to ward off evil spirits that fill the main pagoda. The whole place will be gone in a few years. Fengdu is ancient; my research indicates that it served as a Shang trading post nearly three thousand years ago. The river looked much the same*

then. The Shang dynasty rulers of this region probably picked a site that afforded the most protection from the elements. The geological record I studied shows that even then, this river flooded every ten years or so. The last time it flooded was in 1998. There have been centuries of flood control to keep river floods within their banks, but China's wrecked by floods every year in one or more of its eight major river basins. There've been six major floods since 1931. The 1931 flood killed some 400,000 people and dislocated more than 50 million people in the Yangtze and Huai River basins.

The flood of 1998 was catastrophic. It caused 19 billion dollars' worth of damage, which is a big part of the justification for building the Three Gorges Dam. Flood protection standards on the major rivers are still low, though, so it doesn't do any good to increase economic development that can just get wiped out by water.

A few of the two million people affected by the dam show their disgust for the project by drawing lines on the sides of the buildings where the water will eventually reach, nearly two hundred yards higher than its normal level.

Buildings that will soon be below the water line are already being demolished; homes that have been around for centuries are being torn down, but there were too many homes to keep up with the rising water.

Many of the boat captains skilled in navigating the river are now in a nightmare with all of the obstacles under the water.

Rural China is mostly male—a crisis created by a combination of the government's cap on birth rates and a culture that values sons more than daughters. The result is 200 million more young men than women. Tens of thousands of the men have migrated to the Yangtze, looking for employment.

The 1998 flood nearly destroyed the Chinese government as we know it. Major power shifts took place that we still don't understand. The shifts have created a regime that is willing to sink Fengdu and everything else in this valley forever. I hardly have time here to sketch the lower temple. I must return to my site: Fengdu holds the last remaining clues the Shang provided us. The Fengdu temple contains a map of an underground cave system that has yet to be discovered. The Shang wanted a place that kept their treasure safe—something underground. I thought they went too far, hiding it so well I'd never find it.

The captain of my junk says he's already having trouble navigating the river, because many of the usual landmarks have disappeared beneath the rising water. I think the site we want is very close. My Egyptian obelisk describes much of what I am looking at now, right down to the bull's-horn-shaped rock formation that demarcates the first of the three Little Gorges. If my theory is right, there'll be a rough map of the Shang temple in the Fengdu Ghost Pagoda. Supposedly, it's built over an earlier temple site.

My team is jittery, especially Lin Huan. It's probably because he's been away from home for so long. It took him a while, but he grew quite accustomed to drinking and socializing with Western women back at BU. He's been an invaluable contact with the Chinese government. I'm happy that Vivian found him personable and he's fun to be with. She had really helped him make the switch to life in the States. Maybe that's why he's acting strangely now that he's home; he's out of practice at socializing with his countrymen. No matter, it was so nice to see Vivian finally take an active role in my work again; this is the first project that's interested her in years. I think her time with Lin Huan has helped her see my attraction to the past in a new light. Huan taught her much about the mysticism of Chinese culture and its ancestor worship.

Sam looked up from the journal. "What drove him to push his theory so hard in the first place?"

"My mother, though he'd deny it if he could speak. He loves her. She drove him too hard; nothing he did was good enough. She was only supportive because of the awards and promotions he received and the publicity they generated. She thought she could make him into Indiana Jones, but she ended up with a dedicated scientist who liked his work more than her. And professors are only *middleclass* citizens. They don't have cash to burn on luxuries. She wanted money, now she has it." Danielle stared into her empty plastic cocktail glass. "The doctors say Dad's condition may be partly self-inflicted, Sam. You know . . . from the stress of not fulfilling his research project and then my mother leaving him. They say he is in a state similar to severe combat fatigue."

"But you don't believe that."

"Not after spending the last two years with him. He tries so hard to communicate with me. But all he manages are the same two words. Over and over again, he says, 'Huan' and 'journal.' William thinks that Lin Huan undermined his research and essentially stole it from him. If he's right, it means that his condition was not self-inflicted. I can't cure him, Sam"—she blinked back tears—"but at least I can vindicate his reputation."

"Where is he now?" Sam took another sip of his rum and Coke.

"In a clinic on Cape Cod. William is watching over him for me. He is a great man, my father. My mother still knows that, I think, and that's why she's bankrolling this expedition. She thinks there's something to my father's last theory, too. Maybe she thinks my finding the proof will lend credibility to her life."

"His theory is that there was contact between the ancient Egyptians and the Chinese and you want to prove that by researching his submerged site. And . . . you want to find the proof that this *Vin de Vie* stuff really existed." Sam mentally shook his head. Axelsen wouldn't have cared about old wine. He wouldn't have cared about black-market artifacts, either. He could make a fortune selling state secrets and from what Jonesy had dug up before the mission, his family was very wealthy. Nothing was adding up, but somewhere, somehow, there was a connection."

"I have to finish my father's work. This obelisk is the key. It piqued his interest in China and cemented his first grant request. It's because of this stone that you and I are having this conversation tonight."

Sam looked back at the stone he was holding. "What is it?"

"It's known as the Key of Isis. The inscriptions tell the story of Isis reviving her dead son Horus with her milk, the *Vin de Vie*, or so my father believes. It also chronicles the gathering of a massive treasure to be paid as tribute to the cousins of the Hyksos in the Land of Long Water. It is an established fact that the Hyksos emptied the royal treasury as they were driven out of Egypt. The treasure they took was never seen again, at least not in Egypt. If this obelisk is to be believed, then it's making a reference to the Shang Dynasty along the Yangtze, and not the Upper Nile, as is accepted by most archeologists. My father was so close to proving it, too . . ." Danielle looked up, one hand on the journal.

"This journal makes me feel like I'm talking to my dad, like he's okay again. He wrote down the definition of entropy, and it reminded me of his work." She opened to a well-worn page and read aloud. "Entropy: the tendency for all matter and energy in the universe to evolve toward a state of inert uniformity; inevitable and steady deterioration of a system or society."

"How does that relate to his work?" Sam asked, without looking at her. His interest was waning.

"Dad liked to tie the concept of entropy into his discussions of anthropology. 'Cultures come and go,' he'd say, 'but preserving what they leave behind must be paramount if we are to understand our privileged place in history.' The first pharaoh to die of natural causes must be King Amenemhet III, the first New Kingdom pharaoh. He was the first to live without the *Vin de Vie*; therefore, he died naturally. At least that's my father's theory. First, we have to have a look in the British Museum; then we're heading into China and up the Yangtze.

"The site is near the Three Gorges Dam. My father worked on the site for two weeks, but there's not a single entry detailing his progress in the journal. That's not like him. He was meticulous about recording the progress of a dig." Danielle leaned back to rest on her elbows. "My guess is that Lin Huan must have removed the documents . . . after he poisoned my father."

Sam gave her a long look that prompted her to explain herself. "Huan is still active in China's archeology, but he has abandoned his connections to my father and the U.S. research teams. That only makes sense to me if he was involved in whatever was done to my father."

Sam nodded and said, "The obelisk didn't satisfy the scientific community?"

"Screw the community." The words surprised her and she covered it by replacing the stone into her bag.

"How did your father manage to get the obelisk out of China?"

"He hid it inside a hollowed-out copy of his favorite book, the one that first made the case for the Hyksos-Jacob connection. William and I found it last year while going through his things. Dad's interest in Egyptology grew out of his fascination with the interaction of the Jews and the Egyptians. The biblical stories he learned in Temple never left him. He's always been fascinated by the Hyksos rulers, despite their short rule in Egypt, because they may have been the descendants of the patriarch Jacob, named in the Old Testament."

"If he can't talk to you, how do you know what the obelisk says?"

"I talked to him by phone and e-mail while he was in the field. He was ecstatic, but said he didn't plan to tell anyone about it until he'd made a complete translation." She looked into Sam's eyes. "I don't think he slept the whole time he was there because he could only work on it when Huan and others weren't around. The stone seems to refer directly to the Shang Dynasty. He couldn't translate several of the symbols on the stone. The important thing is that he was positive they were early Egyptian characters."

Sam cast her a sideways glance. "So what are Egyptian

characters doing on a Chinese artifact?"

"My father's convinced the Hyksos influenced early Shang writing and vice-versa. He believes that they were in regular contact."

"So when they were ousted from Egypt, they made the trip all the way to China."

Danielle nodded. "The biggest hurdle was getting permission to enter China and excavate in the right places. The government was in the middle of displacing entire cities to make way for the rising water, a fact they wouldn't allow to be photographed by Westerners. Despite receiving the necessary grant money, it was almost impossible to get in until a few years ago. Lin Huan's exchange program was a major step toward gaining access. Huan and my father were pioneers in such Sino-American cooperation. Dad inspired him . . . at least for a while."

Sam stared at her until she looked away.

At length, Danielle met his gaze again. "There is more than just historical value to the *Vin de Vie*."

When she didn't elaborate Sam was forced to clear his throat. "Value of what kind and to whom?"

"It depends on your motivation, I guess. My father believed that the medical community would benefit the most."

"What did he believe the *Vin de Vie* could do?"

"Extend human life . . . perhaps forever."

Sam finally broke a smile. This had taken a turn into the absurd.

Danielle's face flushed as she seemed to realize that she had lost him. She fished around in her bag and removed a pile of folded magazine pages. "This is the grant proposal my father and William put together that led to the funding of the China dig."

Sam unfolded the pages and was quickly overwhelmed with the technical jargon. He tipped the pages into the light to see more clearly and started reading slowly from the top.

> The Hyksos Dynasty was descended from Jacob, according to the ancient Josephus. They ruled Egypt briefly before being ousted violently.
>
> Almost nothing remains in Egypt to bear witness to their existence. A few tantalizing hints from the same time period have been recently uncovered in China. The following scholarly excerpts help illuminate the necessity that our theory be put to the test as soon as possible.
>
> *Cultural Atlas of Ancient Egypt:* "Avaris, the center of Hyksos life during the Second Intermediate Period, is at Tell el-Dab'a and Pi-Ramses, the delta residence of the Ramesids and Raamses of the Book of Exodus, near Qantir. Tell el-Dab'a witnessed a large influx of migrants from Asia in the Middle Kingdom and the Second Intermediate Period, leading up to the rise of the 15th (Hyksos) Dynasty. An Austrian expedition led

by Manfred Bietak in the 1960s discovered a town and cemeteries. Their discoveries included a local variant of the Palestinian Middle Bronze culture, including temples, perhaps of Seth-Ba'al and Astarte, and similar to those known from Palestine, as well as palaces and other buildings (almost all in brick), and palace gardens."

Ancient Egypt: The Great Discoveries: Page 202. "Tell el-Dab'a has been the scene of several important discoveries over recent years—none more problematic than the remains of [a] striking limestone statue, almost twice life-sized, which was uncovered in 1987 . . . A seated tomb figure, the subject is clearly an Asiatic dignitary of the early 2nd millennium BC, shown wrapped in a multi-colored shawl, clutching a throw stick to his right shoulder. Intentionally destroyed and its features completely obliterated during a subsequent period of political turmoil, the fragments had been buried in a robbers' pit sunk into the floor of a tomb chapel of the late 12th Dynasty. Although fragmentary in the extreme, the original quality of the carving was excellent . . . The Tell el-Dab'a's image is without parallel in Egypt itself, though a very similar, if less accomplished sculpture is known from 18th century BC Elba in Syria. The Tell el-Dab'a statue fragments—as much else at this site—are intriguing, and for at least one historian, David Rohl, of immense significance. According to him, they are the remnants of a cult statue of the biblical Joseph, awarded to him by Amenemhet III for the Hebrew advisor's outstanding service to the Egyptian nation during a time of great trials and tribulations."

But what, I ask you, happened to the Hyksos after their ousting? A newly discovered obelisk points toward a most fantastic possibility: They went back to China! Yes, indeed, BACK toward China. There is now reason to believe, both from the records laid down in this tablet found at Tell el-Dab'a, and from a site in China, that the Hyksos did not vanish after all. Far from it. They began an amazing journey of several thousand miles on horseback, crossing the mountains of Tibet to meet up with their Shang cousins.

What we describe as "afterlife" worship was a very real part of the ancient Egyptians' culture. What modern Egyptology has failed to grasp is that all of the afterlife worship following the exile of the Hyksos was nothing more than a sad tribute to what they had lost: the secret of the production of their holiest sacrament, the *Vin de Vie*. It is only because the records of the New Kingdom in Egypt tell a distorted story, that our current understanding is so deeply flawed. The Hyksos took an ancient secret with them when they fled. We are on the brink of capturing and preserving the greatest treasure Egypt ever produced.

Modern Egyptology focuses on explaining the customs of ancient Egypt, but misses what they themselves were commemorating. Joyful they were not. They were more likely paying tribute to what was lost and praying that their fragile secret would be duplicated for later generations. It was not to be, however. The New Kingdom Dynasty lasted many hundreds of years—from about 1550 to 1070 BC—but the truth of what their burial practices represented faded into myth and legend. By the end of the New Kingdom, the pharaohs themselves no longer believed in the *Vin de Vie*; they regarded it as no more than an old wives' tale.

But the priests knew what they had lost; they went to extraordinary efforts to preserve the story in its full context, a fact highlighted by these discoveries at Tell el-Dab'a. They knew what had been lost, and they understood what the Hyksos had done—a parting blow from a vanquished enemy that would eventually bring down the empire. The

Vin de Vie was the greatest weapon Egypt ever knew. With the elixir, the pharaoh was a living God, immortal to all but the deadliest of attacks, as discussed in the Nag Hammadi Scrolls detailing the murder of one of the earliest known pharaohs.

Our belief is that the wine was preventing cell death from occurring, thereby prolonging the lives of the pharaohs nearly indefinitely. Our neuro-chemical models confirm that this is possible and has been proven in rats. That said, keeping the cells from dying is a double-edged sword. Life can't last forever; body cells don't last forever. They die every day. Brain cells, too. Every second, about 32,000 of our brain cells die. But, if we receive immediate oxygen, we can lower those results considerably. The Egyptian scientists certainly didn't know these numbers and they didn't have the term "cell death" in their vocabulary, but they were on to something. They believed their wine kept the pharaohs alive far longer than if they didn't drink it.

Sam shrugged. "Well, I'll believe it when I see it. Exactly what did your father have in mind, while doing his excavation work in China?"

"He felt he was close to proving that the Egyptian's ceremonial wine held clues to unraveling the secrets behind cell death. The wine was all my father and William could talk about before he left for China." She placed a hand on Sam's arm and fixed her green eyes on his face. "The wine is still William's passion and I know it is my father's, too. I see it in his eyes every time I look at him. He . . . he wants so badly to communicate his thoughts to me . . . and he can't."

The sun had set over Key West and a cold ocean breeze blew over the pier. Sam sat in his worn t-shirt, unaffected by the breeze. Danielle zipped her white-and-yellow Key West sweatshirt up and pulled the strings in close around the hood. Sam signaled the waitress and ordered two more drinks, one rum punch, one club soda. She was buzzed on only two drinks, and he wanted to gauge her reaction to the rest of what he needed to tell her.

"You seem to know a lot about me. Why?" Sam asked.

"William and I did some research on local divers. He thought you sounded like the most qualified." Her answer seemed plausible, but convenient. He hated convenient answers.

"Is that right? Did your friend William tell you anything about why I'm stuck on this fucking island?"

She didn't respond.

Sam took a breath. "There are things you should probably know about me. My SEAL unit was wiped out during a mission to North Korea. I was shot."

"William told me that much."

"Somehow your father and the Three Gorges Dam are involved, I know that now. I only remember bits and pieces of the mission. But I damn sure remember I didn't think the man in charge of our team was trustworthy. I was openly against the mission from the first briefing until we were about to make our jump. And now my men are dead."

Danielle didn't respond at first, she seemed embarrassed. Finally she reached over and put her hand on his forearm. The gesture was the first pleasurable human contact he could remember in a long time and it prompted him to keep going. He stared out to sea, his eyes focused on the failing blue-green light where sky met sea. "Anyway, I've read the official version a hundred times and it's at odds with what little I can recall. The early part of the mission is vivid: We flew into a terrible storm. Despite the weather, we executed a HALO jump, as planned—"

"A what?" she asked.

"It means High Altitude Low Opening jump. We use it to avoid radar detection. Basically, you jump out above the range of enemy radar and then free-fall all the way through it, opening your chute at the last possible second."

"Sounds fun," Danielle said. For a second she seemed serious.

"Anyway, we were in the belly of a Lockheed Martin C5-B, a massive military cargo plane. My commanding officer, Jonathan Axelsen, was struggling in the turbulence to plug a radio connection into his iPod. His music shattered the team's concentration. I remember them looking around at me for guidance, but I didn't know what to do, either. I remember yelling something like, 'Request permission to turn this shit off!'"

Axelsen refused. He just sat there looking at intel pictures of the Pleasure Palace built by Kim Jong Il, now used by his son Kim Jong-un. "Music gets the boys psyched," he said.

"I considered my options. The rules were clear. I had to show good cause to abort the mission, and a commander playing heavy metal hardly qualified. I would have been court-martialed if I'd scrapped that close to our jump. But following Axelsen into North Korea felt like suicide. So, with his crazy shit music blaring inside my helmet, I thought about the detailed follow-up to a formal grievance I'd already filed on Axelsen, which was about Axelsen's behavior, stupid stuff like the iPhone crap—sloppy leadership procedures—but mostly his unnecessary use of force, but I hadn't filed it. I'd hoped to prove he'd stolen equipment; that would have been plenty."

Danielle smiled, frowned and said, "It doesn't sound like you had any choice."

Sam snorted. "I knew I'd look like a bitter second-in-command, eager to get even. I'd made the decision before the mission to wait until I had more. Nothing was more important than protecting the rest of my unit. So I tried to focus on what lay ahead—the Pleasure Palace and the weather modification weapons that Axelsen had told our commanding officers about from his last mission. And just like that, the pilot came over the speakers and told us we were approaching rough weather; it was time for an immediate HALO jump.

"A few seconds later, the cargo hatch opened behind us and the countdown to jump started. Axelsen switched off the music and moved to the edge of the hatch. He turned to face the unit without securing himself to the place as protocol required. One wrong bump and he could have been sucked out of the plane before the rest of the unit was ready to jump, blowing the entire mission before it ever got started. I prayed for some turbulence to shake the plane and even considered pushing him out myself."

"'Let's go have some fun,' that's what the bastard said before he turned toward the open hatch. The unit lined up behind him expecting a countdown. Instead, he ran the final five feet and jumped out of the back of the plane. The rest of the unit scrambled after him. The twenty-thousand-foot descent into enemy waters was over in a matter of minutes.

"The jump allowed us to avoid enemy radar and our raft trip into Pyongyang went fine, other than the fact that it rained so hard we thought our rafts would scuttle. My team had studied the beach terrain and the landing procedures as carefully as we could for a rush mission like this. If there was going to be a surprise, the beach was the surest spot. There wasn't anybody there, though, and we made it fast into the city to a sewer grate."

Danielle's light eyes didn't leave his face for a second, and her hand was still on his arm.

He cleared his throat and continued, "The seven-story building in the pictures looked like any other office building in the world: It had a gray stone façade, rows of square glass windows, and a flat roof topped with radio antenna . . . nothing to betray the horrors inside. We'd studied photos smuggled out of North Korea that showed Kim Jong Il's taste in interior decorating—the gaudier the better. His son hadn't changed a thing. The place looked just as it had when the elder Kim died. The palace was home to the Joy Brigade—young women and girls whose sole function was to entertain Kim Jong Il and his top advisors. It also housed many of North Korea's secret military projects.

"Axelsen lifted the sewer grate alone, then sent the unit into the stinking hole. Once in the sewer, he led us through the labyrinth to the exact spot under the Pleasure Palace where we were to go in. I was surprised that Axelsen hadn't needed to check his GPS unit a single time; he had evidently memorized the route. He set the specialized demolition charges and with a flick of his thumb detonated the device. I was the first man to crawl through the hole it made just after the concrete dust had settled. That's the last thing I remember. I woke up in the hospital." Sam took a long sip of his flat club soda. "What I can't figure out is how Axelsen had known Chris and Mike McCrystal."

Danielle looked up sharply but said nothing.

Sam went on, "I need to find out how and why they had met in Key West. If Axelsen was selling them weapons illegally, I can add that to my report."

"I'll do whatever I can to help," Danielle said, withdrawing her hand from his arm. Something about her tone and the way she had abruptly broken eye contact gave him pause. She wasn't telling him everything, but it didn't matter. Not yet anyway.

Two days later, Sam followed Danielle onto the plane at Miami International Airport and took the aisle seat next to her.

"First class to London's Heathrow," he said, grinning at her. "I'm liking this trip more than I thought I would. Glad your mother provided the bankroll for our adventure into the unknown."

"I'll pay her back, somehow. She was my only hope. Her guilt made her agreeable."

Sam buckled his seatbelt and smiled at the attentive stewardess. "Don't you think it's about time you told me the details, Danielle? You can begin with explaining why we sent our diving gear ahead of us and what we're going to do it after we pick it up in China."

"We won't need it on the first leg of our trip." She reached into her purse and pulled out an envelope, handing it to him.

Sam opened it and began reading through the first of several documents detailing more of the science behind Emanuel Founder's work. The information was fascinating but it didn't answer his question. He looked back to Danielle and cleared his throat.

"The gear needed to go directly to China because I don't have any way to take it through London," Danielle said.

"Got it," Sam said, although he didn't. She was trying to tell him that whatever they had sent ahead to China was illegal in England. That meant that she had someone *in China* that was helping her. Interesting.

"It's better to talk about this once we have arrived safely," she said.

"Sure, no sweat," Sam said. "Let's talk about something else then."

"Like what?"

"Sports?" Sam said smiling. "Knitting? You tell me. I hate flying, talking calms me down."

"You really don't know, do you?" She said.

"Know what, exactly?"

"That I won an Olympic medal when I was in high school."

Sam was taken aback. He thought that he recognized her name, but now that she said it, he realized that she was the Danielle Founder that had taken the silver, years before. "You were just a kid when you won. Why didn't you stick with it?"

"Now you sound like my mother," Danielle said seriously.

Sam smiled in spite of himself. "I always liked women that could swim."

"Is that a SEAL thing?"

"Maybe."

Nine hours later, they shared a roomy London cab on their way across the city to the famous British Museum on Great Russell Street.

Sam couldn't help feeling excited. His missions never included museum time; this was more like a working vacation. It was his first time in England but he had read about the museum many times. He peered out the window and marveled at the bright sunshine. He had been told London was usually gray and rainy. Perhaps it was a good sign. He turned as Danielle removed her sweater and stuffed it into her oversized handbag, and couldn't help admiring her smooth, lightly tanned skin and toned shoulders.

Their cab stopped directly in front of the museum's main entrance. They had landed at 7:00 AM and cleared customs in less than an hour. The cab ride across the city had taken another hour and they were right on time for the 9:00 AM opening of the museum. Danielle purchased their tickets and they strode up the steps and through the entrance, Danielle chattering like a tour guide.

"The museum houses the most extensive collection of Egyptian artifacts outside of Cairo, Sam. This is, of course, a point of contention between the English and Egyptians. In 1882, when the French were forced out of Egypt and the British domination began, the treasures of the ancient pharaohs were deemed too valuable to be left in the custody of the local government. British leaders decided the remains of a culture as splendid as ancient Egypt's deserved preservation in England."

She guided him through the main entrance and directly toward the Egyptian wing. Sam stopped cold at the entrance to the first massive room of the Egyptian exhibit. An obelisk longer than a semi blocked his view of the rest of the room, but what stunned him was the lineup of similar monuments stretching beyond it, and this was only the first room they'd entered. "We need to keep moving, Sam." Danielle pulled on his arm.

"This collection is astounding," he said, dropping into step beside her.

She smiled and said, "It's the premier collection in the world, probably finer than what's left in Egypt. If they'd had enough time, the British scientists probably would have taken the pyramids apart and shipped them here, too. They catalogued and removed as many sites as they deemed valuable, a fact that still forces Egyptologists from around the world to visit the collections housed in London before they go on to Egypt. Their ability to safely move such monuments rivals the splendor of the objects themselves, a fact not lost on the ego of the British scientists and politicians who made the feat possible."

Sam nodded. "Exactly what do you hope to find here?"

"We're looking for a specific display in room number four of the ancient Egyptian wing. This is all New Kingdom, a few centuries after the Hyksos. These are the pharaohs that really started the monument-building that fascinated my father and William." She handed him the journal and pointed to a specific page as she stopped to examine a map of the museum. "Follow me." She strode swiftly through two more rooms, barely glancing at the marvels all around.

Sam started to read the passage aloud, and she dropped into step next to him.

Tears welled up in her green eyes; she brushed them away. "Did you notice those rough edges in the middle of the section, Sam? Several pages have been torn out. My father would always tear blank pages out of journals from the back, never the middle. The journal seems to tell a complete story, and the tone used in the last few pages seems to indicate an impending victory. Dad used phrases like 'only a matter of getting final approval for the site,' and 'so close I can taste the wine,' yet there are no detailed maps. Don't you find that odd? There are only a few rough and very general descriptions of the area of the Yangtze he was excavating. In the text, however, Dad spoke of the wine as if he had proven its existence, at least to himself."

Sam nodded. "You're right, but the site is under water. There may be nothing left. I know that's why you need me and my diving gear, and I'll certainly do what I can to help you, but I'm not making any promises."

Danielle didn't reply. She was transfixed by the contents of the display case in front of them. "This is it," she said.

Sam stared at the case for several seconds. The markings on the small tablet before him were unrecognizable. Danielle scanned the tablet methodically, then began reading it again from the beginning.

"Well, what is it?" Sam asked.

"I'm not sure yet. Give me the journal." She took the journal and began reading to herself from the passage Sam had been looking at. She looked up. "Relics from the false land of long water," She said to herself. "The 'false land' meant Egypt, obviously. The 'relics' must be a reference to this tablet. It's a Hyksos artifact, one of only a very few to have survived. It tells the story of King Amenemhet III and, most importantly, it talks about the *Vin de Vie*." She lowered her voice. "Look here."

Sam peered at the edge of the stone where the text abruptly ended because the tablet had been broken off. "The last part of the tablet is missing," he said.

"Right, but it was not always so," she said breathlessly. "This tablet was broken in 1931 when it was salvaged from the wreak of the ship that was carrying it from Egypt to England. But there was a photo taken of the tablet at the scene of its discovery. My father took me to see the photo of the complete tablet in Cairo when I was ten. He read the inscription to me. It was something that he found fascinating. It described, in Hieroglyphics, 'The three river gorges' that don't appear anywhere on the Nile."

"The Three Gorges are in China, not Egypt," Sam said smiling.

Danielle's face was alight. "Right. And my father knew that I was the only one who could make sense out of the reference. This is the confirmation I needed. He was looking for a place on the river that they obviously haven't discovered without him. The obelisk is part of the map; the rest of it was this tablet. This is why

Huan hasn't found the rest of what he needed. We need my father's maps to find the spot and then the obelisk is the key to finding the cave. We have to get the rest of his journal, and we have to get to his last dig site."

Sam smiled at her. "The journal pages that you *think* exist, and the dig site that's *under* water?"

Danielle gave him a wink and said, "Yep."

Sam was finding it hard not to like her.

11

Entropy

They had been in the air at least an hour. Sam shifted in his seat, once again glad they were traveling first class; he appreciated being able to stretch his long legs. Unfortunately, Danielle wasn't inclined to let him sleep. She cleared her throat and when he didn't respond, shook him by the shoulder.

He glanced at her and she began again, "The original papyrus maps that Dad based his theory on about Sino-Egyptian contact, Sam. I've already told you this, keep up please."

"All right, I remember."

"The copies he made are missing from his journal, but I'm sure they were there before he left for China. I think that's why he wrote me the letter. He knew I'd remember the way he had reinterpreted the maps after the tablet at the museum jogged my memory and I would know they were missing from the journal. My father was convinced that scholars have misinterpreted the originals for hundreds of years. Until his first article on the subject, every other scientist thought the maps were of the Nile and were just crudely drawn. It wasn't until he took tracings of the papyrus and placed them over maps of the Yangtze that his theory gained traction. If the maps lead to something significant in China, it will prove that his theory was accurate and lead me to the truth of what happened to him there."

"You know where his maps are?"

"With the man who stole them, Lin Huan."

Hours later, they both gazed out the small window of the plane again. "I can't believe I'm actually here." Danielle said.

The density of the cities below was cast in stark relief to the beauty of the surrounding land. The layers of rice paddies built into the hills displayed an agricultural technique unchanged for millennia.

Sam leaned over her to catch a glimpse of China from the air. "Look over there," Danielle said, pointing. "It's the Yangtze River. It's snaking its way toward the town of Fengdu."

"I know," he said. "It's about two-hundred miles upriver from Shanghai." He grinned, when Danielle cast him a glance of curiosity. "I did a little homework of my own."

Danielle tapped the window. "See that mass of concrete and steel in the middle? That's the biggest dam in the world."

The concrete structure stared back at them through the haze, a man-made ocean stretching away behind it. "It's destroyed so much," she said, almost to herself. "The key to my father's life work is buried under there somewhere." She stared out the window, oblivious to the tears that streaked her cheeks. "I'm glad you're here, Sam. Thank you for coming with me."

A voice in Chinese echoed throughout the plane, followed a second later by the English translation. Passengers were required to buckle up. Shanghai was less than twenty minutes away. Sam sighed. He wished he had his SEAL team with him. The reality of the task ahead was growing weightier by the minute. Danielle's expectations bordered on delusional. But there was no turning back. At least here he could make a difference. There would be people who did not want them snooping around. He would need to be on continuous alert.

As he and Danielle moved in line through customs, he noticed several Chinese soldiers in dark uniforms eyeing them with interest, their hard eyes taking in every detail of their Western dress. When Danielle placed her passport on the desk of the customs agent to scan into the computer screen in front of him, a look of concern appeared on his face and he spoke into a phone next to him.

Sam grimaced, preparing for the worst. To his surprise, the agents quickly motioned them through.

12

Shanghai, China

Sam helped Danielle from the cab that had taken them from the airport to their hotel. He knew she was trying to say something to him, but he could only hear every third word over the din of speeding cars, thousands of bikes that held up to four people, and hordes of pedestrians. He remembered from his reading that Shanghai was one of the most crowded cities in the world, with a population of around 19 million stuffed into an area of 4,000 square miles . . . or 86 square feet per person, a little bit more than an average-sized master bedroom back in the States. And this was often a space that held an entire family. Casting a quick glance around him at the seething city, he couldn't help but think it looked like a sporting event gone bad, with everyone rushing to find an exit at the same time.

He grinned at Danielle as she joined him in gawking at the swarming populace that seemed to know where it was going. "I feel like an elephant in a bird cage," he said, as he felt someone tap him on the shoulder and hold up a camera.

"He wants to take a picture of us," Danielle said. "They probably don't see many men your height. Maybe they think you're an alien." She laughed and gestured that it was all right for the camera-wielding man to snap a picture of them. She stood closer to Sam and smiled.

"I think he's more into your blond hair," Sam said. He placed his arm around Danielle's shoulders and pulled her close. He noticed that several of the women who had gathered to watch were smiling with pleasure. "They think we're married."

"Then I won't disappoint them by showing my bare ring finger."

Minutes later, they were in front of the hotel's desk clerk. Danielle confirmed their reservation in Chinese.

"Wow," Sam said as he entered his room. "I've had larger quarters on submarines." He reached out his arms. "I thought Japan was the country with tiny rooms."

"Sorry. I didn't want to draw too much attention."

Danielle pulled her suitcase toward the adjoining room.

"Whose attention are we trying to avoid?"

"I'm sure you knew my passport raised a red flag when we came through customs. Evidently, my father's name is on some list. He was quite vocal in his protests about the rapid flooding of the Yangtze in the Three Gorges area. He felt the government should stop the work until all the archeological teams in the area had finished their projects. I guess he made a few enemies."

Sam flung himself onto his bed, his arms and feet dangling off the edges. Her answer didn't add up. Her father had been out of the game for years. His political views had nothing to do with the fact that they were fast tracked through customs. It was Danielle that had a contact here, and she wasn't willing to share with him, yet. He changed course, saying, "I need to know more about the *Vin de Vie*. Why do you think it's real?"

"I thought you military types were used to working on a need-to-know basis."

"Sure, but I still studied detailed mission briefings before going into a hot spot."

"Of course," she said as she opened the door between their rooms. "I am totally indebted to you for being here. Let me freshen up a bit. Then I'll fill you in on our next move."

Sam stared at a stain on the ceiling. Through the thin walls, he heard a telephone ringing in Danielle's room and her soft voice when she answered it.

She was again speaking Chinese.

"Sam. Sam, wake up!" Danielle poked him in the chest. He had dozed off and it was now dark outside. He glanced at his watch and realized that nearly five hours had passed. "It's time to move," she said. "I think we've been followed. I-I want you to meet the men

William sent along to help us."

Sam peered at her through sleep-bleary eyes and blinked several times. Behind her, he saw the shapes of two men in cargo shorts and well-worn t-shirts.

Their identities came slowly into focus. *Chris and Mike.* The two men under the bridge. The two men who knew Axelsen. The two men who had sent him back to the hospital.

He sat up abruptly but otherwise stayed silent, pieces clicking into place.

Danielle was visibly upset, so an explanation would have to wait, not that he expected a very good one. She gave Sam a long look as she removed the leather journal from her bag and set it carefully on the desk, out of the eyesight of her companions.

13

Journal

Inspector Chin Na'Lee kicked open the door to the hotel room, pistol drawn.

Gray-haired and very thin, he was often treated as though he was older than his forty years. Both his enemies and his cohorts were surprised and impressed when they saw him in action. He was far more virile and able than they had imagined possible. His eyes quickly swept the small room. Except for a bed, a bedside table and lamp, and two straight-backed chairs, the room was empty.

Then he noticed the book. It was in plain view on the floor next to the bed.

"Why would they leave anything behind?" he wondered aloud. The occupants had made a hasty escape, but surely they weren't blind.

The inspector frowned. Today had been upsetting, to say the least. First, he had received the early morning call from Lin Huan, the Minister of Public Works. Then he had endured an endless barrage of questions about some so-called suspicious Americans who had arrived the day before. Finally, he had received the curt demand to find the Americans, confiscate everything in their possession, and turn it over to the minister before the end of the day. And what did he have to show for his efforts?

Striding across the room, he snatched up the book and thumbed through it, finally turning to the first page in an attempt to decipher the scrawling inside. His ability to read English was poor, but he could usually figure out a few words if they were printed clearly. The handwritten words made no sense to him, however, and with rising frustration, he motioned to a young lieutenant hovering in the doorway.

"What does it say?" he asked, flicking the page with his middle finger.

He fought to keep his voice even, as the young officer scanned the page with ease. It irritated him that so many of the younger generation knew English. They admired too much of Western culture, beginning with its movies and music. At least his young officer only read and spoke English and hadn't attempted to escape to America, as his own daughter had.

"Sir, it says that it is the journal of a Dr. Emanuel Founder." The lieutenant closed the book and held it out to the inspector.

"Founder?" he asked. That was strange; Founder was the name

that the minister had told him to be especially alert to. "Bag it up and search the room. Be thorough." As Chin Na'Lee scanned the room, he wondered why the minister was so interested in its former occupants. The spineless man had never confided anything of importance to him. All the better that way, if truth were told. That didn't mean he didn't know things, of course. He had his orders, and his team's investigations into public officials were always easier when the target's guard was down.

"There is nothing here but the book," the lieutenant said.

Frowning, Chin stalked to the door. "Get my car ready, lieutenant. You are driving me to the minister's home in Nanjing."

14

Nanjing, China

Minister Lin Huan opened the familiar leather book and gazed at the flowing script without reading any of it. His mentor had easily recognizable handwriting. The journal had been delivered an hour earlier by the insolent inspector, whose attitude never failed to irritate him. Very soon, he planned to demote the man. He didn't completely trust him.

Mingli Tsang, his newest recruit, opened the intricately carved door to his library without knocking, and strode confidently to his side. "You called for me?" he asked.

His thick northern Chinese accent put Huan on edge. It reminded him too much of his mother's accent. "Come and sit with me, my friend," Huan said. He held up the journal. "My inspector recovered this little gem from their hotel room in Shanghai."

"So you were right," Mingli said. "I still don't like it. We have foreign nationals running around with weapons that we allowed through customs. Both our careers are finished if we are unable to contain them."

"Keeping their presence unknown to others will serve us all." An uncontrollable twitch over his right eye caused him to blink rapidly several times.

"But why would she leave the book behind?" Mingli asked.

"She probably panicked,"

"You seem confident, I am less so. Let's assume that you are right," Mingli said. He eyed the journal in the older man's hands. "What hope has she of finding the cave without the book?"

Huan glanced up. "She would have studied the book to the point of absurdity. There's nothing left in it for her to discover. She hopes to throw us off the trail, no more." He said opening the journal and thumbing through several pages. "Listen to this entry in Founder's words. Listen carefully." He placed a finger on the page and read Emanuel's handwritten notes slowly, almost reverently: "'Scenes depicting the richness of the culture and the homage paid to certain priests are key themes running through the temple sites. A cask of wine is the centerpiece; the priests surrounding it suggest that it is at the center of an important ritual. The significance of the wine cask is highlighted by the following scene, in which the body of a sick pharaoh is shown drinking from the cask and regaining his strength.'"

Huan snapped the book closed. "This rambling journal is all well and good, Mingli, but it's incomplete. I have the missing pages and maps that Emanuel counted on when he came to China. I only gave him half of what I had discovered." He smiled broadly, enjoying his deception. He rested his head against the back of the sumptuous red leather chair.

Mingli Tsang sat stiffly in his chair and dismissed the rhetoric with a wave of his hand. "If the structural problems with the dam are not addressed soon we are going to have a nightmare on our hands. And you're saying that you believe this . . . this nonsense?"

"It *isn't* nonsense. Give me your support in my endeavors to unearth the proof, and I will honor both our families. Imagine proving that the Hyksos brought the wine to China. This is the greatest archeological discovery of the century."

"It's just old wine. Even if it exists, it can't be anything more than a stain on the inside of a broken pot."

"Emanuel and I thought otherwise, and we were close to proving it. If we are right, it's so much more than wine. It's the sacred elixir of the ancient pharaohs." Huan shook the journal at Mingli Tsang. His eyes flashed his resolve. "We can't let outsiders make this discovery for us!" He rose and paced the room. "All I need you to do is use your military rank to secure the site. We need to dedicate highly specialized ground-piercing radar to a fairly small area for a just a few weeks and we'll have it. It has taken all my patience to refrain from going back to America to find this journal, but my long wait paid off. I have it in my hand."

Mingli Tsang shook his head. "Shouldn't we be focused on the problems with the dam?" He pursed his lips and eyed Huan through narrowed eyes. "You really think they discovered . . . eternal life?"

"Yes, or something very close to it." Huan flipped through several pages of the journal. "Here. This is the draft of an article Emanuel was working on. Read it. You won't be so cynical then."

Mingli Tsang handed the journal back to Huan. "I do not know Dr. Founder, but you have worked closely with him on his project. If you believe there is truth is what he says, I must accept it also. What now?"

"Now that I have Emanuel's complete works in my possession, not even the Three Gorges Dam will stop us." Huan strode to his desk, pulled a handful of papers from a drawer and turned back to Mingli. "These are the missing maps and notes that Emanuel and I worked on at the end of the dig. I thought that they were all we needed to locate the final spot. But I was wrong. I needed the knowledge amassed in this journal as well. The tie to Egypt is the key."

"More on Egypt?" Mingli groaned, interrupting him. "I hate history lessons."

"You know the cliché about history, don't you?" Huan asked, glancing up from the book.

"Those who forget the past are doomed to—"

"No, no, no," Huan said, waving his hand to quiet him. "The *key* to our future resides in the past." He gestured toward two chairs by an elaborately tiled fireplace. "Let's make ourselves more comfortable. I want you to hear this. I removed the maps and drawings of the river just before Founder sent the journal away. He tricked me into believing that the maps were the key to finding the site. His final act of deceit was carried out when he mailed the rest of the journal back to the United States, robbing me of the other information I needed. The maps we worked on together were only half of the puzzle. The information he harvested from the town of Fengdu before it was destroyed in the flooding of the reservoir was vital. He was clever to avoid electronic recording of his data. A computer file or email would have been easy to find. But everything I needed was in this filthy book. Now that I have the journal back together with the maps, we can move toward uncovering the final resting place of the *Vin de Vie*." Lin Huan stretched his arms over his head in a casual gesture. "All that remains is the support of your father."

Mingli Tsang sat up straight in his chair. He was on high alert now. "My father?"

"Yes," Huan said casually. "We will need someone of his immense international stature to complete the final steps of a project this ambitious. Your father is a commander of the Nanjing Military Command, Mingli. He controls one of the seven largest regions in China. The troops at his disposal are as numerous as the entire enlisted army of the United States. He can have the radar we will need in a matter of hours, if he cares to help."

"I am aware of what my father is capable of."

"The radar technology he shared with Kim Jong-un is what we need. It will be useful in diagnosing the issues with the dam and it will help us scan the cave systems with the level of accuracy we need. He will help you, if you ask for assistance, will he not?"

"For the right price, he'll help anyone," Mingli Tsang said. He gazed into the fireplace, where the logs still produced bright flames. "You align yourself with a very dangerous man, Minster Huan." He peered intently at the public works minister. "I must admit my father is a stabilizing influence on North Korea. He claims to be the main reason Kim Jong-un listens to China but—"

Huan held up his hand to stop his rhetoric. "Yes, and that *is* a good thing. A very good thing." He returned to his desk and sat in the high-backed chair behind it. It had taken him months of behind-the-scenes maneuvering to get Mingli Tsang appointed to his staff. He had high hopes for their relationship, but so far he was finding him a disappointment. His father—the powerful Major-General Tsang—was, indeed, a dangerous man, but he was also the key to the success of his own plans. He needed Mingli Tsang to intercede on behalf of the project. He needed him to insist the general return to China. He'd been enjoying the hospitality of the North Korean's for months.

Examining Mingli Tsang through narrowed eyes, he decided he was a cowardly sort, one easily swayed. That was just as well, but he seemed incapable of exerting any influence on anyone, least of all his power father. Huan would suffer the insult of associating with him, for now.

Perhaps if Mingli Tsang's career were in jeopardy, though, his father could be compelled to intercede.

15

Poseidon

"You must think I'm a fool," Sam said.

"Look, I couldn't think of a better way to get you involved. I had to have you here. I knew that Mike and Chris were working with Axelsen. He sold them weapons and gear for this trip. We knew that you were in his unit." She paused and seemed on the verge of crying. "I have to help my father, even if it means working with people I don't trust."

He glanced at them as they paced the room like caged tigers. It didn't seem plausible to him that they had merely been roughing up Danielle because they didn't want her to make the trip to China without them. She explained that they were the nephews of Emanuel Founder's best friend and project collaborator, William McCrystal. She had always disliked and distrusted them, but

William had insisted they would be valuable to her in China. But they were just a pair of Boston thugs, petty criminals, by their own admission. The trip from Shanghai to Nanjing had taken less than ten hours but it had felt like days. Sam didn't dare broach the subject of how these two came to be a part of the mission. Once he started asking questions, he would have answers, or there would be violence. So he had kept a careful eye on everyone and spoken only when necessary. Until now. Now they were safe inside another tiny hotel room in the industrial city of Nanjing.

"Why do you trust me?" he asked.

"Once I saw the way you handled yourself under the bridge, I knew that I needed you. William was fine with it; he wanted someone along with your skills as well. Maybe this will help you uncover what was going on with Axelsen. I never met him, only Chris and Mike did. We were trying to get him involved in this project. That was what William wanted to do, anyhow."

"Well, you got me here. Now what?"

"Now we need to get moving."

Aware for the first time of how complicated a task he had agreed to undertake, Sam looked at Danielle with a new appreciation. Was she finally telling him the whole truth, or was she still not completely trusting him and his motives for agreeing to be her diver? He couldn't blame her, if the object of their mission was as valuable as her father's documents indicated. But he didn't like being taken for a fool. He believed most of her explanation for hiring Chris and Mike, but it was still far too convenient.

They were a liability, no question. But Sam was not in charge, at least not yet. He would have to stay alert to them, but not give away his complete distrust. Danielle was in over her head.

Sam cleared his throat. "What of it, you two?"

He was met with dumb stares.

He met Chris's eyes and said, "Axelsen. Tell me what you know about him,"

"Guy's a freak," Mike, the larger of the two said. "Uncle Willie hooked us up with him. He sold us a few things off the base. Willy was trying to get him to come on our little field trip. He said no, he had something better working."

The answer was not forced. These two seemed too stupid to lie well, so for the time being, Sam would accept the answer. "What did he sell you?"

Mike unzipped a large black duffel bag on the bed and opened the flaps for Sam to peer inside. It was about what he had expected; he recognized the weapons and hardware that had been missing before the mission was launched into North Korea. Some poor staff sergeant had been put under investigation with a court martial around the corner.

Danielle had apologized profusely the night before for the beating he had suffered on her behalf and assured him that it wouldn't happen again. She couldn't know how right she was. She had touched his arm, and said, "I'm sure William doesn't know it, but I believe they plan to confiscate any historical relics we find and give them to my mother to sell. She's always been strangely fond of the jerks."

Again, Sam couldn't keep from wondering if Danielle's explanations were created to satisfy his shock after waking to find Mike and Chris hovering over him in Shanghai. "How do you know where the journal's been taken?" he asked from his position near the window of their luxury hotel room. He kept his gaze on the tree-lined streets of Nanjing. The late afternoon light was softening the otherwise bright hues of autumn. The calm afternoon did little to change the explosive atmosphere in the hotel room.

"I'm sure the journal is in Lin Huan's possession by now," Danielle said, not the least bit nervous. "Huan has become quite a powerful minister in the Chinese government, but he was my father's student and worked with him closely on the research project. He . . . he knew we were coming to China."

"What do you mean he knew?" Chris asked. He stopped pacing the room and glared at her. "You a retard or something?"

"He knew, because I told him, Chris," Danielle said.

"Stupid cow!" Mike hammered his fist onto the top of the dresser. He crossed the room to Danielle's bed and grabbed her by the arm.

Sam was on them in a split-second. He swung his left hand around in a quick slicing motion, careful not to strike too hard. He wanted Mike stunned, not suffocating on the floor with a crushed larynx. The blow was adequate; Mike clutched at this throat and crumbled as Chris fumbled with the zipper to the black duffel bag on his bed. Sam had assumed he would try for a gun, and had grabbed a small lamp off the bedside table with his right hand. He hurled it at Chris's hands and succeeded in making him lose his grip on the half-drawn zipper. Sam took two large steps and swung his foot into Chris's groin with the third. He too crumpled to the floor.

"Stop!" Danielle howled. Sam moved to the bag and re-zipped it. "Listen up, Mike." She spat. "I need Sam's expertise. I can get William on the phone if you want me to, but you know he told you to follow Sam's orders, remember?" Danielle sighed and rubbed her neck. Turning to Chris, she said, "I had to tell Huan some of what I was planning. It was the only way to find out if he had betrayed my father."

"How's that prove anything?" Mike croaked through a bruised wind pipe. The baffled expression on his beefy face spoke volumes.

"If he cared about protecting my father, he would have told us to stay *out* of China, but he was delighted to hear we were coming." Danielle looked past Mike and directly at Sam. "In our conversation, I told him where to find us."

"Chink cops might kill us," Mike said. "Or worse. I'm not rotting in gook prison."

Sam watched the exchange closely. He didn't want to contradict her in front of the idiot brothers, but he had to know more. "Exactly why did you leave the journal? I thought it was invaluable to us."

"I left it because I've memorized it. What's written down has no more value to me; it's what's missing from it that I need." Danielle perched on the edge of the bed. "Lin Huan has the rest. He's had it for the last two years but never been able to use it."

"You've taken quite a gamble." Sam said. He leaned forward to rest his arms on his knees, and turned his head to watch her talk. If she were lying to him, he hoped to be able to see it in her face or hear it in her voice.

"Maybe, but I don't think so. Huan always keeps his work structured and precise. The first thing he'll do is reorganize the completed set of documents. My father's lack of order made Huan crazy." She watched as Mike and Chris stopped their continuous movement to listen. "Unless we have the hand-drawn maps, the rest of the location data in the journal is useless. Huan will read and reread the completed journal, gloating while he studies the materials. He's risked his life and reputation on this project and he'll want to celebrate." She took a deep breath. "Then, hopefully, he'll add the missing maps to the journal, to make it complete. I'm counting on it."

After a moment of staring into space, Danielle continued. "Huan destroyed the person who believed in him most to take personal credit for an unprecedented archeological discovery. He'll put the journal together and relax, thinking he's won. That's when we'll have our best shot."

"Shot at what?" Sam asked, straightening.

"At getting the journal back," she said. She reached into her duffel bag and removed a military device Sam recognized. Known as a Poseidon, it looked like an iPhone, but slightly larger. The device was satellite enabled and highly encrypted. It would work anywhere in the world. The Poseidon was especially coveted because not even the U.S. government could track them when they were set to stealth mode. The thinking had been that if the U.S. couldn't track them, enemy forces couldn't either. The catch was that several of them had gone missing over the years in failed missions, and their existence was no longer a secret. Worse, it was rumored that the Chinese had already reverse engineered one and were in high level negotiations to sell the technology to the Russians. But the fact remained that the devices worked undetected behind enemy lines. They would be invaluable in China.

Sam raised an eyebrow and said, "Axelsen get you that?"

Danielle removed the Poseidon and glanced at Mike as she tapped the Internet icon.

"Yeah, me and Chris got it from him," Mike said, answering Sam. "We got other goodies, too."

"Here we are," Danielle said, peering intently at the screen. "Huan's family has lived in the same home for ten generations. I have a virtual tour of it from this website." She tapped the screen several more times and started to read aloud. "'Like most of the cities in China, Nanjing has an ancient past. It is surrounded by hills on one side and the Yangtze on the other. Its first historical records date from—'"

"Get to the point," Mike said.

Danielle cut her eyes at him and skipped ahead. "The city flourished again during the Tang dynasty. Marco Polo may have visited the city in 1275."

"Wicked boring," Chris said, flopping onto the bed behind her and Sam. "We here for a fucking history lesson?"

"Ah-ha," Danielle said to Sam. "'The historical home of the Huan family—an architectural marvel with treasures from all around the globe incorporated into its design—may be toured by appointment. It is one of the last fully functioning historical homes of its kind in China. The home is currently occupied by an heir of the original builder.'" She held the screen closer to Sam so he could read with her. "Here's the tour we need," she said, opening the video.

Sam examined the text on the screen. He had been silently watching the odd group interact. "A tour is a horrible idea," he said.

"Why?"

"Think about it, Danielle. You want to break into the home of the minister of public works, search the premises, and then reclaim your father's journal using only a map you found on the Internet and in the presence of other tourists?" His eyes darted from hers to Chris and Mike's, who were both lying face up on the bed behind him. "With Marco and Polo here as our support?"

"Screw you," Mike said.

"Well, maybe we should simply plan a break-in. No tour. Mike and Chris have burglary experience," Danielle said. "William had to bail them out more than once. Mike actually did three years." She glanced at Sam with a sheepish look on her face.

"My point exactly," he said, shaking his head. "I wouldn't want to attempt the insertion you're suggesting with less than a six-man SEAL team. These two will either get us killed or arrested."

Danielle turned toward Mike and Chris. "Would you two mind going to your own room for a few minutes? I want to speak to Sam alone." As they left, she reached back into her bag and withdrew a rubber-banded roll of $100 bills. "Here's another twenty thousand if you'll take the lead on this." She tossed the bundle into Sam's lap. "I know it's dangerous, but I need the journal with the additional pages and I can't do this without you."

Sam grimaced as he fingered the money. He hated to take it, but he couldn't afford to turn it down, either. He wasn't drawing a Navy paycheck until he was cleared for duty. It was an impressive amount, and the destruction of his unit was clearly tied into all this. What was disturbing was that Danielle honestly believed the four of them could fend off members of the Chinese military if their presence in Huan's private residence were made known.

Danielle's robbery excursion needed his expertise, and he needed to stay in her good graces if he wanted to gain any more understanding of the demise of his SEAL unit.

"There's something you have to understand, Sam," Danielle said, crossing the room to open a bottle of Chinese rice wine on the dresser. She poured them each a glassful and turned to examine Sam's gloomy face as she handed him his. "Have you ever known the answer to something but not been able to convince anyone else of the truth of what you knew?"

Sam nodded.

"My father wasn't only a victim of the flooding of the Yangtze and the theft of some of his research. Someone, I think Huan, purposely destroyed his life. That is more personal than an archeological dig. I just can't imagine what they must have been onto, other than the *Vin De Vie*, that would justify what was done to him." She took a sip of her wine and fell silent.

"Dad and Lin Huan shared the same tent for months. Huan could have administered the poison and forced my dad to leave China. An attempt was made to confiscate the whole journal the day he was leaving and the search must have been ordered at Huan's request. But Huan didn't bank on Dad mailing his journal back to the United States to my mother the day before that. Then a year after my dad was forced to leave, Huan was appointed to his current position. Instead of slowing the rate of fill, he sped it up. I think he knew where the final site was likely to be and so he destroyed the landmarks that could point other teams to it. The entire site is submerged now, which is where you come in."

"What does the Three Gorges Dam itself have to do with this?"

"Everything comes back to the construction of the dam. Huan allowed the destruction of the only landmarks that would mark the site. The fact that he was helping displace millions of Chinese citizens probably didn't even enter into his thoughts."

Sam nodded again. "He did it because he thought he already

knew where to dig. All he had to do was eliminate the competition."

"Right. But he was off his mark. He wagered everything on his ability to outsmart my father."

Sam smiled as he said, "Wait until he gets a taste of you."

16

Mansion

After a restless night, the four Americans packed up their few belongings once more and left the hotel for their next destination—a site near Lin Huan's family mansion.

Sam saw that lines of anxiety had become etched into Danielle's forehead. "It's not too late to change your mind," he said.

She shook her head. "I can't," She said. "I won't. The site is under water, but I can still find it from the landmarks, which I'm sure will be described in the journal . . . if Huan reinserted the maps of them and we get the journal back into our hands, of course. He will be working hard to put together his own team, if he believes he has really put together the rest of the clues to the final site."

"That's assuming your father was in the right place, too." Sam opened the back door of a Mercedes taxi and waved her inside. As he piled their bags into the trunk, he noticed how heavy and cumbersome two of them were—the two that belonged to Chris and Mike. "You sit in front with the driver, Mike." He handed the driver a card with an address written in Chinese.

"The site needed to be independently authenticated by experts at the scene of its discovery. Huan was supposed to provide that for my father, but he obviously lied to him. He left my father babbling to his peers about the find of the century, without being able to provide enough physical proof." Danielle focused on the blur of images behind Sam. "His proof was this obelisk *and* the site on the Yangtze. That's why Huan has stayed quiet. This obelisk," she said, pulling the familiar black stone from her bag, "is an important clue to finding the site, but it's not the only way. With my father unable to object, Huan can take most of the credit if he finds the site without the obelisk. He will barely have to mention Dad's theory."

Sam stared out the window to mentally photograph the route the driver was taking to their destination.

At that moment, the driver pulled the cab over to the curb and gestured to the card in his hand to indicate he had taken them to the right place.

Sam pulled several bills from his shirt pocket to hand to the driver, who immediately hopped out to open the trunk. They were in the heart of downtown Nanjing. Sam strolled to the rear of the vehicle and motioned to Mike and Chris to take custody of their bags. Then, as the cab drove away, he glanced up in time to see that the driver was talking on his cell phone.

Danielle stood in front of the bell tower, which evidently marked the center of the city, and read aloud from the screen of her Poseidon. "'The hexagonal Bell Pavilion, built in 1338, houses a huge one-ton bronze bell and a memorial hall. The hall is dedicated to the two daughters of the artisan who was ordered by the emperor to cast the bell. Legend tells how, after the craftsman had made several unsuccessful attempts to produce a correct blend of metals for the bronze, the two girls threw themselves into the smelter, whereupon the composition of the alloy was miraculously perfected. As a result of this filial sacrifice, he was literally saved by the bell from certain execution.'" She glanced at Sam and grinned. "That's my new mantra: Saved by the bell. I think this is where we should meet, if anything goes wrong tonight."

She shaded her eyes from the harsh morning sun. "Huan's home is two blocks to the north. I rented office space across the street." She removed a key ring from her bag and pointed to a building across from the bell tower. "That's the one. Huan's home is behind it, near the river."

Mike shivered. "It's freezing out here, Danielle. Didn't you know the temperature this time a year? I should of worn long pants. Let's get inside." He headed across the street without waiting for her approval. Chris followed closely behind him, both hands gripping the handles of the heavy duffle bags.

Danielle continued to read from the Poseidon, as she unlocked the door to the unfurnished office and moved inside. "'The Huan home is a large pagoda-shaped building, facing the Yangtze on the northeast side of the city. A ten-foot wall surrounds the entire complex, which was built by the original owner over a thousand years ago.'" She glanced at Mike and Chris and frowned when she realized they hadn't heard a word. She gave up on them and handed the Poseidon to Sam. "Here. Maybe you'd better read this yourself."

Sam read the rest of the article:

> It's a forbidding and complex structure, even by Chinese standards. Built to stand the test of time, a great love of ancestors comes through in every perfectly preserved and cared-for detail of the massive house. Ancestor worship is a key element of Chinese culture. The notion of ancestor worship, or "filial piety," embodies a deep reverence for the honor of family. Don't miss the intricately carved wooden inlay throughout the home, the priceless jade artifacts, and especially the hand-painted urns. The Huan estate houses many prized relics of Chinese history. A

perfectly preserved set of patriarch urns containing the ashes of ancestors dating back a purported one hundred generations is on display in the home's main library. The intricately detailed urns represent a deep and lasting connection to those who helped forge the Chinese empire.

The Huan home is built around the massive library housing the relics. Each of the six entrances to the room comes from sections of the home designed to make the person moving through them feel a sense of tight security, as if the structure were there to protect those inside. Upon entering the library, the tight halls give way to fifty-foot ceilings, creating a sense of personal insignificance. Bright overhead lights draw attention first to the urns, then away to large tables surrounded by stiff-backed chairs. Oversized octagonal windows mimic the shape of the room, providing a view of the award-winning Huan family gardens.

Sam glanced at Danielle, who was staring out the windows.

"We have a good view from here," she said. "That's the south wall of the Huan home. I can see a bit of the garden behind it." She squinted. "It looks like it hasn't been tended in years. Huan's family would be disgraced to see it like that, but it may give us some cover."

"Not a bad idea," Sam said. "But how do you think we can get into the house itself, without being seen or heard?"

"Not sure," Danielle said. "That's why we're here today. To figure it out." She sank onto the floor and leaned against the wall, pulling her bag closer to her.

"You mean we're supposed to sit here and stare at Huan's wall all day?" Chris whined. "I'd rather be out in the wind."

Mike scratched at his thick beard and didn't offer comment. He watched as Sam went to the window and checked the view with that on the Poseidon. Then he leered at Danielle. "Must really make you happy that your mom takes Emanuel's theory so serious." He stood and stretched his bulky frame, bending from side to side and swinging his arms.

Danielle sucked in a deep breath. "I couldn't care less what my mother thinks about my father anymore. She was willing to come up with the money to get us here because she needs to feel better about what she did." She glanced at Chris and then back at Mike. "Don't you ever wonder why a woman like my mother helps you two?"

"Well, now, I just might be able to enlighten you on that one," Chris said, smiling at Mike. "She's been screwing my Uncle Willy for years."

Danielle blanched and Sam turned from the window with a frown.

"William would never touch my mother! He and my father are like brothers."

Mike grinned. "Old Willy's been laying pipe there for years. Might even be that he's *your* daddy,"

Danielle locked eyes with him. "Can't you see that my mother is exploiting you morons the same way she does everyone around her? As soon as she gets what she wants she'll abandon you too."

Sam found her response troubling. She wasn't addressing the fact that William might be sleeping with her mother, a reality that would taint any advice or help he was giving her. Sam didn't like the smugness he saw from Mike and Chris. Their statement about William and Vivian seemed plausible, and worse, unforced.

Mike crossed the room and Danielle recoiled from him. "Quit acting like I'm stupid," he said, his face an inch from hers. "Show some fucking respect or you'll regret it."

Mike glanced at Sam to gauge his reaction.

He obliged him with a simple statement: "If you touch Danielle again, I'll kill you myself."

Sam's decision as to the brothers best use was an easy one: Bait.

17

Silk

Sam returned to the window and stared down at the garden behind the wall surrounding the Huan estate. "I'm going down there to do a little reconnaissance," he said, turning to face his suddenly quiet partners. "I'll be back in a few minutes. All of you stay here. I'm going to get a closer look at the wall. We don't need to call attention to ourselves any more than we have already. We're probably being observed." He held up his hand to halt Danielle's protest. "I'm going alone. I don't want complications."

Several minutes later, he returned to find a solemn group waiting. Ignoring everyone but Danielle, he made his report. "I know how to get in without being detected. But once I'm inside, I'll need help to find the journal. I'll take only one of these guys with me."

"What do you mean 'one of these guys'?" Danielle jumped to her feet to confront him with her hands on her hips. "I'm the one who knows what we're looking for, so I'm the one going with you!"

"No way," Sam said, meeting her glare with narrowed eyes. "If this goes badly, we need you on the outside making decisions." He glanced toward Mike and weighed whether or not he could trust him enough to stay with Danielle alone.

"I'll go," Chris said. "Mike's not as fast."

"All right. Speed might be necessary. We leave in ten minutes. What weapons are you carrying?" Sam looked directly at Chris.

"Glock .45," Mike said, answering for his brother. "We got a few stun grenades too." He grinned.

"Leave it all here."

"Screw you, Sammy." Chris laughed nervously. "No way I'm going in there without heat!"

"The perimeter is rigged with metal detectors. Old school, but effective. Leave the gun," Sam said, annoyed by Chris's resistance to his orders. "Take off your belt and anything else metal. We'll have to leave the Poseidons here, too."

The change in Sam's voice and attitude seemed to command a modicum of respect. Danielle threw him a thoughtful look and then slid down the wall to a sitting position, without further protest.

Sam removed a coiled climbing rope from his bag and headed for the door. "You are to do exactly as I say, Chris. No going off on your own," he said.

Chris snorted and gave him a condescending smile.

"We have only one mission—to retrieve that journal. Nothing else. Don't touch anything in any room. If we run into trouble with security, get out quick. Keep your eyes on me at all times. I'll make the first entry."

Chris removed his belt and threw it next to his gun. Muttering obscenities, he handed his Poseidon to Danielle and followed Sam down the emergency stairway that faced the dark wall of the compound.

Sam moved quietly up to the crumbling wall and dropped to one knee. He could see his breath with each expiration as it hit the cold air. He glanced toward Chris, who was only a few paces behind him. After surveying the area to ensure they weren't being watched, he turned and jumped straight-up, catching the lip of the stone wall with one hand. Without pausing, he hoisted himself to the top and motioned to Chris that he was going to jump down and then toss him the rope to help him over. Seconds later, he was on the ground in the overgrown garden. He uncoiled the rope with well-practiced hands and threw one end over the wall. When he felt Chris grab hold of it, he pulled on his end, hand over hand, until he could see Chris at the top of the wall. As soon as the lumbering figure hit the ground next to him, he pulled him into the shadows and held a finger to his lips. After another quick scan of the garden, he headed for the house, pushing through waist-high brush and overhanging tree branches.

Danielle glanced from the window and across the room at Mike and saw him smirk at her. She averted her eyes and pretended not to notice when he removed his Poseidon and paused before entering his code, struggling to recall it. Unbeknown to him, she could see him in the reflection of the window mouthing his temporarily forgotten password. She had no trouble deciphering the code as he mouthed the letters S O X. He finally entered the letters and gained accesses to his e-mail account.

Brilliant, she thought, smiling to herself. *His password is his favorite baseball team.* She focused on the garden across the street and thought she could see Sam as he moved carefully from tree to tree. She fought a nervous twinge in her stomach.

Mike scanned a message from William and blinked several times as he reread it.

His confusion was slowly replaced by a grin. He tapped out a reply to William and sent it. As he pocketed his Poseidon, he chuckled aloud, knowing he was annoying Danielle.

Sam listened for any new sounds and assessed the final fifty feet of garden between their location and the house. Then, creeping as close to the manor as he could, he inched quietly from window to window, door to door, looking for one that would open. A sharp metallic click from a door in front of them froze him. Flattening himself against the stone of the house, he waited without breathing. After several long seconds, a paunchy Chinese man stepped into the garden. A flash from a cigarette lighter blinded Sam momentarily. The new arrival stared up through the swirling smoke, silent.

Sam felt his heart pounding against his ribs. He remained motionless. Only half his body was covered by shadows and bushes. Any movement could give him away. Where was Chris? He didn't dare turn his head to look for him. Shifting his eyes slightly, he took a closer look at the man. His heart beat faster with recognition. It was the face of the man whose picture Founder had stuffed into the journal, *Lin Huan.* He wore a monocle now, but his features were distinctive. He was garbed in a suit that buttoned almost to his chin and he stood ramrod straight, not moving except to bring the cigarette to his mouth and to exhale the smoke. When he finished, he tossed the butt onto an aging pile of similar smokes and ground it into the dirt with his boot heel. Then he yawned, as though he were exhausted but didn't turn to go back into the house. Sam wondered if he would leave the door unlocked and considered his options. He remembered the way Danielle had described Huan: "He's from an important military family, but he got caught up in the Western curiosity of the late 'eighties. He was at Tiananmen Square and brought disgrace on his family. It was a relief for them to send him to America to study, but he returned to China and took a menial position as the undersecretary of public works for the Hubei Provence, overseeing parts of the Three Gorges Dam project. Now he's the minister of public works. He has put himself in a position to continue the search for the truth about the Shang

Dynasty and their connection to the Hyksos."

Sam's thoughts were cut short as Huan took a step toward him. Had he heard something? Sam held his breath when he heard what sounded like a muffled sneeze near the wall. Huan's head snapped around, instantly on alert. Was it Chris? The fool. He should have left him with the others.

Out of options, Sam took advantage of Huan's distraction. He inched his way along the wall of the house, until he was within a few feet and almost directly behind the Chinese minister. He closed the final feet without a sound, slipped his arm under Huan's chin and placed the crook of his elbow over his windpipe. In one smooth motion, he cut off his air supply. He held him firmly against his body for what felt like an eternity, finally dragging him into the deep shadows behind a hedge as he went limp. Huan would live, but the headache might make him wish otherwise. Perhaps when he awoke in a few minutes, he would remember that his assailant had been generous with his life.

Sam turned the intricate bronze doorknob and pulled the heavy door open only a crack. From his earlier reconnaissance of the wall, he remembered seeing several people moving about in a room that looked like a library or study. The journal was most likely to be there.

He placed his ear to the space he had created with the slightly opened doorway.

It was quiet.

The library was down a long hall, just outside the bedroom he was about to enter. He moved noiselessly into the outer perimeter of the huge bedroom, swimming through the shadows. Every surface of the cavernous room was draped with red silk. The light breeze from an overhead fan caused the thin membrane to billow in a silent dance.

Sam hoped he could locate the journal quickly; a novice like Chris would eventually create a problem given enough time, a fact he was banking upon.

Sam circled the massive bed taking up most of the room's center and headed directly into the long hallway that would take him to the library. He didn't have much time. Huan would be awake soon. Ten more yards. He was out of practice, but the training was in his blood. From around the corner, he heard the deep voice of a man speaking rapid Chinese. When he stopped barking orders into his radio, a quick reply was transmitted back. Then total silence.

Sam ducked into a deep alcove and melded himself into the wall. He heard the speaker come into the hallway, not twenty feet ahead of him. Within seconds, he heard the familiar sound of well-worn leather against steel. The speaker had pulled a revolver from its holster. He knew someone was in the hallway with him.

The ancient floorboards moaned under the man's boots as he inched forward. His movements were measured and sure . . . probably those of a professional soldier. Ten more steps and the man would see him. Then what? He had no gun. His adversary did. All hell would break loose and he didn't have the journal yet.

Somehow, he needed to reach him before he could shout a warning or fire his weapon. Sam counted off the steps. One. Two. Three. Four—

Someone on the radio was shouting, "Mingli Tsang!" snapping the words out with an unmistakable military crispness. The man, apparently Mingli Tsang, listened to the conversation on the other end of the device without speaking. Just as quickly as he had appeared, he turned on his heel and disappeared the way he had come.

Sam sucked in a breath and moved with the same deliberation toward the library. He didn't have much time to find the journal, if it was even in the library. Lin Huan might be awake already. Maybe he was the one speaking with Mingli Tsang on the radio. Just as he was about to slip into the library, he heard a muffled but familiar voice.

Sam moved closer and put his ear to the door. It was Chris. The lumbering idiot had gotten himself captured sooner than Sam had hoped.

"I don't know what you're talking about," Chris said. "I was at that hotel across the street for a couple a days and I seen this place from the window. Thought I could slip in and get myself a souvenir. It looked like a fancy joint . . . you know, rich man's place. I don't mean no harm."

Sam chewed on the inside of his bottom lip. Chris was giving him a nice distraction, but that didn't help him if the journal was in the library. At least he was speaking loudly enough to be heard.

"What is your name?" the man who had been called Mingli Tsang asked Chris, in crisply annunciated English. "How did you get in here?"

"C-Christopher. I . . . I came in through that open door behind me. I didn't take anything, see? No weapons. Nothing. You can check me out. Why don't you six guys just let me go back to the hotel? I won't come back. I promise."

Six men. Probably security guards. Maybe Chris was smarter than he'd thought. He'd managed to slip in several clues as to his predicament. Sam crept back to the red bedroom and out the door into the overgrown garden. Hugging the deep shadows, he cast a quick glance and saw that Huan was still unconscious. Then he made his way toward the outside of the library and the open door Chris had mentioned.

Lin Huan opened his eyes to see tree leaves and sky, not the red silk billowing over his bed. It took him a full minute to remember stepping outside to gaze at the sky while smoking a cigarette. When he attempted to swallow, he felt the pain in his throat. Bringing a hand up to stroke it, he realized an intruder was on the premises. He had been choked until he passed out. Where was his security? Why hadn't they found him? Why hadn't they detected someone entering the compound? *The journal. She was after the journal.* He struggled to his feet and stumbled through his bedroom. As soon as he entered the long hallway leading to the library, he heard the voices. Good. The intruder had been caught.

Frowning with frustration over not being in full control of his body, Huan barged through the doorway and into the library, still rubbing his sore neck. He fixed his gaze on Chris. "Who is this man?" he whispered. "Wait a minute . . . don't I know you?" He squinted at Chris.

He was met by the blank stares of the guards. Chris didn't take his eyes off the floor.

A second later he rushed out of the room, moving unsteadily toward his personal study, which was located adjacent to the library. At the very moment he reached the door and placed his hand on the knob, he heard the unmistakable sound of breaking glass. He staggered into the room and switched on the overhead light just in time to see a man slipping out the broken window. He opened his mouth to shout for help but merely produced only an agonizing croak. He turned his back on the window and began searching the desk frantically, but it was too late. The journal was gone. He focused instead on fishing his keys out of his pocket. His gun was locked away in his bottom drawer.

18
Fountain

Mike had watched the capture of his brother through night-vision binoculars from the window of the office space overlooking the garden. He had seen enough. Without a word to Danielle, who still stared out the window, he quietly wrapped several ammo belts around his shoulders and stuffed as many loose shells into his cargo shorts as his pockets would hold. Without a word he slipped out the door of the office room and charged down the fire escape stairs.

He carried both his Glock .45 pistol and the M-249 Squad Automatic Weapon, or SAW. When he reached the area of the wall where he felt he had the best chance, he tossed the rifle over and scrambled his way to the other side, dislodging bricks and mortar in the process. He didn't care if anyone on the other side heard him or if the metal detectors nearby were ringing every alarm in the compound.

Chris was in trouble and it was Sam's fault.

A look of murderous rage contorted his face as he turned toward the house and his breaths came in short gasps.

Once over the wall, he grabbed his rifle, loaded the first long belt of bullets, and then dashed in a low crouch through the maze of brush, completely oblivious to the security cameras that were recording his movement. He headed directly for the tall windows that matched those on the Poseidon's screen shot of the house. Behind them was the room they called the library. Creeping behind a massive stone fountain, Mike faced the windows and tucked his Glock securely into his waistband. "This ought to wake up a few gooks, Chris," he said. "Hope I get to you in time." He set up the SAW on the fountain lip, aimed at the upper half of the windows to avoid hitting his brother and squeezed the trigger.

He swelled with satisfaction as round after round pumped out of the barrel, first smashing the glass windows and then destroying whatever was hit inside the room.

Mike fired for nearly thirty seconds before the belt emptied. He fumbled behind the fountain to reload and dropped his second ammo belt into the cold, stagnant fountain. His inexperience had cost him precious seconds. Two of Tsang's guards pinned him down with pistol fire. The trained soldiers were excellent shots and nearly hit his exposed flank as he fished his ammo out of the putrid water. He squinted through the puffs of concrete dust erupting off the ruined fountain and worked at maintaining his cool.

He raised his weapon again with shaky hands; his first brazenness replaced by a sinking fear. Several men inside the room were returning his fire. He kept his bulky frame as close to the ground as possible, while deciding to be more sensible with his remaining ammo. He fired randomly, but when one of the guards showed himself at the window, he took careful aim and saw the body collapse in a mist of blood.

Seconds after the shooting started Chris ducked behind a couch, praying he wouldn't be killed by one of the guards. They took no notice of him. The maelstrom of automatic weapons fire reverberated off the walls, and the sounds of windows breaking and furniture and vases and light fixtures blowing apart was loud enough to pierce his eardrums.

It was Mike. He was sure of it. He was opening up on these monkeys with one of the SAW's they'd brought with them. His shots were aimed into the upper half of the room; Mike didn't want to risk hitting him by mistake. He used the chaos to crawl toward the right side of the library and out of danger. The man named Mingli Tsang was returning fire blindly, shooting over the windowsill and keeping his head down. The guards had appeared from the rest of the house and were taking cover behind furniture, dumbfounded by the attack.

Chris crawled unnoticed across the floor, through the doorway of the library and into the dim hallway. Maybe he could get to another room and make a getaway before anyone realized he was gone. He climbed to his feet and dashed the final fifteen feet down the hallway toward an open door. Another volley of automatic gunfire erupted behind him. Spurred into panic mode, he slipped into the room and crouched down once again. He scanned the walls of the space and saw immediately that one of the huge plate glass windows at the far end of the room had been smashed.

A commotion at the other end of the room snapped his head around. He made eye contact with the man and recognized Lin Huan from the photo in Emanuel's journal. Huan looked back down and continued fumbling with the drawers of his desk. Chris kept his eyes on Huan as he edged toward the window, not wanting to find out what it was he was looking for. He and glanced toward his objective every few seconds, until he saw Sam motioning to him from the shadows outside. Then he ran.

Lin Huan slammed his hand on the top of the desk with a curse and tried another key. The journal was gone and his pistol was locked in his desk. He glanced up just in time to see the man from the library sliding out the window. That must mean that the shooter in the other room was the one who had stolen the journal. He was now laying down cover fire for his friend's escape. The final key on the ring opened the bottom drawer. He removed the chrome revolver that had been his father's and began loading shells. He looked back at the smashed window before him. He clicked on his radio and screamed for a report. There was a garbled response, drowned by another long volley of weapons fire.

The gunfire had stopped by the time he got to the library. Still, he opened the door cautiously, peering around it to make sure it was safe to go in. His mouth fell open in the face of the destruction of his treasured library. The random shots had spared his most important artifacts, but bullet holes in the mahogany cabinet that housed dozens of urns dating back nearly a thousand years revealed a ghastly sight.

His stomach turned and he nearly retched, but his anger bubbled to the surface and he dashed over to the nearest breakfront. He hoped to rescue some of the remaining urns, but instead had to dive to the floor as another wave of gunfire erupted from his left. The remains of his forefathers drifted like spring snow, first into his hair, then over his face. His monocle protected one eye from the falling debris, but the other filled with ash and involuntarily clamped shut.

He fought the urge to stand up and protect the sacred urns with his own body, but knew he would be cut down. Far more than his own death would be needed to appease the spirits of his ancestors now.

With wrenching clarity, Huan knew what had happened. The realization tore into him like the bullets that had slammed the urns above his head. He could feel his face flush with the heat of his anger. The Americans, again. He was still voiceless and paralyzed.

Americans were dogs; as bad as his father had said they were, and worse. Resolve hardened in him as he crawled through the falling ash and intricately painted ceramic shards. They would all pay for this crime against his family.

Huan rose to his feet and ran across the room toward the smashed windows, a seething hatred driving him to action. He had never killed before, but he hoped to change that. Covered in the dust of his ancestors, he dove out the broken window, rolled to his feet, and sighted a huge man armed with a rifle and a handgun. He was trying to reload the pistol and he looked scared. Leveling his own weapon, Huan fired one shot after the other. The shots tore into the man, spinning him like a dancer. He stood still for a moment, then crumbled into the fountain.

Huan walked to the fountain and stood shaking. "That's one down," he said as he rolled up his sleeve. He reached into the dark water and began a methodical search of the body. He stopped moments later and spat at the floating dead man.

19
Bronze Bells

Sam and Chris sprinted up the stairs of the office building to their rented space and found Danielle at the door.

"Are you hurt?" she asked.

Sam shook his head.

"Did anyone see you come here?" Her eyes swept over their bodies, fear radiating from them before they came to a halt on Sam's face.

"We're fine," Sam said, "but I don't know where Mike is. His move was reckless but effective. He distracted the entire security force and gave us time to get away."

"Where's my brother?" Chris demanded, running to the window facing the Huan compound.

"I . . . I'm sorry, Chris." Danielle said.

Chris remained silent, a bad sign. They needed him to move. Sam considered killing him on the spot but realized he could serve a better purpose.

He glanced at Danielle and could tell by her paleness that she had probably just watched Mike die. "This place isn't safe," Sam said, looking out the window. "Let's move out. Keep the rendezvous plan at the bell tower. We'll wait for an hour to let things cool down. Your pal Huan knows you're the most likely one to go after that journal, Danielle."

Danielle came closer and raised her mouth to his ear. "There's no reason to wait at the bell tower, Sam."

Sam nodded and glanced at Chris. "Your brother saved your life, Chris, but if we don't move now, his sacrifice will be for nothing. You don't have time for grieving yet."

Chris cast him a look that spoke more effectively than words. "We should make a stand here," he muttered.

"Do what you have to," Sam said. "But you won't last long alone. If you move with us, you'll have a chance at vengeance later."

Chris shrugged, a blank look on his face, and turned back to the window.

"Get your gear together. We're leaving here in the next two minutes," Sam said. He pulled Emanuel's leather journal from under his shirt and handed it to Danielle. "Mission One accomplished." He rummaged through Mike's duffle bag, selected the other Glock .45, and worked the action a few times before tucking it into his waist band. It was the first pistol he had touched since leaving his SEAL unit. It felt right in his hand, but its undersized six-shot capacity was unsettling. He would have to ensure every shot found its mark.

Within the two-minute allotment, the three were on their way down the exit stairway again. Sam went out the door first and checked the street for Chinese soldiers. The mansion guards had probably gone across the street to the hotel that Chris had mentioned. But they'd soon check out the office building and every other building adjacent to the mansion's walls. They would find no obvious sign of any Americans, but detailed forensics would surely turn up more than enough evidence to condemn them if they were captured.

Thankfully, it was almost dark and they would have an easier time slipping through the city without being seen. He opened the exit door and motioned for Chris and Danielle to follow him. According to his Poseidon map of Nanjing, the Yangtze River was less than a hundred yards to his right.

Danielle touched his arm. "I don't hear any police sirens. That's a good sign, isn't it? Huan wants to keep this quiet. It's personal with him, not a government thing."

He nodded. Stepping into the freezing rain that seemed to appear out of nowhere, he, Danielle, and Chris moved quickly down the street, crowded with swarms of Chinese citizens on their way home from work. Many carried umbrellas, but most braved the inclement weather as though they were accustomed to it.

"Let's head for the river," Sam said.

Chris glanced vacantly over his shoulder at the inhospitable wall that kept him from reaching his fallen brother, oblivious to the rivulets of rain that dripped off his chin.

Danielle tucked her hand into the crook of his arm. "Mike was a brave man, Chris, but don't make his mistake."

"He's dead because of me," Chris said, shaking free of her hand.

Sam felt a brief sense of satisfaction when they reached the Yangtze River without any difficulties. He paused to wipe his eyes and examined the rain-dimpled surface of the water. Turning to survey their immediate surroundings, he recognized three of the guards from Huan's estate pushing their way through the hoards of late afternoon foot traffic. They were heading directly toward them.

"Listen to me, Danielle, Chris. We don't have time for any discussion. Huan's guards are heading this way. We have to break up. I'll distract them and head for the water. You two stick together and stay out of sight. Stay in the shadows and make your way to the pavilion. I'll come back for you once I've lost the guards. Go now. No arguing. And Chris . . . no stunts."

Chris locked eyes with Sam and snorted. He was useless as a guardian and Sam knew it. But she was still better off with him than she was alone and Sam could buy them time. As soon as they were away, Sam walked toward the guards and made sure they saw him. He took off at a slow trot toward the river. As they closed within pistol range, he dove off to his left into the unnaturally warm—and filthy—water of the Yangtze.

The water was the dirtiest he had ever experienced. The Chinese allowed chemicals from mile after mile of factories and coal-burning power plants on both sides of the Yangtze to discharge unchecked waste into the river. Sam had read somewhere that a new coal-fired power plant opened every four days in China. Some nights, the surface of the water stayed warm even in the cold air, a result of too many chemicals freely mixed.

Sam opened his eyes momentarily, but quickly squeezed them shut when they started to burn. He clamped his mouth shut, too, but water leaked through his nose and into his sinuses and throat, bittersweet and revolting. He had trained and worked in the harshest waters in the world, but this was like free-diving into a septic system. He surfaced under a bridge and heard yelling from above. He had no choice but to swim downstream and then try to meet Danielle and Chris at the bell pavilion.

Without delay, he began the well-rehearsed routine of hyperventilating to saturate his lungs with oxygen. Thirty seconds later, he took one large breath and slipped under the water again, diving beneath the warm chemical slick floating on the surface. The water under the bridge was pitch black and icy cold. He wasn't wearing his usual diving suit and his limbs tightened against the frigid temperature of the deeper water. Five feet under, he opened his eyes and found the water was relatively clean.

He swam along the bottom of the channel with the swift

current, feeling comfortable with the familiar embrace of the water. It had been some time since he'd been on a SEAL mission and it was gratifying that his body remembered what to do. He gauged his speed to be around three knots, a trick he had learned from swimming hundreds of hours through training tunnels. He dreaded having to resurface through the chemical cocktail above him, but it was a necessity every few minutes.

Recalling the map he had studied on the flight between Shanghai and Nanjing, he estimated he needed to travel about three miles downriver before heading west to reach the center of town.

He pushed useless thoughts of Danielle being hurt or captured out of his head. He needed to focus on making his strokes as efficient as possible. His lapse in concentration had caused him to scrape his leg on a sharp piece of metal underwater. The foul water burned in the open wound but the pain cleared his head. It would do him no good to spend even a minute thinking about the details of the mission he couldn't control. Right now, he needed to put several hundred yards between himself and the bridge to ensure that Huan's security guards couldn't follow him.

Finally, Sam had to admit he was out of practice. The daily bike rides had kept him in shape, but he hadn't spent enough time in the water. The inside of his skull felt wet . . . a sure sign that he was dangerously close to blacking out. As a red curtain started to disorient him, he headed for the surface again. The putrid film washed over his face and neck as he grabbed hold of a floating board. Resting his body across its length, he peered about him.

Thousands of twinkling lights lit up the skyline. As his vision cleared, he could see that the bridge was several hundred yards behind him. He was safe . . . for now.

He had no time to waste, though. He needed to swim ashore and get to the bell tower as quickly as possible. Danielle was in more danger from Chris's irrational behavior and hot temper than she would be if she were alone. The man's mental state could cause him to do something unpredictable at any moment. Cold and wounded, Sam used a strong breaststroke to propel him to shore. Although he met and swam around many small fishing boats along the way, he was quiet enough not to attract attention. Thankfully, it was dark on the water and most of the boats had only one lantern swinging from a pole.

As he neared the shoreline, Sam headed for a dock built far out onto the water. It would provide adequate cover. Minutes later, he felt like a half-drowned rat as he crawled onto the bank under the pier. There was no sense in wasting time trying to wring the water from his clothing. It would dry fast enough in the air. The rain had finally stopped. He broke into a slow jog, heedless of the undue attention he'd draw. Climbing out of the Yangtze had taken most of his remaining strength, and if he were confronted by the police or Huan's soldiers now, his only option would be to use his weapon. He didn't relish killing, but he was good at it.

Winded, he paused in an alley opening and heaved several deep breaths. Every exhalation made plumes of steam. If the guards didn't take him down, the cold night air would. *"When you let the training take over, you live longer."* Unbidden, he heard his old SEAL commander lecture him. With shaking hands, he activated the Poseidon and peered closely at his map. He was on course but a nagging doubt enveloped him. It was Mike. In his haste to lay down cover fire for his brother, had he thought to discard his Poseidon? Sam thought not. That meant that Huan probably had it now. All he needed to do was look at the bookmarks in the map application and he'd know that the Bell Pavilion was their rendezvous.

Trucks making night deliveries lumbered through the streets and the clamorous noise of their diesel engines masked any other city sounds. Sam dashed across the potholed street and headed toward the bell tower. Without warning, a black Navigator roared around the corner from a side street, not fifty feet in front of him. Once again, he ducked into an alley and hugged the wall.

His hand automatically covered the handle of his pistol as he waited for the vehicle to pass by him. He sucked in a deep breath and held it as he was bathed in the stark light of headlights and then just as quickly plunged back into darkness. The engine of the jet black SUV idled for a moment and then roared to life again, as though the driver weren't sure where to head next.

Then the vehicle made a sharp U-turn in the street and headed directly toward the bell pavilion. Sam was alone and still over a mile from the giant bell.

High inside the ancient wooden bell tower, Danielle and Chris huddled in nervous silence, afraid they would be heard if they spoke or moved. Five minutes seemed like an hour.

Danielle stared at the giant bell and wondered if her eardrums would survive the cacophony, if it were to toll the hour. She glanced nervously at Chris and knew he was thinking about Mike.

Although the brothers were the ones who had insisted on accompanying her to China despite her protests, she still felt responsible. Perhaps if she hadn't needed the additional information she was sure Lin Huan had in his possession, she could have chosen a different plan. She sucked in a long deep breath and exhaled slowly through pursed lips to fight her growing malaise.

Once again, she thought of Sam's insistence that Chris leave his Poseidon with her. If he had carried it with him into Huan's compound, they would know about the tower hideout plan. With a shiver she realized that Mike had most likely carried *his* with him.

"Come on, Sam," she whispered to herself.

She slid over to a small hole left by a knot in the ancient ash wall of the octagonal tower, and pressed her eye to it. She didn't dare show her face in the large openings the builders had left on each of the eight sides of the tower for those looking in from the street to see the bronze bell. She scanned the street but couldn't see enough to make any worthwhile judgment. She glanced at Chris again. He was staring trancelike at the giant bell. He wasn't going to be much help.

At the sound of a fast-approaching vehicle she returned to the peephole.

"So they threw themselves in for their family, huh? Those women?"

It took Danielle a few seconds to interpret Chris's musings. He was remembering the story she had read aloud hours earlier about the making of the bell. "Keep your voice down," she said, in a whisper. "We're not safe." Her heart missed a beat as the purr of an idling engine died. The vehicle had stopped in the street directly below them. She peered through the hole again. "They're here, Chris. They found us."

"Fuck it," Chris said calmly. He rose to his feet and pulled the pistol from the holster strapped under his arm.

"Oh, god," Danielle said, taken aback by the all-too-real predicament. Sam was right. Chris was as dangerous to her as any of the pursuers. She could hear men talking as they examined the room below the ladder to the tower. How many were there? Quickly, she sent a text message to Sam on her Poseidon, before stuffing it into her pants' pocket. Then she crawled out of sight, pulling her duffle bag with her. It contained the journal and she had no intention of letting it out of her sight again. *We need you, Sam.* She thought, *I need you.*

Chris stomped to the area of the floor that opened to the ladder. He peered into the room below, leveled his pistol and opened fire.

Danielle stared open-mouthed at the unfolding crisis. They were trapped. Chris was beyond stopping now, he was deaf to the world. He didn't care if they died. The mission in China was meaningless; his life was about killing as many of the Chinese guards as he could.

Her only option was to stay hidden and hope the Chinese would be satisfied that Chris was a lone assailant.

The first volley of shots from Huan's men sent a hurricane of splinters into the upper room. Bullets ricocheted off the bell, creating a deafening noise that reverberated over and over again. She covered her ears with her hands, but it didn't do any good.

Despair replaced her fear. *I tried my best, Daddy,* she thought.

Chris ignored the head-splitting noise from the bell and the bullets that landed within inches of him. He turned away from the havoc below and withdrew his own M-249 SAW machine gun from the duffel bag. While studying the numbers on the side, he remembered the only time he and Mike had used the weapons before flying to China. It was right after they had bought them from Axelsen. He grinned at the memory of Mike unleashing round after round from the deck of William's boat.

"For you, Mike," he said, the words lost in the din of the firefight.

He spun around, tipped the barrel of the gun over the edge and squeezed the trigger. Hearing the shouts of agony below, he laughed aloud.

He released the trigger only after his ammo ran out. He flopped onto his stomach to peer down the shaft and saw several dead guards, but he reloaded the M-249 just in case more were on the way. With a bag of ammunition at his feet, his high position in the tower, and the excellent cover offered by the bell, he felt certain he had a good chance of defeating the overwhelming force outside. He reloaded and shot at the mangled doorframe below to discourage any other guards.

What he didn't expect was tear gas. Between bouts of fire, he saw the canister whip past him and immediately emit its crippling vapor. Out of the corner of his eye, he saw Danielle crawl from her cover toward their other black duffel bag and frantically dig in it for the masks they had packed inside. He felt a moment of calm expectation, but it was replaced a second later by the searing pain in his eyes. He stumbled to his feet and reached for the mask Danielle held up for him. He could see she had already pulled hers on, but that was the last clear image he had.

Too late, he pulled the mask over his face.

He lurched a few more steps and stumbled over a rope that curled on the ruined wooden platform. The trip propelled him toward the opening overlooking the pavilion. Feeling himself falling, he reached madly for the giant bell. His fingers clenched its outside edges as he swung out over the chasm. The slope of the rim was impossible to hold onto for long.

"Help!" he shrieked.

The bell swung back toward the edge of the wood platform and Danielle grabbed the back of Chris's shirt.

But as the bell swung back, she lost her grip.

Chris held for a moment, and then fell. He landed on top of a dead guard, the fight gone from him. He opened his eyes for a second and saw that Danielle had grabbed the rope that was attached to the huge striker inside the bell.

Sam heard the familiar sound of automatic gunfire and was certain it was another of the weapons carried by the McCrystal boys. The guards must have reached the tower and cornered both Danielle and Chris. At that very moment, he felt the vibration of his Poseidon. The text message from Danielle confirmed his fear. They were being fired on by several of Huan's guards. They wouldn't last long.

Summoning his strength, he sprinted toward the sound of the shots. He saw the bell tower minutes later. The geometric structure appeared totally different against a dark sky than when he'd first seen it that morning. Now it loomed, menacing, and seemed to mock him as it imprisoned Danielle and Chris. The black Navigator that had chased him and finally given up was parked directly in front of the entrance, its motor still running and its halogen lights backlit a group of soldiers pulling on gasmasks.

Hiding behind a delivery truck parked in front of a grocery store, Sam took in the scene and realized what had happened. As his eyes pierced through the fog created by the remnants of rain, he saw the smoke of what must be tear gas pouring from the tower door. Glancing up at the bell, he saw the same blue cloud swirling out. Huan's men had finished pulling on their masks and were about to enter the tower with flashlights.

He remained where he was and waited, realizing the hopelessness of his attempting to take on so many with only one pistol in his possession. Moments later, the solders came out, dragging Chris between them. He was limping, but otherwise seemed to be alive. Where was Danielle? Even if she were dead, wouldn't they carry her out, too? Maybe . . . He didn't want to speculate. He'd wait. If they came out with Danielle, he'd move on them.

Sam watched the soldiers haul out several more bodies and toss them into the rear of the SUV, but none looked even remotely like Danielle. Chris must have gone berserk. When the vehicle finally pulled away with Chris inside, he waited and watched. Huan must have left the police out of his little venture and the local citizens knew to stay away from the military.

The streets were abandoned. As the last tendrils of tear gas retreated from the entrance to the bell tower, he crossed the street and slipped inside. There was evidence of violence everywhere, but no bodies. "They're gone," he said aloud. "Danielle? Are you in here?" He started to climb the ladder to reach the bell. "It's safe to come out. Danielle!"

"Sam! In here," Danielle shouted. "I'm in the bell."

Just as Sam reached the top of the ladder, he saw her swing down from the massive striker and hang in mid-air fifteen feet above the floor. "Drop down," he said smiling. "I'll catch you."

"Can you even hear me?" he asked as he set her down and helped her remove the gas mask.

"Barely," she said, shaking her head. "I'll never enjoy the sound of bells again. They . . . they took Chris."

"I know."

"Is he still alive, then?"

"He was being dragged, but his limbs were moving."

"He went completely nuts. It was all I could do to stay out of the way."

"You did the right thing. I'm sorry for leaving you with Chris, but it was our only shot." Sam looked at the blood on the floor. "We need to get out of here. Chris will tell Huan you were with him and the local cops are sure to start an investigation of their own."

"I have a car stashed in the garage attached to the office building. So much blood," she said, blanching.

"Don't look at it." He herded her toward the door. "Let's get moving."

20

Family Ties

William McCrystal stared at his Rolex Submariner without seeing it before fixing his gaze back out to sea. His yacht, where he had been living for the past week, felt like a prison.

The call from his nephews was overdue. Even *they* should have checked in by now. Neither had been known for punctuality, but this was too long. He hadn't heard a word since receiving Mike's cryptic text message hours ago. Something had gone wrong.

"Goddamn those bumbling idiots," he complained aloud. "I should have left them to the orphanage when I had the chance." He glanced at Emanuel, who stared vacantly at him from the wheelchair. He moved his lips, but produced no words. "No good deed goes unpunished, does it?" he sneered, focusing a blank stare on Emanuel. "None of us would be enduring this if you hadn't made so many selfish decisions. I just want what's mine, what I've earned."

Emanuel struggled to speak again, but William didn't move from his spot in the captain's chair. "I've had so much on my mind I've forgotten to give you today's dose of antidote," he said, smirking. "Well, perhaps a little later."

His mood darkened. If his nephews didn't call in the next twelve hours, he would have to resort to his backup plan. He didn't relish the idea, but without control over the operation, he would not only lose the *Vin de Vie*, he would be exposed for his role.

Actually, he was glad. He was tired of waiting.

He turned the key in the ignition and felt the engine grumble to life. Smiling at Emanuel he said, "Enough of the Cape, warmer waters await."

William gunned the boat forward, steering with his right hand. Once he hit his cruising speed, he reached into an inside pocket and freed a chrome Smith & Wesson .357 revolver. He opened the cylinder and twirled it rhythmically with his thumb. With a quick move of his wrist he snapped the gun shut and put it into the pocket of his parka. He allowed his eyes to go out of focus as he stared at the bleak winter coastline of the Cape. With the sun shining like this and his eyes half closed, he could pretend that he was already gazing at the perfect blue water of Key West.

After three days in Key West, William found that he missed Cape Cod. His boat reeked of cigarettes and rum. He and Vivian had tried to share an intimate rendezvous, but neither had been up to it. The excitement was gone. Without the thrill of getting caught, sex wasn't titillating enough to interest either of them. Vivian's new husband didn't care what she did on her own time and William was beginning to see why.

Vivian couldn't stop talking about Mike and Chris. She wanted to know what he had heard from them and if they had said anything about Danielle. She'd gotten irritated when he'd insisted that he hadn't heard a thing since his last text message from Mike before he left the Cape. It was the truth, but she hadn't believed him. William had never seen Vivian so aggravated, as though what his nephews did was his fault. He had even caught her stroking Emanuel's hand while she sat with him. At least she was keeping careful track of the injections Emanuel required, which made for one less thing he needed to deal with.

Whiny women really turned him off. He wished Vivian weren't involved, but he had needed her. He was relieved when she finally left the boat to drive back to Miami. William's work bored her, she said.

Apparently, the board of regents at Boston University felt the same way. He had been passed over by the review committee . . . again. He thought for sure that his latest grant request to study the neurological effects of ancient wine would be approved. If the illustrious Emanuel Founder had written it, it surely would have been.

What mattered now was how to convince Sam Drake that it was in his best interest to bring him the *Vin de Vie*. It was the only way to salvage the situation. The ancient wine was worth a fortune and if he had control of it, his position and prestige would be assured. Best of all, he'd have something to share with Horst Mendelbaum. The wine was his way in, his shot at immortality.

In order to succeed, however, he needed convincing leverage. He knew something about Sam's sister, Sharon. Her father-in-law had pulled strings to have her treated aboard Mendelbaum's hospital ship, the *Pura Vida*. The treatments had failed, but Sam couldn't know the extent of what the admiral was keeping from him.

21

Pyongyang, North Korea

Major-General Tsang, commander of China's Nanjing military region, was a regular guest at Kim Jong-un's Pleasure Palace.

The seven-story Pleasure Palace at Pyongyang, North Korea, was the refuge of Kim Jong-un's inner circle, as it had been for his late father. Decadence and corpulence swirled into a stunningly vile synergy. In every room, Persian silks and fine furniture from around the world filled the spaces. Rare works of art had been chosen more for price than decor; they appeared out of place on the marble and gilt inlaid walls. Pornographic murals painted high overhead proclaimed the North Korean leader's lack of sophistication and taste, as did the great numbers of scantily clad young women he kept as pleasure slaves in his Joy Brigade.

The western sensibilities of visiting dignitaries found the idea of such abject human bondage offensive, but the women and girls in Pyongyang viewed themselves as lucky. It was a great honor to have the opportunity to serve the North Korean leader. No one mentioned that they were also avoiding a fate of poverty and suffering in their villages. In their North Korea, the army ate first, the Joy Brigades second, and the people starved. Sexual slavery was a small price to pay to live in the Pleasure Palace, surrounded by a failed and dying population.

As overseer of a military force as large as the entire standing army of the United States, General Tsang should have been preoccupied in China. But his influence over Kim Jong-un allowed him to spend as much time as he cared to in North Korea. As was his custom on such visits, he was being kept dutifully occupied by a beautiful young girl.

The Pleasure Palace was his favorite place to escape to when the tedium of life in China overwhelmed him. There was no finer place to relieve the stresses and complexities of his life than in Pyongyang with his young friend, Kim Jong-un, who understood his appetite for young women, unlike those fools in Beijing. General Tsang was like an uncle to Kim Jong-un. He and the late Kim Jong-Il had been friends since childhood. They had risen to power through different military organizations, but they had always stayed close. Because of his close relationship to the late Kim, and his influence on his decisions, he had been successful in preventing his own enemies in Beijing from removing him from power . . . even after his true political motives had become clear to them. They needed him to keep North Korea in line. His influence over the young Jong-un was delicate, but intact. He was one of the few outsiders that Kim Jong-un would still listen to.

General Tsang had been in North Korea for less than ten hours and the ringing of his cell phone was more than annoying. He squeezed the volume button on the device much harder than necessary when he saw the number. He hated being disturbed here, but he was one of seven major-generals in China, and only a small number of men in the Beijing government had direct access to him; he couldn't ignore the call. He pushed the girl away and rolled over to perch on the edge of his immense opium bed. Another dose of narcotics and several hours of copulation were slipping away, but he would not give up without a fight.

"Hello," he said, schooling his voice to its customary tone of authority. He activated the speaker phone function and rolled back onto the girl without missing a stroke.

"Major-General Tsang, you are needed in China." Zhu said. The sniveling bureaucrat made the comment with no introduction and no semblance of respect.

"And why is that?" Tsang asked between thrusts.

"There are serious issues surrounding the defector."

"That again? I have the defector here, you know that. I have seen to his asylum request, Beijing has no involvement."

"It must not be made public. You cannot allow the U.S. to know what you have done. We may own the majority of their debt, but we risk an act of war if they know that we have facilitated something like this," Zhu said.

"Do not lecture me on international relations. I am the only reason Kim still listens to Beijing at all. Do not forget that. Now, you have caught me in the middle of my massage. Is there anything else?"

"As a matter of fact there is. It concerns the radar system your son has requested on behalf of Minister Huan."

"Huan?" Tsang grunted. He stopped the rhythmic thrusting of his hips into the prone girl before him. "What does my son have to do with him?"

"The minister requested his reassignment and I granted it."

"You did what?"

"It is well within the purview of my office to reassign a lesser military official. He is acting as the minister's assistant. He may even be enjoying himself."

General Tsang bit back his response with great effort. This was too much. The girl looked up at him questioningly, and then reached out for his shrinking penis. He smacked her hand absently and pushed her away.

"Watch your tone, Zhu," Tsang said.

"And I have reports that Americans are exploring restricted areas without proper clearance. To what end do you imagine they are here? My guess is that they are after the defector. We have reports of a shooting. This is in your military jurisdiction but I will gladly step in if you are unable to contain the situation. I believe your son is in the middle of this with Lin Huan. He has once again interfered with our decisions regarding the Yangtze project. He has filed a request for ground-piercing radar systems on behalf of Minister Huan that has already been denied several times. I have granted his request conditionally, but I require your authorization as well if I am to postpone convening the tribunal to determine whether he has overstepped his authority."

"Alert my son that I will be back tomorrow."

"Alert him yourself."

General Tsang loosed a string of obscenities into his cell phone before he realized that the connection had been severed. When he glanced up at the bed, his girl was shrinking away from him into the huge silk pillows. The gesture made him angrier. He would be dangerous to be around tonight.

He reached for a plate next to his phone and dug around in the grayish powder with a tiny mother-of-pearl spoon. He lifted a heaping pile to his nose and inhaled hard. His eyes watered and he closed them tightly. As he exhaled he found the calm he had hoped for. Perhaps the American defector was right after all. He had predicted that there would be more to the dam project than the minister had let on. The defector's warning about the secret raid into North Korea had saved Tsang immense embarrassment. Even his close relationship to Kim would have been tested by a successful assault on the Pleasure Palace. The defector had sacrificed his own men to gain their trust. His demands were steep but not unreasonable for the benefit he had provided them. It was so rare to get an American defector anymore, they were all so brainwashed by the western media, they couldn't appreciate the quality of life enjoyed by the elite of their government's enemies. Poor fools. But this man had seen through it. He recognized that true freedom came only with power, like that enjoyed by the North Korean leadership.

He opened his eyes and looked around his lavish room. Everything was available in the Pleasure Palace; the American was particularly taken with the act of sex killing. Tsang had come to find it quite boring, but there were many who still found it to be the height of sexual release. He glanced at the girl and considered killing her for sport. No, she was still too fresh for that. He used the act only as a weapon to terrify; his gratification came from simpler pursuits.

What was interesting was how hard the minister was working to get the radar systems. Minister Huan had tried for months and been turned down. Now he had involved Mingli. Enough was enough.

"My son's military career cannot be tarnished in this way," he said to the now bored-looking girl.

Things were going to get out of hand if he didn't step in directly. Minister Huan would have known that and yet he had done it anyway. He could not simply kill the man. His family was too important. But perhaps his focus on these artifacts was worth something after all. No matter. If they were worthwhile, he would take credit for them, if they were not, he would use the failure to destroy the meddling minister once and for all.

"To think that he can intrude on my pleasure time," he said as he struggled to pull his pants over his wet legs. When would his son learn to listen to him and not fools like Lin Huan? Huan was assigned to oversee the Three Gorges Dam project, and he was completely transparent to General Tsang. Huan had personally requested that Mingli's assignment be changed from military affairs to preservation of artifacts and Tsang had denied the transfer. And now that bastard Zhu had granted it to spite him. His son had done enough damage when he leaked information to the western press on the problems with the dam. The article was etched in his nearly photographic memory: He could remember every word of it even though he wished otherwise.

> A senior Chinese official has revealed this week that cracks have appeared in the controversial Three Gorges hydroelectric dam being built on the Yangtze River. Qian Zhengying, the former Minister of Water Resources who heads an expert group on the dam, returned from a week-long inspection of the project, demanding that the cracks be "repaired fastidiously," according to the state-controlled *China Daily*. The cracks measure a maximum 1.25 millimeters across and 2.5 meters deep. Cracks had also been found in the project's permanent ship-locks and ship-lifts.
> There have been persistent rumors that the 185-meter high dam, which entails the removal of entire villages to

higher ground, is being shoddily constructed, amid reports of endemic corruption by those involved on the project. But the *China Daily* report represents an unusually frank admission that the dam has serious shortcomings and some leaders are now critical of the project. "During the past three years, concrete placement in the project has not been first class, causing a variety of related accidents and drawbacks, though the concrete process has improved, compared with previous years," Ms. Qian stated.

The Chinese government's prestigious project is costly. Officially, it is expected to exceed 24 billion dollars, but unofficial estimates say it could cost at least three times that amount. In 2000, ninety-seven officials were convicted of embezzlement from the dam fund. Activists have criticized the enforced resettlement of those whose homes lay in the 300-mile area that will form the Three Gorges reservoir. They say the flooding of the area will destroy many historic buildings and artifacts. The dam is intended to control China's notorious flooding problem, but engineers have questioned whether the dam will be effective, citing problems with sedimentation and the construction itself.

The Chinese Dam

Tsang frowned. Zhu and his other political adversaries in Beijing had used the dam reports to undermine him, forcing him to play his trump card: North Korea. His arms deals with Kim Jong-un enabled him to exert influence over the rogue nation, when it was most needed. But it rarely came to arm-twisting between him and Kim Jong-un. The boy could be volatile, like his father, but he could be made to see sense when necessary. Without their friendship, Beijing feared his godson would disrupt their lucrative relationship with America.

His own son's leak to the foreign press had been difficult to contain, but he had tied off the damage years ago and gotten Mingli's career back on track. The boy was standing on his last nerve, though, and Minister Huan had no idea the super storm he was bringing down upon himself. Old wounds would be reopened if too much digging into the dam project were allowed. Tsang had to admit the 1998 flooding of the Yangtze had been far worse than he had planned. The weather modification technology he used had been in its infancy and he had been unprepared for the level of damage he had caused with it. It had come so far since then. He knew the flood would force the construction of the dam, but the price was obscenely high, even for him. But the dam cemented his power. It was the crown jewel. The outside world knew very little about the severity of the flood, but it was widely suspected that it had nearly toppled the Chinese government. Twenty million people had lost their homes and tens of thousands had died.

"My son doesn't understand that I built the dam for him," he said shaking his head. The girl looked up at him expectantly. "It's already considered the greatest accomplishment in Chinese history . . . a marvel for the ages." Her eyes glazed over again. "Sometimes we must destroy what we love, to build what we need," Tsang said to the girl. She ignored him and instead crawled across the bed to the small plate of powder. She helped herself to a small blast, then looked at him suggestively over her shoulder. Tsang considered disrobing and joining her but he knew that things were out of control at home and it was time to go. But there was no use in letting her go completely to waste. "Be sure to visit the room of my American guest," he said. "Let him know he has one hour with you before we depart."

22

The Three Gorges

Sam and Danielle stood at the rail on the top deck of the half-empty ferry as it departed. They had been out of Nanjing for less than twelve hours and were exhausted, but not ready for sleep. "I rented a cabin," Danielle said, breaking the silence that had lasted for at least an hour. The trip from Nanjing to Chongqing had progressed smoothly, compared to the past forty-eight hours.

After removing their rental car from the garage without incident, they had driven out of the city and onto the ferryboat that was carrying them up the Yangtze, through the Three Gorges, and into the burgeoning industrial city of Chongqing. The Three Gorges Dam had opened up major shipping lanes into the inner reaches of China; Chongqing was expected to rival Shanghai as a center of commerce and shipping over the next decade.

"Why don't you grab some sleep, Danielle," Sam said, "I want to read some more of this." He held up the journal.

"I'm too wound-up to sleep. Let's change your bandage. You can't afford to get an infection." Danielle glanced at the hole in the leg of his black pants. "And you're the one who needs sleep."

"I'll be all right for the next few hours." He had to admit sleep sounded great, but they weren't far enough out of Nanjing to relax.

Danielle nodded and yawned, but she didn't move from the rail. She peered over it, toward the far bank. Sam followed her gaze.

"We're getting closer to the dam," Danielle said. "We should be there within the next few hours. I'll try to sleep, if you promise to wake me the second you see it."

"Sure thing," Sam said. He took Emanuel's recovered journal out of his pocket and flipped to a passage written when the professor had first traveled the Yangtze.

"It's the biggest dam ever built," Danielle said over her shoulder, as she headed back to her cabin. Sam's eyes lingered on her until she was out of sight and then returned to the writing in the leather book.

Sam remained on the deck a few more minutes, before stuffing Emanuel's journal into his backpack. The view of the river had improved as the fog lifted. Sounds came back muffled and close, like children whispering in an empty church. Sam inhaled deeply and exhaled slowly, watching his warm breath form a visible plume in front of him as it clashed with the cold afternoon air.

His thoughts drifted to Chris and he wondered if he was dead or alive. If the soldiers who held him captive believed he had useful information, they would keep him alive, at least for a time. He didn't really care. It was Danielle he wanted to help.

He headed down a stairway into the belly of the ferryboat boat and toward their car.

Through the window of the vehicle several hours later, Sam noticed a porthole that was either painted over or blocked by something on the other side. Frowning, he slid out of the car and strode across the space, until he was within three feet of the aperture. The window was not dirty, but he couldn't see through it. Leaning close enough that his head almost touched the glass, he realized the window was normal, but the object on the other side defied explanation. Pressing his face against the porthole, he could see the top of the Three Gorges Dam.

The cranes working at the top of the structure looked like toys. Lines from the journal played through his mind like a combat briefing:

The cranes were the largest in the world.

The dam required more cement than was needed to build entire cities.

Forty billion cubic yards of water were held by a lake two-hundred yards deep—an artificial body of water the size of Lake Michigan, formed in just a decade.

Sam remembered promising Danielle to wake her as soon as the dam was visible. He opened the door to her cabin slowly and peeked into the room. Danielle was awake. She was crying. Striding to her side, he said, "We can see the dam from the portholes, Danielle." He placed his hand on her back, but it took her a moment to acknowledge it.

She turned to him and met his gaze. "I knew we were close to it. There was no way I could sleep knowing how much this place cost my dad." She blotted the tears from her cheek with her sleeve.

Sam glanced at the porthole. "I understand."

"The ferry has stopped?"

"It's waiting for entrance into the shipping locks that will get us to the other side of this dam."

"We'll probably be here for a few hours. Are you sure you don't want to grab a short nap?" She peered at him with a quizzical look and then patted the bed. "Have a seat. Looks like you have something on your mind."

Sam settled himself on the mattress and realized he was nervous for the first time in years.

She met his gaze but stayed silent.

"I came to China with you because I wanted to get closer to Mike and Chris. I know, now, that you and your father weren't involved with Mike and Chris in the rest of their activities, Danielle. You only wanted them to help you get to China. I'd have killed them myself if I thought that it would have helped me."

She recoiled from him but he didn't care. He kept his gaze on the floor between his shoes. "I don't believe for a moment that your father's condition is an accident, Danielle. Someone close got to him and I don't think Lin Huan is the only one culpable. William McCrystal hasn't told you everything he knows. I'm not sure you can trust him. Somehow this is all wrapped together. Your father, the dam, my unit. Axelsen is the key."

"William warned me you might do this." Danielle said, rising from the bed. "He was the one who convinced me to hire you . . . because of your training. He said it was very important that I get the trip under way."

"Why? Why would he be so eager to get you involved? You don't have any training. You're putting your life at risk. He was willing to let you do that."

"William worked with my father on the article that led to the China trip. He knew as much about the research as Lin Huan and the others who accompanied my father. He wants to finish my father's dream."

"Are you sure he doesn't have another angle? Can you trust him, after what has happened?"

"I-I don't know anymore. He was my father's best friend."

"Huan was your father's friend, too."

"I know, but my dad had him figured out at the end." Danielle peered out the porthole.

"Just not in time to stop him from ruining his expedition." Sam watched her carefully.

Danielle threw him a look of desperation. "You're confusing me."

"Maybe your father was wrong about William as well."

"I don't think so, Sam. William . . ." She stopped speaking and stared at him.

"What is it?"

"You're just so . . ."

"So *what?*"

"Never mind." Danielle turned toward the porthole again.

"Finish your sentence."

"I . . . I paid to have your dive operation shut down, Sam."

"I don't care."

Danielle returned to the bed and did something unexpected: she draped an arm around his shoulders.

Sam felt Danielle's breath on his cheek. Her arm seared his shoulder, but he didn't consider pushing it away.

Without warning, Danielle leaned closer and kissed him on the mouth.

He didn't respond at first.

Then, slowly, he wrapped his arms around her and kissed her back. Their mutual need removed their inhibitions and they fell into each other as though they were longtime lovers.

Very quickly, they forgot the concrete goliath outside their window.

"The dam ruined him," Danielle said. She turned away from Sam for the first time all afternoon. "Dad was forced to float his theory to his peers before it was ready. If he waited until his research was complete, the sites would have been lost under this inland ocean. He had to come when he did, and he wasn't ready for what he found."

Sam sucked in a deep breath and tried to refocus. "We can still help your father," he said. "Tell me about the landmarks I should keep in mind once we get off this ferry."

Danielle buttoned her shirt as she crossed the room back to the porthole again, peering out at the dam before she answered. "Let's take another look at the journal, Sam. We should be able to see the first landmark right after we clear the dam."

Danielle flipped through the worn pages until she found the right passage. "There are three Gorges along the Yangtze: the Qutang Gorge, the Wu Gorge, and the Xiling Gorge. The Wu Gorge is the second one and is famous for its towering and misty mountain peaks. It says we need to look for the 'elephant trunk at the Wu Gorge.' The entrance should be directly beneath it. Dad was sure of that. But my father's radar scans from the site turned up no evidence of tunnels."

Examining his Poseidon, Sam nodded. "According to this map, the Wu Gorge is an hour up river from the dam. What type of tracking equipment do we have?" When Danielle didn't answer him, he threw her a glance to see if she were all right. "Did you hear me?"

"Yes, I heard you, but there must be something Dad missed." Danielle frowned. "There are a few GPS receivers left. Do you think we should throw them overboard when we're getting close to the Wu Gorge?"

"I have a better idea." Sam stood and tucked his shirt into his jeans. "How much cash have you got left?"

"Plenty. Why?"

"We'll need to entice the captain to make an unscheduled stop at the Wu Gorge."

Back on deck moments later, Sam located the captain's nook and gave Danielle a thumbs-up signal. They had reached the steep-walled beginning of the Wu Gorge and both were eager to spot the elephant trunk Emanuel had described in the journal.

Minutes passed slowly and they saw nothing but the bare walls of the gorge looming on either side of the ferry. A dense fog swirled overhead. The ferry moved steadily into the ever-narrowing gorge, quietly cutting through the strong currents.

"I don't see anything even remotely resembling an elephant's trunk," Sam said. "The fog may be too thick." He frowned and cast a glance at Danielle to see how she was coping. "I'm going to find the captain. Will you be all right here by yourself?"

"Of course. Bring the captain here; I'll find out how much this will cost."

Ten minutes later, Sam returned with the captain in tow. Very thin and not much taller than Danielle, he peered at his passengers with both interest and suspicion. "You wish speak with me?" he asked.

Danielle smiled. "It is very important that we stay in this position for about an hour. Would it be possible for you to stop the

The Chinese Dam

ferry, if we made it worth your while?" She pulled a wad of bills from her pocket and handed it to the seemingly flabbergasted man.

He counted the number of bills before peering up at her. "This money . . . it keep ferry operation running a few more months, but changing course very bad." He gazed off into the distance. "The rock formations . . . my father teach me to navigate by them, but most under water now. Very dangerous." He examined the money again and then stuffed it into his pants pocket. "I do as you ask. One hour." He turned and hurried back to pilot the ferryboat.

The boat slowed and then stopped closer to the western side of the gorge. The Wu was barely visible through the fog that engulfed the ferry. Only the steady lap of the Yangtze against the side of the ship broke the monotonous silence.

Bored, the other travelers on the deck shuffled about, unconcerned. Others returned to their cabins. Sam studied the fog, willing himself to see into it. Thirty seconds later, he sucked in a deep breath. He was sure he had caught a glimpse of a silhouette that could be an elephant trunk. He signaled to Danielle and pointed toward the ship's pilothouse. With only a cursory glance at the uninterested passengers, Sam slipped off his shoes and leaped over the railing.

Battling the current of the Yangtze, Sam moved slowly toward the sheer cliff walls a hundred feet from where he hit the water. He was grateful that the Navy-issue Poseidon in his pocket was waterproof. Even better, the water was clean, compared to that of the Yangtze near Nanjing.

As he reached the cliff wall, he grabbed hold of a protruding rock and peered up for the distinctive shape of the elephant trunk. It wasn't easy to see anything at first because the fog obscured most of what would be considered the body of the elephant. Moving slowly hand over hand along the cliff, though, he finally made out the shape he had seen from the ferry. He reached into his pocket for the GPS transmitter.

At that moment, Sam heard a sound no Navy man wants to hear. He didn't need to look to know what had happened. The captain had piloted the ferry into the newly submerged rocks that were once visible to navigators on the Yangtze. The hull was scraping over them. Even beneath the water, the metal on rock made him cringe.

Quickly, Sam installed the GPS device he had taken with him and started swimming back to the ferry. He emerged near the wounded boat and swam hard toward it, barely able to reach its side as the captain gunned the craft in reverse to juggle it loose from its temporary perch on the rocks. He waved at Danielle, who was leaning over the railing with a rope. She tossed it to him, secured it to the rail, and smiled as he hauled himself out of the water.

He shook violently in the cold air as Danielle wrapped a blanket around his shoulders. He was accustomed to pushing his body to its limits, and he knew he was in dangerous territory.

Below deck, he sat next to Danielle on the edge of the bed in her cabin. Dangerous assignments were nothing new, but having

Danielle with him added an element of peril he wasn't accustomed to.

Recovering the artifacts didn't seem important anymore. Protecting her was all that mattered.

He reached down and touched the area around his wounded leg. "I could use a little medical assistance, if you're up to it."

23

Northern Military Headquarters, Shanghai, China

As he prepared to enter his ice-carving studio, Major-General Tsang opened the top of a small vial containing his preferred drug cocktail. The mixture of powdered tiger bones for virility, opium for relaxation, and cocaine for clear-headedness had been carefully mixed according to his strict specifications. Well aware that widespread addiction to opium had been a significant cause of his country's downfall historically, he found deep irony in his personal love affair with the drug.

The pain it caused him served as a constant reminder of his need to stay the course against the opportunistic West.

The pleasure it evoked kept him from getting caught up in the misery he caused others.

Holding the vial to his nose, Tsang paused.

He wanted to take full pleasure in the upcoming interrogation of the American prisoner. Snorting too much of the potion would lessen the thrill. He chose to inhale only a small blast of the gray powder out of his long pinkie nail. It stung the raw membrane of his nose and caused his eyes to water, before the cocaine numbed the pain. The tiger bones quickly produced just the right amount of hallucinogenic euphoria he required.

Holding his head high, he opened the heavy door to his freezer.

Chris lifted his head with difficulty and fought another violent shudder as the man known as Major-General Tsang paced the freezing room. He peered through his puffy, bruised eyes at him and saw that the general still seemed lost in thought. He had been tied to a chair in the massive marble room for the last hour; the general had been pacing for the last ten. The room was colder than an industrial meat locker, and he was well past feeling the pain his beatings had caused. He couldn't feel his nose and his teeth chattered incessantly. He had been covered with a thick wool blanket just warm enough to keep him from dying, but now his fear of this new arrival had momentarily driven away his physical discomfort.

Ornately carved ice sculptures loomed from the walls of the room, creating a grotesque Siberian statue garden. Their smiles mocked him. Chris stared at the casually clad man who had yet to address him. He was the only one in the cooler not wearing military garb; instead, he was dressed in a dark purple, velvet jump suit. It appeared stained and seemed offensive and inappropriate.

Everyone around him snapped to attention. Although Tsang's stature seemed unthreatening, he exuded a kind of menace, because the guards avoided his gaze. Before the general had entered the room, Chris could hear his captors shuffling their feet, coughing, or even farting. Now the general's ice sculpture room was deathly silent.

The guards were in his private refuge and being here obviously upset them.

Again, Chris shuddered and fought the urge to empty his bladder.

Tsang sauntered past Chris, still ignoring him. A guard scrambled to bring a silk-covered chair to him. After seating himself, Tsang removed a thin cigar from the front pocket of his velvet suit and held it to the small gold lighter in the guard's gloved hand. Only then did he make eye contact with his prisoner through a veil of smoke.

He held Chris's gaze for a moment, then exhaled smoke into his face and glanced away. When he finally spoke, he leaned forward and whispered, "I've never liked anything conventional. Not in weapons or in sex." Chris found the comment oddly unsettling. A moment later Tsang continued in a conversational tone, "The real pleasure in killing comes from close combat, like sword play. Sex is the same way, yes?"

The guards in the room remained perfectly still, none daring to move lest they draw the general's attention. Tsang motioned to a large man in a dark trench coat that Chris had not noticed before.

As the big man approached Tsang, he ignored the other guards. Chris couldn't see his face, but his presence in the frosty room was as unsettling as that of the queer in front of him. Normally, he would relish the opportunity to jeer at a chink wearing a purple velvet jumper, but he quashed any impulse to make things worse. He had an idea of what was to come. If he were lucky, he'd pass out immediately and not have to endure any more pain.

The man halted a few feet from Tsang and pulled off his overcoat, exposing broad tattoo-covered shoulders. Even in the dim light of the cooler, Chris recognized the well-muscled arms at once. So, the bastard had survived the mission after all. He must have realized that there was a lot more to be gained playing for the other side altogether. A sense of dread like none he had ever known washed over him. He knew he was not to leave the room.

The tattooed man pulled a long sword from the sash around his waist and handed it, still sheathed, to Major-General Tsang. He smiled at Chris but said nothing.

"This sword has been in my family for five generations," Tsang said, holding it in front of him. "It took nearly fifty years to grind the blade out of jade. Four generations of a family worked on this piece as a gift to honor my family. It was presented to my great-great-grandfather.

"His ashes were stored at the Huan compound to honor both families—an honor you and your compatriots have since stolen. A sword like this . . ." Tsang paused and moved behind Chris, ". . . defies monetary worth. Many in my country would say that its value can only be measured in blood. How many would have to be sacrificed to pay for such a magnificent sword?" Tsang paused again.

Chris felt bile rise in his throat and tried not to choke on his own fear. He wished he could make himself pass out, but he had to admit the general fascinated him. He wondered if the Chinese guards could understand English.

"Of course a barbarian like you would have no problem placing a price on such an item," Tsang said, continuing his uncontested monologue. "But to a culture of more refined taste—a culture with a true appreciation for history, family honor, and an unblemished ancestry—such an item could never be sold."

Tsang grasped the ornate ivory scabbard in one hand and the gilded hilt of the long sword in the other and slowly pulled the blade free. Then, walking around Chris to stand directly in front of him, he leaned in so close Chris could feel his breath. The words stung the skin of his ears. "Many heads have been removed with this sword. I'm not sure your flesh is worthy to touch the blade. My father once told me a story about a grave robber captured at my family's burial plot."

He smiled broadly with the memory, white spittle showed at the corners of this mouth. "My father was only a boy at the time, but he was allowed to watch his uncle exact the punishment for the thievery. 'Like cutting the air itself,' my father said. To use it for an execution must seem foolish to a Westerner. But the effect on the psyche of the common man can never be overestimated. Grave robbery is a dire offense; one that must be met with the utmost intensity. That was the last time this sword was used, nearly fifty years ago."

Tsang lifted Chris's chin with the top of the blade. "Your face has lost what little color it had. That is good. You understand that your next words will decide whether you live or die."

Chris couldn't keep the tears from rolling down his cheeks. The gesture sent Tsang into a fit of laughter. "Crying like a woman will not help. You must understand, it is bad luck to sheath the blade dry. It must have blood one way or the other now. Explain what your friends hope to find in the Three Gorges and perhaps a more worthy victim can be found to soothe my ancestors."

Chris couldn't think. His brain felt scrambled. What did the man want to know? He stared at him, tongue-tied.

Tsang was calm. "Nothing? *Nothing?*" He jeered at Chris, with his face only inches away. "Are you here because of the dam?" Without waiting for an answer he said, "Building the dam was my ultimate tribute to the ancestors. Like the Great Wall, you can see my dam from the moon!"

Tsang's focus was no longer on Chris. He lowered the sword to his side and removed a red silk handkerchief splotched with dark stains. He dabbed gently at the corners of his eyes. Holding the dirty silk to his face, he spoke once more to Chris. "The dam," he said, speaking calmly, "*must* be your objective." Then, switching tactics, he spoke more forcefully. "You think you have the right to take artifacts out of China?"

"We . . . we just need wanted to make some m-money." Chris said.

"Money?" Tsang repeated, with genuine amusement. "Money from stolen artifacts? Who could possibly provide enough cash to satisfy Minister Lin Huan? Don't look so surprised, I know all about his little plot. But he wouldn't touch a black market artifact sale unless it was a ticket out of China. He's in this for fame, not money." Tsang raised his gaze to inspect the ceiling of the enclosure. "Huan must know I will have him shot on sight. Why are *you* here?"

Tsang raised the jade sword and looked at it silently.

Taking two quick steps, he swung the blade in a full arc, stopping less than an inch from Chris's throat. Winking with his right eye, he swiveled to his left, leaving the sword perched near Chris's neck. Then, in another instant, he skillfully whipped it to the right in a vicious semicircle. It made contact with an ice sculpture of a young girl. For a second, the sculpture appeared to be untouched, but before Chris could utter a sound, the visage of the innocent-looking ice-girl crashed to the hard marble floor and shattered.

Chris swallowed. "We're . . . we're trying to find the . . . the Water of Life," he said, his voice croaking with each word.

Major-General Tsang stopped in his tracks and turned to face him. "*Vin de Vie?*" he said, clearly stunned. "The American archeologist," He said to no one in particular. He turned to his cigar-lighting guard. "Get Minister Huan in here."

24

Fengdu, China

Sam and Danielle huddled on the rusty deck of the ferry. Sam knew that the next stop would probably be the last for the damaged craft and they'd need to find alternative transportation for the rest of their journey up the river. The smooth rocking of the boat lulled him, but he fought the urge to fall asleep by massaging the area around his wounded leg. The pain kept him alert to their surroundings. The remains of the ancient town of Fengdu appeared out of the mist, with only a few of its original red tiled pagodas still visible above the water.

From his reading, he knew that the Yangtze had always been the center of life in Fengdu; all commerce and visitors, strife, and even wars had come to the city from the river. Fengdu, like almost every other small fishing village on the Yangtze, had depended upon the river for its economic stability.

But the water had ultimately taken far more than it gave.

The central government in Beijing had cracked history's hourglass over the edge of the massive Three Gorges Dam, scattering the sand of countless villages like Fengdu over a man-made ocean. Only the main temple remained intact. Ugly state-built concrete houses replaced the former ancient dwellings, which were now submerged by the lapping water.

Sam closed his eyes and recalled Dr. Founder's journal notations. Fengdu had long been known as the City of Ghosts—a title the rising Yangtze had reinforced. Founder had written extensively of the popular tourist attraction high in the hills surrounding the town called the Underworld Temple. His visits predated the dam, but reflected the deep sadness he felt at the loss. He had explored the area often and had been intrigued by the grotesque statutes spread around the hills.

As the ferry neared the small town, it was clear from the new buildings that life in Fengdu was not the same.

"We'd better gather our things," Sam said, pushing himself to his feet.

Minutes later, they were on land. The first thing that caught their attention was a dead dog lying in a ditch while they were jostling with the other debarking passengers and figuring out when their car would be driven off the ferry. Several fairly young children and teenagers ran about, attempting to act as guides.

Then, a man of indeterminable age smiled broadly at Danielle, while tugging on her jacket sleeve. "You want see temple of ghosts, lady?" he asked in clear, if somewhat broken English.

Danielle smiled back, but shook her head. "Not today."

The guide tugged on her arm anyway and pulled her onto the flat stone paving that led into the village. Danielle glanced at Sam for assistance, but he merely shrugged. "Why don't we have him take us somewhere to eat? We can come back for our car." He pulled up his pant leg and examined his bloody bandage; it was in definite need of attention, a bad sign. Without warning, he shivered. He felt his forehead, noticed that he was unusually hot, and realized he might have an infection.

They made the ten-minute walk up to the temple, their guide walking briskly before them. "My name Deshi," he said. "Fengdu is city of ghosts. Temple keep spirits happy." A smile spread across his wide face again. "That and plenty rice wine!"

Sam listened to the chatter and was amazed that he could walk under his own power. The wound in his leg was throbbing now. He needed antibiotics quickly, but they could not risk entering the small clinic in the center of the town. Several Chinese troops stood guard at the entrance, scrutinizing each person who approached it. If their pictures had been distributed, they would be no match for the alert men.

They chose instead to explore for other options, and headed toward the largest building in the center of town. The outside of the Temple of Fengdu was designed as a traditional red pagoda. Its ornate carvings and graceful structure failed to warn visitors of the horror show inside. The temple's main attraction was a garden of ten-foot tall ghoulish underworld figures, an impressive display of Chinese demonology.

Sam stared at the intricate figures, impressed by the detailed craftsmanship. Some of the statues looked as though they could walk off their pedestals at any moment. He stopped in front of one—a massive male figure holding the severed heads of fallen soldiers, the sick grin on its lizard face split by a forked tongue between sharp teeth—and stumbled back into Danielle.

"Are you okay, Sam?"

Sam mumbled an explanation to her, but knew it was incoherent. His eyes rolled and he knew he was about to pass out. "Need to sit," he said, and did just that.

Faintly, he heard Danielle yelling at him. Was she underwater with him? He couldn't see her.

"Sam! Sam, can you hear me?"

Sam opened his eyes and stared directly into the eyes of the Fengdu temple's demons. Then he saw Danielle. "I . . . I think I have an . . . infection," he muttered.

Deshi helped him to his feet. "You come with me, mister. We fix. We get you Underworld Tea. Good medicine."

Deshi took them to a small hut on the edge of the village. An attractive woman was sweeping the hard-packed dirt floor. She rushed to greet Deshi and his guests and then ushered them into the one-room home. Sam perched on the edge of a cot, too weak to protest Danielle's fussing.

Deshi brought him a cup filled with something smelling of turpentine and rotten milk. "What . . . is this?" he asked, repeating the question several times.

"It called Underworld Tea," Deshi said, for the third time. "This girl, she my sister Feng. She make good tea. You feel well. Make fever go away."

Sam glanced at Danielle. "Thanks, but I don't—"

"Drink it, Sam," she said. "We don't have any other options. It can't be *that* bad. Hold your nose, if you have to."

Sam held his nose and sipped from the cup. The stinking liquid felt surprisingly soothing on his throat. As long as he couldn't smell the tea, he could manage to drink it. He gulped down the rest of it and handed the cup to Deshi.

Feng had retired to a corner of the hut and was grinding rice on a sea turtle-shaped stone.

Sam pointed at it. "Is that a rice stone?" he asked.

Deshi nodded. "It four hundred years old. Rest of old village under water now."

"You moved the stone?" Danielle asked.

"River spirit angry we move it," Deshi said, "but good rice stone hard to find."

"We need a guide to Chongqing and then back down the river," Danielle said. She turned to face Sam. "We have equipment to pick up."

Sam nodded and rubbed at his eyes. "Did you find what you

came for?"

"My father used the temple as his second landmark, just as the Shang did three thousand years ago. He knew it was high enough up the embankment to defy the rising water."

Deshi seemed to be listening.

"The ghost pagoda was built over the Shang site. The original temple site and the Wu Gorge were the markers for the cave entrance where the Shang hid the Egyptian artifacts." She looked out the door to the river. "My father sent me the pages that described Fengdu. I left a GPS transmitter inside the door of the temple. The cave entrance is halfway between the temple and the Wu Gorge."

"Sounds too easy," Sam said, pulling up his pant leg to examine his bandaged wound.

"Many scientists along Yangtze before river get too high," Deshi said. He knelt beside Sam and peered at the bloody gauze dressing. "I take you to Chongqing." he added. "I get you where you need to go. No problem."

"Looks like we've got ourselves a guide," Sam said. He felt better, almost giddy, until he burped some of the tea up. "If he can get us back to the GPS receiver with the diving gear, we may have a shot at exploring whatever is down there." Sam didn't add that if it were a trap, at least he'd have a shot at whomever had set up his SEAL unit.

"I get you there," Deshi said again. "No one know Gorge like me. I drag junk up down river all time."

"Junk?" Sam glanced sideways at Danielle. Maybe this Deshi had beaten them to the punch.

Danielle said, "They use ropes to drag their boats against the current."

"How much do you want for your help?" Sam asked.

"I do it for. . . ." Deshi darted a look at his sister, but she wasn't paying any attention to them. "I do it for a thousand U.S. dollars."

"Done," Danielle said, before he could change his mind.

Deshi didn't answer at first. He seemed to be in shock that his first offer was accepted so quickly. He peeled off the bloody and pus-coated dressing on Sam's leg and spoke to his sister.

"When can you be ready?" Danielle asked.

"I ready now," Deshi said. "Unless he want more Underworld Tea."

"I'm all set with the tea, thanks." Sam said.

Feng approached the trio and knelt beside her brother with a basin of steaming hot water. She also handed him a jar. Deshi soaked a cloth in the hot liquid and dabbed at Sam's wound. "First we clean. Then we use healing herb. Then we go to boat," he said.

Sam winced and suppressed another burp. "Thanks, Deshi. I hope you know what you're doing."

25

Northern Military Headquarters, Shanghai, China

Lin Huan stumbled into the arctic sculpture room of Major-General Tsang. He looked back at the guard who had pushed him, but said nothing. He held himself erect and smiled warmly at the general, who scowled in return. Before he could utter a word, however, another guard shoved him unceremoniously forward.

"Explain yourself, minister!" Tsang said. Then, without waiting for a response, he continued. "You have disgraced your family. You knew why the Americans were here. That Founder woman is the daughter of your former professor!"

Lin Huan peeled his eyes away from the captive American and focused on his boss. He sucked in a long, shaky breath. The memory of his forefathers' ashes sprinkling down amid the shards of priceless pottery replayed in his mind. The joy he would take in seeing Tsang's prisoner die was immeasurable. He and his comrades were responsible for breaking into his office and confiscating Founder's journal. Now, however, he needed to find a way to diminish Tsang's anger.

"This American tells me you seek more than artifacts," Tsang said.

"General," Huan began, "this man was responsible for the destruction of *thousands* of years of history. He must not be allowed to return to the United States."

Tsang's eyes widened. "This man is never leaving China." He smiled and visibly relaxed. "*You,* however, may be headed back there on murder charges."

"Murder?" Huan repeated. "Of whom?" The image of his first shooting flashed through his mind.

"This man's brother, of course," Tsang said. "Unless, that is, you have something you would like to share with me." He held the jade sword casually, opening and closing his hand on its hilt. "Perhaps you should start with the details of the *Vin de Vie*."

Huan's mind reeled as he tried to work through his options. Perhaps he could stall. "It is a long story, general; perhaps we could excuse ourselves and talk somewhere else."

"Nonsense. We will remain where we are. Our guest has been enticed to tell me some of your story. Why don't you tell me more about the work of your old professor, Emanuel Founder, and his wife."

"Of course, general." Huan could not refrain from wringing his hands, but managed to conceal the anger he felt over having the story he had hoped to use to curry favor already exposed. At this point, he needed to aim for damage control. He adjusted his monocle. He smiled. "You already know that I was a student of Emanuel Founder at Boston University, in the state of Massachusetts. I was one of the best students he had." He avoided meeting Tsang's riveting gaze. "I helped him make sense of the stories from ancient Egypt referring to the Hyksos rulers leaving for China. The Hyksos ruled in Egypt for only a short time, but they were very powerful. Historians theorize that they were descended from Jacob, who took control after Pharaoh Merneferre Ay died."

"Get to the point, Minister Huan," Tsang said. He rubbed Chris's shoulder, while eying Huan. "What does this have to do with your treason?"

Huan winced at the harsh word. Tsang was growing impatient. Somehow, he had to appease him. "The inscriptions we researched could have referred to Shang dynasty sites along the Yangtze, which would explain why the vast treasure of the Hyksos exile was never found in Egypt."

"Are you saying that you believe there is more in the Yangtze than dusty pottery shards?" Tsang appeared intrigued. "It sounds to me like you're more interested in pursuing another of your attempts to preserve archeological sites from the dam project."

Huan peered about the room and fought a shiver. The guards were standing at attention and not looking at either him or Tsang. They, too, were afraid of riling him. "My desire, General—to save the sites from the dam—stems from this project with Dr. Founder. If there are antiquities to be found, they should remain in China."

He made himself look directly at Chris, who was staring at him through angry, puffy eyes.

"It is my belief, General, that the McCrystal brothers came to China because Vivian Goldfarb, Founder's ex-wife, is bankrolling their operation." He cast another quick glance at Chris. "She knew that her husband was brilliant, but told me on several occasions that he lacked the follow-through to make a discovery of the magnitude proposed in his study. Mrs. Goldfarb showed me how weak Dr. Founder was. I knew early on that such a man should not be associated with a discovery as important as the *Vin de Vie*." Huan shifted his weight and finally met the general's stern gaze. "I worked hard to get your son appointed to my staff so I could one day bring my plan to you, but it appears that fate has brought it to you sooner."

"It is fortunate for you that this expedition brings more than dusty archeological finds, Minister Huan," Tsang said, dabbing at his eye. "I have followed your attempts to get my attention with some amusement, but involving my only son has very nearly brought you to your end." He paused to think and then smiled again. "You have actively spoken against my dam project, and for that alone you might have paid with your life, but now you shall lead me to the *Vin de Vie*." Tsang fingered the hilt of his sword and then carefully placed it on a worktable where he carved his ice figures.

With elaborate gestures, he removed a small amount of gray powder from a compartment in the orange hilt and rubbed it into his gums. Almost immediately, a dull expression clouded his eyes. Then, before Huan could even blink, Tsang giggled like an idiot, whipped the jade sword free of its sheath, and with one swift movement ruined another perfect ice sculpture. Casually sheathing the blade again, he said, "Yes, I am familiar with Founder's work. I know about the wine. What else did the Hyksos take with them, Minister Huan?"

"Surprisingly little, other than a famous black obelisk, The Key of Isis." Huan cleared his throat and decided he had been granted a reprieve. "The inscriptions tell the story of Isis reviving her dead son Horus with her milk, the *Vin de Vie*. It also chronicled the gathering of a massive treasure to be paid as tribute to the cousins of the Hyksos in the 'Land of Long Water.' Dr. Founder and I believed this referenced the Shang along the Yangtze and not the Upper Nile residents, as accepted by most archeologists."

"It seems to me that the professor was quite brilliant and certainly passionate about his studies. Tell me exactly why you switched your allegiance from such a scholarly man to his ex-wife."

Huan knew he had to speak carefully. Tsang must never know of his romantic relationship with Vivian Goldfarb. He had been unable to resist her charms. She was available to him and, indeed, quite eager to establish a secret liaison. He had learned a great deal from her and, at one time, he had talked of working with her to uncover the treasure and share the proceeds with her when they were sold to underground dealers.

That dream had died the moment gunfire erupted in his garden. He trusted no one, but would use all the means at his disposal to acquire the prize. His need for the *Vin de Vie* had become an incurable disease. Nothing else mattered, especially the petulant general.

"I'm waiting, Minister Huan. Exactly what was your relationship with the former Mrs. Founder?"

Huan felt his heart speed up and cleared his throat to fight his rising fear. He spoke as if he were addressing an academic peer review committee: "My research with Dr. Founder clearly indicated that the obelisk contained the inscription necessary for access to the cave where the antiquities are presumed stored. I thought Emanuel was very close to discovering that entry, so, while we were on-site, I had his food prepared with a rare neurotoxin provided by Mrs. Goldfarb. He knew something was amiss, for some reason, and hid his notes and the obelisk by sending them back to America with a departing research team. He gave his journal to his ex-wife. She knew it was incomplete. I removed several pages of maps under the pretense of updating the detail work."

"Perhaps that made him suspicious," Tsang said.

"For the past ten years, I have been using advanced oil exploration techniques to study the banks of the river for the entrance to the cave system, but there are, unfortunately, hundreds, if not thousands, of caves in that area. And the Hyksos were very clever; if they wanted the *Vin de Vie* to stay hidden, they were a culture eminently capable of secreting it away. I needed to remain in contact with Mrs. Goldfarb in order to get hold of Founder's journal."

Major-General Tsang was pacing in front of him, sometimes glancing at him and sometimes examining the ceiling of the room. Huan took a deep breath. How much more would he have to reveal before he was satisfied that he wasn't treasonous? "The description in the first cave Founder and I discovered during our excavation along the Yangtze describes a substance that moves like water, but reflects all light."

"Mercury." Tsang said.

"Yes, probably. If the cave entrance were somehow flooded with mercury, my seismic equipment would think it was looking at solid rock. I had almost given up hope, until Vivian Goldfarb contacted me. I had thought I would never see her again after leaving the United States." Huan shrugged and stopped speaking.

"What did she want? And don't leave anything out of your recounting," Tsang ordered.

"Mrs. Goldfarb didn't care if Dr. Founder had proved his theory that the Shang and the Hyksos were once in contact," Huan said. He shifted positions and wished he could be seated somewhere. "She is not academically inclined. She was only interested in the antiquities and what they might earn in the marketplace. She wanted to live a life of luxury, to make up for all the years she has spent as a poor professor's wife. She suggested that if she were to give her daughter the journal, Danielle would be disposed to finish her father's search." Huan looked directly at Chris. "She used her friend's nephews, who were very capable criminals and as greedy as she for money they hadn't earned, to persuade Danielle that they were needed on the trip to China. That way, she would have her allies in the field."

When Tsang didn't say anything, Huan hung his head, hoping to appear shameful. "And I deeply regret to say that she used me, too," he said. "She spoke about the nephews of Founder's best friend and colleague at the university—William McCrystal—like they were her own sons and with a greater depth of feeling than she did her own daughter. The daughter had too much of her father in her, she said. Danielle is an idealist and will do anything in her power to prove her father's theory has merit. Even though Founder has been—shall we say—incapacitated these past ten years, Danielle is determined to substantiate his theory. That is why she is in China, General. I believe we can use her passion and determination to lead us to the treasure, if there is any. She is eager to confirm Founder's lifework and erase the academic world's belief that he is a failure." He paused for a moment, a thought forming in his mind. He continued slowly, cautiously. "I don't think she knows it, but she is in love with McCrystal. I could see it in her eyes when she was around him. Proving her father was not a fraud and vindicating his and McCrystal's theory will bring her closer to him than she has ever been."

"You are astute, Minister. Some might go so far as to say manipulative, as well. Bringing my son into this scheme of yours may yet cost you your life. It is now beyond my power to remove him from his post without destroying his career, a fact you were no doubt aware of when you made your appeal. He has been formally appointed by that bastard Zhu and I will need a highly compelling reason to reverse his decision." His mouth twisted around the words and Huan felt his sphincter tighten. This was not a man he had angered lightly, but the reality of his rising fury was still awful to behold.

"I understand, General," He said. He swallowed hard. At least he was not going to die today. The connection that Danielle Founder must have been in love with William McCrystal had occurred to him only that very second, literally as he was saying the words. Why else risk so much over her father's theory? Her whore of a mother provided her with money; she didn't need to do anything as risky as steal artifacts from China.

Huan glanced at Chris again and wished he could choke the life out of him. "Danielle Founder knows her father's work better even than I do. If she can make sense of the notes he left behind, then the treasure will be ours for the taking. All we have to do is follow her to the cave."

Huan waited for the general to react to his suggestion. He

hoped the subtle distortions of truth and the parts of the story he had omitted hadn't given him away. It was imperative that the general believe him.

"It appears I have underestimated your political skill, Minister Huan," Tsang said, finally. "How can my army be of assistance in this endeavor?"

"The army?" Huan repeated, shaking from more than the cold. "General, with all due respect, we have the situation well in hand with my security forces. What we need from you is restricted seismic equipment and the government go-ahead to carry out our plans without interference."

"Is that so?" Tsang said, narrowing his eyes. "Bring my son to me," he ordered curtly, still staring at Huan.

A moment later, Mingli Tsang entered the frozen room. He bowed politely to his father and then stood at attention.

Tsang nodded and turned back to face Huan. "Your idea of having the situation under control got my only son involved in a gun battle. You will use what the army has to offer, and, in the process, I may have the opportunity to try out a new toy."

Tsang turned his attention to his son, whose gaze remained on the marble floor. "Are you embarrassed to face me, Mingli?" he asked. "Look at me, when I speak to you."

Mingli lifted only his eyes.

"You will accompany Minister Huan aboard our new watercraft and oversee the final tests prior to delivery to North Korea." He smiled at his son and said, "I have a demonstration

215

planned that should put Zhu and the rest of his sycophants back in their places."

"How are the Joy Brigades?" Mingli asked, ignoring his father's words. His tone did nothing to conceal his revulsion.

"Fresh, as always," Tsang said, with a smile. "Perhaps you will join me one day." Without warning Tsang twisted his hips like a dancer and spun around in a small circle, his sword whistling through the air behind him.

Blood spurted from the stump of Chris's neck, then an arterial geyser quickly drained the life from him, soaking Lin Huan. Tsang wiped the jade sword on his filthy sleeve and said, "Minister Huan, you will complement your security force with these men. You are ordered to locate and catalogue any finds of significance to the people of China at the Yangtze site."

Mingli became violently ill but Huan didn't acknowledge it. He didn't dare move or show his joy other than to allow his tongue to slide over his blood-soaked lips for the briefest of tastes.

26

Long Distance Calls

"Where were you planning on docking this thing?" Sam asked.

Deshi gestured absently into the grey before them.

The well-worn junk was making headway, but sloshed violently with every wave produced by the larger vessels passing them. Sam glanced at Danielle, who was quietly mortified and clutching the side of the boat. He smiled at her.

She grimaced.

"Using Deshi to navigate seemed like a better idea yesterday," she said weekly.

"Take us in before Danielle gets sick," Sam said.

"I know best place," Deshi said above the din of motorboats and smog. "We there very soon."

"Thank god," Danielle said.

The cliff walls of the Three Gorges were far behind them now; the Yangtze was as wide as the Mississippi here. Thick smog hung just above the water as massive barges and high-speed Russian ferryboats moved freely in the obstacle-cleared stretch of river leading to Chongqing.

"I have reservations at a five-star hotel in the heart of the city's commercial district. I thought we might need a good night's sleep and a decent shower," Danielle said. She glanced at Sam. "You've probably seen pictures of Jiefangbei, known as the Liberation Monument Square. It's a famous monument built to commemorate the Sino-Japanese War in 1940. The hotel is adjacent to it." She grinned. "It's called The Harbor Plaza Chongqing and it's connected to the Metropolitan Plaza Shopping Mall. The thought of stable ground, a hot shower, and a new outfit has kept me going all day."

"I know where hotel is," Deshi said.

Sam watched him with interest, as he navigated through the marina. He was good at what he did. His insistence upon showing them around his city had turned out to be a stroke of luck. He followed the direction of Deshi's gesture, as he pointed toward a dock and then gunned the small outboard motor. Within a few minutes, the junk bumped against the designated dock.

Sam climbed out, secured the rope to a dock post, and then helped Danielle climb up beside him. "You look like you could use some Underworld Tea," he said.

"I make strong batch at hotel room," Deshi said, jumping up next to them. "Hotel just short walk that way." He pointed toward a stone staircase built into the concrete floodwalls.

The putrid odor of industrial fishing and chemical production filled their nostrils.

"Let's get away from the water," Danielle said. "Underworld Tea is starting to sound pretty good."

The Harbor Plaza Chongqing was a massive 32-story hotel.

"Busy city," Sam said. He scanned the unchecked urban sprawl. The city had grown too quickly. There didn't seem to be any room for the docks and the old houses crowded next to the mindboggling array of shipping containers, cranes, heavy trucks, and construction crews.

"I spent six months planning every detail of this trip," Danielle said, regaining her composure. "I paid top dollar to be sure that all our gear and a car are waiting for us. We'll collect both as soon as we're settled in the hotel, and then enjoy one night of luxury." She glanced hungrily at Sam in spite of her sea-sickness. "If we're lucky, we'll have a good head start. I don't want any more run-ins with the police."

"Police?" Deshi asked. He stopped walking.

Sam gave Danielle a hard look and answered for her. "We had a small altercation in Nanjing, but we should be all right now. Other men—evil men—want the same thing we're here to find."

"No problem," Deshi said. "Cost you extra thousand."

"Done," Sam said. Deshi watched with wide eyes as Sam

counted out the money and handed it to him.

"How many police?" Deshi asked, pointing to where they needed to turn to reach the hotel.

"It's more like the *army* than the police," Danielle mumbled.

Sam bumped her with his elbow. "It's too complicated to explain now," he said. "Get us to the hotel and then out of the city, and you can leave, Deshi. We'll make it worth your while."

"Sure thing, boss." Deshi said. He turned down an alley to their left, smiled and pointed straight ahead at the clearly marked entrance to the Harbor Plaza Hotel.

Danielle heard the chirping of her Poseidon and glanced at it with surprise, recognizing William's number on the screen. She hadn't spoken to him since Mike made his shocking comment about his involvement with her mother. Since then, she had become suspicious of William's possible involvement with Lin Huan, too. The phone shook in her hand. Maybe he wanted to find out what had happened to Mike and Chris. She didn't know what to tell him, but she answered the call anyway. "Hello, William," she said.

"Tell me why Mike and Chris haven't answered my calls or text messages."

Danielle tried to speak but couldn't. William was the one who had insisted they come with her. His tone was oddly unsettling, but he deserved to know what had happened. "I'm sorry. Mike was killed in Nanjing. Chris was captured by Huan's guards. I don't know if he's dead or alive."

She heard a string of obscenities. Then nothing for several seconds.

His voice was a cold whisper when he said, "Listen carefully, Danielle. You have one opportunity to salvage this situation." For the first time in her life, his voice made her skin crawl.

"S-salvage?" she asked. She motioned to Sam. "What do you mean?"

"Bring me the *Vin de Vie* and I'll give you the antidote to your father's poison."

She sucked for air as if she had been struck. "The *what?*" She said, nearly dropping the phone. Her hands were shaking as she activated the speaker on her Poseidon so that Sam could listen.

William laughed. "I know you heard me, you little slut. I have the antidote to the neurotoxin Lin Huan gave your father ten years ago."

"How?" She asked, refusing to accept what she was hearing.

"Don't be stupid. I designed the toxin." He said it matter of factly with a hint of smugness that made her squeeze the phone so hard her hand hurt. He continued, "The neurotoxin is slow working and produces symptoms very similar to advanced Parkinson disease."

"You son of a bitch!" Danielle managed, feeling the breath explode out of her. "You—"

"There's no time for pleasantries, my dear," William said. "For now, you need to focus on exactly how you'll get the *Vin de Vie* to me. I can restore your father or I can throw him in the ocean. I assume Drake is listening by now. I wonder how long Emanuel can stay afloat? He doesn't seem like much of a swimmer these days."

Sam buried his face into his hands for a moment, and then snapped his head back up. His eyes were on her but his gaze seemed to be focused on a far away object. He cleared his throat. "Where do you want it delivered?" He said flatly.

"Have it in Cape Cod within four days. If I don't hear from you, he goes in the water." He paused.

"I'll make this worth your while, too, Drake," He said. "Do you know where your sister was treated at the end?" He asked.

Sam blinked in confusion. "Sharon? What does she have to do with this?" he asked.

"The admiral. Lawrence Lantana never told you what he did. The way he tried to save her. He didn't even tell his own son; I guess it's not surprising that he kept the truth from you too,"

"She was treated in an undisclosed private clinic. Lawrence...I mean, Admiral Lantana, wouldn't tell me where it was. I didn't press the point. How in the hell do you know about that?"

"I know about it because I want the same thing. The *Vin de Vie* is my price of admission to a clinic that will allow me to live forever. Bring it to me and I'll tell you all about the ship and the man that runs it. We'll all be waiting. Keep in touch."

Danielle broke into silent tears and fell against Sam. He held her firmly and she drew strength from his calm resistance to the unfolding horror. She sat up a moment later and scrolled through the numbers in her phone. "I'm calling my mother," she said dryly, "Let's see if she'll answer."

27

William's Yacht, *The King George*, Key West

Vivian felt the vibration of the cell phone against her leg. When she pulled the phone out of her pocket and saw the number, her stomach lurched. She couldn't talk to Danielle. Not yet. It was too much. She screened the call with a shaky hand and glanced at Emanuel. For the first time in years, she felt a swelling of compassion for him. There was a nauseating sensation she couldn't place immediately. Shame.

"I think something has changed in Emanuel's condition," William said.

"How do you know? He hasn't moved in months." Vivian asked. She'd been below deck while William made the phone call to Danielle. She was seated on the deck with him, ignoring his well-maintained boat. She hated boats, regardless of how fancy there were.

"True," William said, "but something about the way he keeps looking at me is different." He glanced at Emanuel, who sat immobile in his wheelchair, staring into space. Over the past few days, there had been several little changes. William was less sure about his condition. Emanuel was more alert, and he seemed to be trying to move more often.

William fingered his cell phone. "The call went well. It should make everything worthwhile." That's why he had ordered Vivian to return to the yacht. His plan was in motion. He moved to the far side of the deck.

Vivian heard her cell phone ring twice and looked down again; she was getting a voice message from Danielle.

"Who is it?" William asked.

"A message from my daughter," she said, avoiding looking at Emanuel.

"She and Drake should be near the excavation site by now." William said. He could have been discussing navigational charts. "Fetch me a coffee," he said.

Vivian dialed her voicemail and listened. "How could you do it, Mom? How could you destroy Dad like this? William will kill Emanuel, what do you think he'll do to you? This is your fault. Mike is dead and Chris is missing. Did you know about them, as well? I bet you knew Lin Huan was a traitor. How could you look me in the eye and send me here?"

Vivian's phone was slick with sweat as she deleted the message. William was not supposed to kill anyone. He had always said he could make them rich beyond their wildest dreams by pulling the right strings. It had seemed like such a good plan.

But that was years ago.

She had stopped thinking about those days and had no personal interest in William. She was remarried and had more money then she could spend. And William had changed since his trip to the Keys. He wouldn't let it go. She was afraid of him.

"No one was supposed to die," she mumbled to herself, while removing a pill bottle from her purse.

She swallowed several barbiturates without water and thought back over her actions since meeting Lin Huan. She had enjoyed getting caught up in the deception he and William had cooked up. All in the name of revenge and greed. They were ugly words, but nothing compared to the newest addition. Murder.

A wave of nausea swept over her: William intended to murder the father of her child regardless of whether Danielle brought the *Vin de Vie* home. She had been able to ignore it, at first. He had told her about it in a calm voice, as though it were something ordinary . . . as if it were the most natural thing he could have done, given the circumstances. She turned her face toward the sea and became violently sick.

William smirked at her. "Get yourself some Dramamine why don't you? And get my coffee while you're down there,"

The Chinese Dam

As she knelt at the edge of the boat, she couldn't get William's face out of her mind. He had told her that the only way to control events in China was through leverage over Danielle. Somehow, she had to stop him. How could she have loved him? Had she ever, really? She wasn't sure if it was love or just her resentment of Emanuel. It seemed like a whole other life.

Vivian glanced at Emanuel and smiled wistfully, remembering a time when she had loved him. It was a different life in those days. He was young and full of energy and ideas. His love for academia hadn't blocked her out yet. He had been spontaneous and had showered her with affection.

But then the notion that he could prove a link between ancient cultures more profound than any ever considered overwhelmed him and swallowed up their lives. Everything she had done after that was to punish him for abandoning her.

She had openly cheated on him with both William and Huan, and he hadn't noticed.

He only had time for Danielle and his work. Running around with William had been the easiest thing in the world. His life had been consumed by his hatred of Emanuel's success, as well.

But this was far more than payback for being abandoned.

Vivian sighed. She knew what to do. Over the past few days, she had carefully diluted the neurotoxin that William administered to Emanuel every evening on the boat. After William turned in for the night, she had also been slipping Emanuel a dose of the antidote, slowly tipping the balance of mobility back into

Emanuel's favor. Emanuel knew what she was doing and he played along, making sure not to move too much in front of William. Although he couldn't speak yet, he thanked her with his eyes.

Sometimes, the tears would roll down his cheeks. This morning, however, William's comments about a change in Emanuel had brought fear close to the surface. He could tell by the expression on Emanuel's face that something was different.

God help them both if he figured it out too soon. With that thought in mind, she knew that there was something else she could do.

She crept below decks and located the vial that contained the toxin. She drew a small dose into her syringe, listened for William, and carefully injected the cup of coffee he'd commanded her to prepare.

28

Harbor Plaza Hotel, Chongqing, China

Sam moved quickly past the doorman into the polished hotel and waited until both Deshi and Danielle had stepped inside the lobby. Several uniformed bellboys rushed to take their few bags and one ushered them to the reception desk. Danielle fumbled with her Poseidon and finally located the confirmation for the clerk.

"Ah, yes, Ms. Founder," he said. "We have been expecting you. The vehicle you requested is waiting for you in the garage. Here are the keys." He passed Danielle a car key with a large Porsche logo and a room key. He turned and reached into a room box on the wall behind him and pulled out an envelope. "This message arrived for you last night."

Danielle took the envelope and turned to Sam. "I wasn't

expecting a note from anyone. This wasn't part of my plan." Stuffing the note into her pocket, she added, "I'll read it later. I'm ready for a long, hot shower."

As they headed for the elevator, Sam caught a glimpse of a man who turned quickly away as they passed near him. Instantly on edge, he made a methodical search of the faces in the lobby. He nudged Deshi and leaned close to whisper, "Check out the people in the lobby. Carefully."

"What's the matter?" Danielle asked. She reached for the twentieth-floor button.

Sam stopped her and punched the garage button instead. "There was too much security in that lobby. They are on alert already."

"What do you want to do?" she whispered. "How could they already know we are here?"

The elevator opened onto a pristine parking garage.

"We in trouble?" Deshi asked, nonplussed.

Sam scanned the rows for the slot marked 16F. "Here we go," he said, striding toward the vehicle.

The second bank of elevator doors chimed and opened behind them. The hard faces of three Chinese policemen fastened on them. They stepped out slowly and began walking forward.

"Yes, this is the one," Danielle said, standing in front of a gleaming red Porsche Cayenne Turbo.

"Inconspicuous," Sam said smiling. She really was a rookie. The vehicle was a knockout, but it stood out like an apple in a pile of potatoes.

Danielle tossed him the keys and peered over her shoulder.

"Get in the front," Sam said to Deshi, who quickly followed orders. "Can you get us out of here?"

"Sure. Head back to water," he said.

Sam cast a quick glance into the area behind the back seat. It was packed with gear and his black SEAL duffel was on top.

"Hope it's all here," Danielle said.

Sam backed carefully out of the parking spot, slipped the transmission into drive and rolled past the guards. They were still standing in front of the elevator, watching but not moving. "They're herding us," Sam said.

The exit to the garage was two levels down. Sam scanned each level as he drove through it, watching for any vehicle that might try to block him in. He pulled up next to the automatic gate, and waited impatiently for it to lift and allow them to pass through. "Do you see that black Navigator behind us, Danielle?"

Danielle turned her head to peer out the back window. "Yes. Two men. Both in uniforms."

"I assume Chris and Mike stuffed more guns into the equipment bag. Dig one out and get ready to use it."

The driver of the Navigator didn't attempt to keep his distance; he sped up and tailgated their rented vehicle, following it through the first traffic signal.

Danielle hung over the back seat and rummaged through the bags. "Yes, there are several."

"Got a gun for me?" Deshi asked.

"Not this time, pal," Sam said. There was a slight change in Deshi's voice. Sam cast him a sideways glance. He didn't appear nervous at all.

"Okay, Sam, I think I've got a couple of them loaded," Danielle said. Her voice cracked as she said, "I don't know if I can do this."

"You'll be fine. Keep your head down. When I tell you to shoot, aim for their tires."

Just as he was about to give the order, the Navigator slowed down. Sam watched in the rearview mirror as the black SUV signaled and then turned left.

"What the hell? Get us out of the city, Deshi. And stay alert for an ambush."

Deshi had stayed calm throughout the chase. He seemed to have a criminal streak after all.

A half hour later, they cruised to a stop next to a dilapidated filling station. "Deshi, I need your help here. You know this city. We don't. We're being followed by people in the highest echelon of the government. They are not on an official government mission. They want us to lead them to the archeological site that Danielle's father was about to locate before they poisoned and paralyzed him. We're being blackmailed into finding the antiquities. Danielle's father is being held hostage." Sam expected him to ask for more money but instead Deshi dutifully jumped out and filled the tank.

Sam was distracted by Danielle's gasp.

"Sam . . . look at this!" She handed him the contents of the envelope she had finally pulled from her pocket. "It's from William. I—"

Sam examined the letter and then the photograph of Emanuel Founder holding a week-old newspaper. "This is a desperate move, Danielle. It explains why he thought that I should come along with you," He met Danielle's watering eyes. "You had no way of knowing. He fooled your father, too."

"What now?" Danielle asked with a shaky voice.

Deshi returned to the front seat and sat silently, aware of the change in mood.

Sam shook his head. This was no time for Danielle to have a meltdown. He had to keep her head clear. She reached out and held his arm. He blinked away the rush of emotion and looked back at the photo.

This was the most important mission of his life and there was no room for error. "We do the only thing we can do. Get the *Vin de Vie*."

He poured out the rest of the tea Deshi had purchased from the station owner's wife. "He won't hurt Emanuel unless he thinks we won't give him what he wants. Call him and tell him everything is on schedule. We'll have it in the States by next week."

"But . . . how can we get out that quickly, Sam? I was right about Huan. He never intended to let us out of China."

"None of that is important now, Danielle. We have to focus on what we can control. Right now that's finding the final site. I need you to prove your father was right. Can you do that with me?"

"Yes, of course. But, what if William is working with Lin Huan? Why don't they just arrest us now? Why did they let us leave the city?"

"If William were working with Huan, he would have told us to turn ourselves in. He's on his own. Huan isn't sure where to look; he needs you for that. He knows the only way you'll lead them anywhere is if you continue to believe you can prove your father's theory."

Danielle finished her tea and handed Deshi the empty cup. "I don't understand how they can be following us. We've been so careful."

"There are military technologies they could be using. China's a superpower. The military or something very similar to it must be involved, if they can let us go and still track us," Sam said. "For all we know, our vehicle is bugged."

"Military?" Deshi had been listening, but not reacting to their conversation. "If military involved, you in deep trouble. I get you through, but why try, if military want you?" He examined them both closely. "Can't you go home?" he asked. "Military kill you and not think twice." Deshi fell silent for a moment. Then, looking off into the distance, he said, "They move many thousands of Chinese from banks of Yangtze at the end of bayonet. All for dam project of Major-General Tsang. He wicked man. You try to stay, they *force* you to leave. Whole families on banks killed when they fight back."

"We're walking into a trap," Danielle said quietly.

"Probably," Sam said. "We'll give them more than they bargained for, though. I know something they don't."

"I help you," Deshi said. "Family most important thing."

After loading the Cayenne, Danielle, Sam, and Deshi headed out along the southern bank of the Yangtze. They had only fifty miles to cover, but the narrow road was barely passable. Travel in this area was usually accomplished on water, not land. They followed deeply worn animal trails, sometimes losing site of any pathway whatsoever and resorting to using their GPS and Deshi's impressive sense of direction.

Locals gawked at the shiny vehicle as they rumbled past. Sam smiled and waved at them, but made no attempt to communicate verbally. The last thing they needed was to make more of a spectacle of themselves than they already were in their bright red Porsche.

Deshi, for his part, seemed at ease in the Cayenne. He stretched out in the front seat next to Sam and calmly provided information about upcoming road conditions and changing topography. "We close to elephant rock you show on map," he said, suddenly sitting upright and peering through the windshield. He pointed. "Over next rise, you see long water and elephant rock."

"How can you be sure?" Sam threw him a glance, once again amazed at their good fortune to find him in Fengdu.

"I grow up here," he said.

Sam steered the SUV around a large hole and rounded a thicket of sharp brush. The brown waters of the Yangtze snaked beneath them. The weather had changed drastically; a warm wind blew through Sam's open window. He scanned the skyline as he pulled the SUV clear of the brush, and noticed a familiar pattern in the clouds ahead of them. "Damn!" he said. Beads of sweat dampened his forehead as he studied the cloud formation. They swirled and changed direction several times, coming together and then parting like massive wraiths.

"What is it?" Danielle and Deshi asked together.

"See those clouds up ahead of us? That's a SIMS weather pattern."

Sam fought against the flood of memories he had tried for months to sort out—images of his mission in North Korea, the Pleasure Palace of Kim Jong-un, and the SEAL's attempt to intercept stolen technology. He blinked back into reality just in time to steer the Cayenne away from a tree and slam on the brakes.

"Sam! What's wrong?" Danielle shouted. "What do those clouds mean to you?"

Sam brushed the back of his hand over his eyes. The clouds were forming directly over the area on the river near the elephant rock. "Did you feel that warm wind that blew into the windows a minute ago? Do you smell the ozone in the air, like right before a rainstorm?" Neither answered him. "Someone is using weather modification technology."

"Someone's making it rain?" Deshi asked. He leaned forward far enough to stare up through the windshield. "How can you tell?"

"It's more than rain, Deshi. It's a super-storm used to disrupt enemy troops." Sam glanced at the man next to him, noting the change in his accent. "We're in serious trouble."

Miles ahead, the dark clouds swirled in strange patterns, still high above the river. Lightning forked between the clouds, but didn't make contact with the ground. The overpowering sweet smell of ozone forced Sam to make a decision; he pushed the Cayenne into PARK. "Let's camp here for a while," he said, opening his door and climbing out of the vehicle.

After building a campfire and helping Deshi brew a pot of tea, Sam sat with his back to the growing wind and watched Danielle unpack diving gear. He had to tell her about who and what they must be dealing with, but she wouldn't look at him. Perhaps she already knew. He cleared his throat. "I believe Major-General Tsang is involved in this. Ever heard of him?"

Danielle nodded. "He's the driving force behind the dam project. My father tried for years to reason with him, but he's impossible to contact . . . unless he wants you to find him."

"Did Emanuel realize he was dealing with a monster?" Sam scrubbed his face with shaking hands, as the images of his last mission played on his memory again. There was more this time. Pieces were gliding toward each other in his mind, joining up and creating a fragmented narrative. "The clouds are part of a stolen

U.S. technology meant to destroy the communications and morale of an enemy. It's going to be used against us." He rubbed his eyes vigorously, to clear the disjointed combat scenes. He opened them again and fixed an icy stare on her. "The cost at which Major-General Tsang procured this technology is staggering. My entire unit was killed over it."

Another memory danced just out of reach . . . a memory that would explain all the rest. *"It's Axelsen!"* he thought. "Axelsen is here with Tsang," he said aloud. The realization turned his stomach.

Axelsen couldn't stop looking at the pictures on the plane, and his mannerisms had been uncharacteristic throughout the mission. They all made sense now. The documents from the various island banks he had seen on that trip to Axelsen's office must have been in preparation for his defection. They had nothing to do with "research," as the official report had suggested. Axelsen had planned to desert his unit all along. His real goal, from the early planning stages of the mission, had been to gain access to the foreign superpower that would be willing to harbor the most dangerous fugitive possible—an American traitor. Axelsen had willingly participated in annihilating his own troops, in order to gain access to the general's obscene lifestyle.

If this had all been part of a defection plan, then he was still alive. Something had never felt right about the reports of his death and now he knew why. *They were wrong.*

"Axelsen?" Danielle said, baffled by his comment.

Deshi didn't say anything, but watched Sam's face and waited for an explanation.

Sam paced in front of his listeners. "I woke up in the hospital, after what was left of my unit had been sent back into North Korea to finish what we had started. I heard later that every member of my SEAL team had been killed." Sam kicked at the dirt with the toe of his boot. "Their deaths are . . . mine."

"Let's find that cave," he said, re-zipping his duffle bag. He peered one more time toward the dark super-storm gathering in the west. It was moving steadily toward them.

"It won't be long now."

29

Yangtze River, China

Major-General Tsang stood at the bow of his new hovercraft and admired the handiwork of its primary weapon. It would be impossible for Zhu to deny its existence to the watching American's now. That should teach the meddling bastard a lesson. Earlier that morning, while enjoying time with a passably beautiful young village girl, he had realized that this was the perfect way to disentangle his son from Lin Huan and to harass the Americans at the same time.

By creating a display that was sure to be picked up by the watching satellites, he had created a situation from which even the slippery Zhu could not extricate himself. Beijing had already promised to sell the technology to North Korea secretly; that would be impossible now. As soon as the North began testing, there would be no argument as to where they got the technology. And best of all, he had personally delivered ten of the hovercrafts to Kim Jong-un the week before. They were scheduled to begin testing any day. Zhu would have to beg him to intercede with North Korea or risk an open violation of the agreement he had personally negotiated with the filthy Americans. Perfect.

"Amazing, isn't it?" he commented, turning to Mingli Tsang and Lin Huan, who stood on the large deck behind him. Neither replied.

In less than an hour the weather modification systems aboard the craft had created an intense storm. Swirling winds had closed in on the small fishing village the general had chosen as his testing grounds.

In places accustomed to tornadoes, alarms would be wailing, but there was no audible sound other than that created by the force of the wind.

Huan's response was interrupted by the sudden appearance of an enormous tornado. The swirling mass of debris settled near the center of the small village and swept across it, leaving a path of destruction. Within seconds, it had torn away a wall of stones and hurled them like cannonballs into the surrounding structures. Then, as quickly as it descended, the storm subsided. Light broke through the clouds and the intermittent rain stopped completely.

Major-General Tsang strode into the main cabin and suppressed a chuckle. He opened the compartment on the hilt of his sword and scooped at the gray powder with his polished pinkie nail. He closed his eyes, snorted deeply, and waited for the drug to take effect. When he reopened his eyes, he peered about him and pointed at Lin Huan, who stood just inside the entrance. "Where is my son?"

"I'm right here," Mingli said, entering the cabin.

"Did you see that display, my son? Wasn't it impressive?"

"Yes, I would have to admit it was impressive."

"It's time to send a storm up the valley," Tsang said.

Mingli's head snapped around. "You plan to send this weather toward the dam?"

Tsang only smiled in reply and took another snort of power.

"I have to get back to Beijing." Mingli said looking at his cell phone. "Could you wait with the storm until I am safely out of the area?"

"You will miss the best part. I insist that you stay," he said with a knowing smile.

Mingli shook his head. "This is your project, Father. Zhu has ordered me to report at once for reassignment. If I ignore the summons it will bring dishonor upon you. Surely you wouldn't want that."

Sam was the last to scramble back into the Cayenne as the second tempest swirled in around them. In a matter of minutes, the man-made clouds had gone from gun-metal gray to pitch black. "They're using weather-seeding technology—illegal weapons controlled by satellites," he explained. "They must have a focal point somewhere down there, something like a tank or a large truck that the satellites are triangulating on. The fixed location on the ground directs the course of the storm; the satellites send directed energy beams into the upper atmosphere, and massive storms erupt." He took a deep breath and shouted over the wind. "These are basically space weapons and they're highly fucking illegal. It's not an overt act of war because they're using them on their own people. The villagers have no idea this isn't natural." He grabbed the door handle but turned to Deshi before he opened it. "Wait for my directions," he yelled.

Deshi nodded and gave him the thumbs-up sign.

In a single motion, Sam opened the door and dove into the storm and tied the end of their climbing rope to the tow hitch. "Drive up to that tree in the middle of the field," he yelled.

Deshi nodded again.

Sam squinted through the gusts and held onto the rope with an iron grip. He motioned to Danielle, who had followed him into the storm and was working to maintain her balance.

Deshi drove to the designated spot several yards away, parked, and then slid out into the storm. He held onto the Cayenne for balance, but appeared to be unafraid as he watched Sam move to the edge of the cliff.

Loosening his grip on the rope, Sam leaned over the edge and surveyed the uncertain waters of the river far below. He shouted at Danielle, who stood ready to follow him. "This is the spot on the GPS." He yelled. "We'll repel down and try to secure our raft."

A sudden gust blew Danielle into the door of the Cayenne. She grabbed onto the handle to steady herself, her expletive lost in the wind.

When Sam saw that she was all right, he yelled at Deshi. "You stay here and get ready to pull us back up if we get into trouble."

Danielle leaned in to within a few inches of Deshi. "Are you okay with that?" she asked.

He nodded and waved her on, glancing up at the sky again. "Is the army making it rain?" he shouted at Sam.

Sam nodded. He stared at Deshi for a moment, but said nothing. Then he faced Danielle. "Get into your gear. I need to speak with Deshi alone."

Several minutes later, he braced himself against the swirling wind while securing one end of the rope to the black bag that contained a self-inflating raft. He used a slipknot so that it could be easily released when the rope was under pressure. He rolled the heavy bag over the cliff and, with one gloved hand, expertly controlled the descent of the raft down to the water. Satisfied, he turned to Danielle. "Let's hope your father's notes were accurate." He moved away from the cliff and quickly pulled on his own gear. The familiar snap of the pressure lock on his dry suit helmet sent a rush of adrenaline through him. He was back.

A hundred feet below him, the water swirled viciously, whipped to a frenzy by the force of the man-made storm. He turned to ensure that Danielle was ready to follow him. He clicked the intercom switch on his arm and spoke to Danielle. "The storm has supercharged the river. The currents will be more dangerous than usual. Once we're in the water, make sure you stay with me. Keep this line in front of you at all times."

Just as he was about to repel off the cliff, he heard the sound of a far-off swarm of locusts carried on the wind.

"What's the matter? Why are you stopping?"

"Do you hear that buzzing?"

Danielle strained to hear. "Sounds like jet skis."

"Not standard jet skis," Sam said. "Military. They burn a mixture of ethanol and hydrogen. We've got fast-moving company. Keep close to the wall when you head down to the water." He peered over the edge of the cliff and examined the swirling vortex of water far below them. The hellish scene below was familiar. The storm that blew in before them made gooseflesh stand up on his arms. There was no reason to deploy a weapon of this scale against his small team. International weather monitoring services would be going insane; the information would be on the top of intelligence briefings in Washington, London, and Pairs within hours. While not an overt act of war, this was more than saber rattling. A thought occurred to Sam that he wished he could dismiss, but once conceived, it refused to budge. There was nothing he could do about it now. Danielle was coming down the rope above him, they were committed. But what if the target of the super storm was not his team at all; what if the target was the dam itself?

"Can we do this?" Danielle shouted into the microphone.

"We'll be fine," he said evenly. "Once we hit the water, stay with the equipment." He turned his back to the river and stepped out over the water.

He released the rope with his right hand and dropped fifteen feet before catching himself. The wind blew him against the cliff wall and he crashed into it with his shoulder before he could brace himself with his boots. He glanced up at Danielle and saw her repel over the edge after him. The smell of ozone was even stronger. They were committed; it was time to find the *Vin de Vie* or die trying. He couldn't ignore that both Lin Huan and Major-General Tsang were formidable adversaries and neither one of them wanted Danielle or him to leave China alive. But he was calm.

Focusing up again to ensure Danielle was all right, he increased his speed down through the gathering fog, covering the last fifty feet to the water in a few seconds. He kept the rope as taut as he could for Danielle and held his position just above the surface of the river.

She was working her way carefully down the precipice, the strong wind rocking her from side to side against the rock wall. She dropped a few more feet and was pulled away by a stiff gust of wind. Sam watched in horror as she hung suspended fifteen feet from the cliff for several seconds. The wind abruptly changed direction, blowing her back to the wall. Her scream was lost in the wind as she hurtled toward the stone, landing with a thump.

For a few long seconds she hung limp, the climbing harness holding her in place against the wall. Then she reached for the rope and steadied herself.

Sam clicked on his intercom and asked, "You okay?"

"Yeah, great."

His smile was cut short by the buzz of approaching jet skis.

Sam jerked at the cord attached to their raft; it inflated instantly but hit the water at an odd angle and nearly overturned in the tumultuous water. He tied the end of the rope to the raft and dropped in. A few moments later, Danielle was at his side.

No sooner was she settled than a jet ski cut across the water, slicing through the fog toward them. The rider turned sharply, kicking up a huge wake on the already churning water, before disappearing into the dark. The storm was forcing large waves to crash into each other at odd angles; the combination of fog, spray and wind eliminated visibility beyond fifty feet.

Sam stared after the jet ski and saw a large black shape sitting on the water's surface, seemingly unaffected by the raging storm. Cocking his head at an angle to listen, he heard a dull whooshing that was barely audible above the tempest. The rider circled the shape once and was joined by a second jet ski.

"Ready for a swim?" he asked Danielle.

She gave him the thumbs-up sign, adjusted her mask and pulled on her fins.

Sam unpacked their underwater propulsion vehicle, known as UPV, and checked his spear gun. With a final glance at the jet skis circling the black mass obscured by the fog, he started the flow of oxygen to their helmets. When he looked back up, a jet ski was charging toward them. Sam couldn't bring up the spear gun in time to get off a decent shot, so he shoved Danielle over the side as the high-speed craft ripped between them, shredding their raft. Sam's helmet caught the side of the ski, his radio fizzled in his ear, and went silent. Communications were dead.

The swirling madness above them was replaced by an eerie calm as they slid quickly into the dark water.

Normally, the undertow of the river would be dragging them hard downstream, but the unnatural weather had forced the river into a kind of standstill. By Sam's calculation, the water was nearly forty feet deep and very murky. He activated his Poseidon and searched for the signal from the beacon he had left days before on their Yangtze cruise upriver. A strong signal to their left showed him where to guide their UPV. He grabbed Danielle by the shoulder and gestured toward the spot below. The water was very cold, but Sam didn't mind. The lack of ambient noise soothed him. He would live underwater if he could.

As the UPV pulled them deeper under, he felt Danielle tug at his vest. He turned toward her and saw that she was motioning for him to head closer to the cliff wall. The markings blended into the stone at first. But when he studied the area she was pointing at closely, he saw the patterns. He flipped the familiar yellow light switch on the side of his UPV and illuminated the area. The small propeller on the UPV spun to life and pulled him forward. Danielle grabbed onto his diving vest and descended with him. Keeping one eye on his Poseidon, he followed the signal, until Danielle tugged at him again, indicating he should stop.

She aimed the beam of her flashlight at the markings just above what appeared to be a stone shelf carved into the rock face. The well-worn pathway had clearly been above the water until the flooding from the dam project and was probably used as a footpath for the men who pulled their junks up the river. Submerged and useless now, Sam thought it fitting that he and Danielle would be the last to use it. Danielle gestured toward specific markings. Sam nodded and glanced at his oxygen meter. He had almost his entire share of oxygen left, a trick learned as a SEAL—extreme oxygen conservation. He pulled Danielle closer and peered at her gauge.

She had used nearly a quarter of her oxygen. Her collision with the wall had damaged her regulator. Small bubbles escaped with their precious cargo in tow. Time was not on their side. Sam led the way down, confident despite the darkening of the water around them. The deeper current was unaffected by the storm above and it pulled them strongly down river. With every foot they traversed through the river passage, he knew Danielle's excitement was increasing. Although he couldn't speak with her, he could sense the strength of her anticipation.

Sam hovered thirty feet below the river's surface, pondering their next move. The dial on his oxygen meter was slowly moving toward the three-quarter mark. He examined Danielle's again and saw that it was down to nearly the half-tank mark. She was inexperienced and didn't know how to preserve her supply. He should have practiced breathing techniques with her.

Sam maneuvered close to the wall and stopped again to peer up through the murky water at the remains of their raft. A chill passed through him when he saw that a black shadow had crept to within fifteen feet of the floating rubber.

It was a massive military hovercraft, a vehicle he had spent too much time aboard to misidentify. With his pulse racing, he took one long and slow inhalation of oxygen and regained his composure. Although other divers must be close at hand, he needed to focus on Danielle and will her into making some progress in their search.

She was moving hand-over-hand along the shelf, intently studying the rubble-strewn area. Dr. Founder would have been looking for small caves and depressions in the stone wall.

Danielle motioned to him. Pointing at an area just above her, he saw that a piece of fabric had caught on something near a slight depression. It billowed outward in the current like a warning flag. He moved closer and reached for it. After inspecting it himself, he held it in front of Danielle's helmet.

It was a piece of heavy-weight tent canvas. Danielle attempted to clap her hands and he saw her smile at him. Then, with almost giddy anticipation, she pulled at a metal stake put in place by her father when he had set up his final camp. When she had freed it, she held it up triumphantly to reveal the stamp: BOSTON UNIVERSITY ARCHEOLOGY DEPT.

Teetering on the shelf, Danielle ran her gloved hand over the spot on the stone last touched by her father and willed herself to think like him. She made small circles on the wall, feeling for any hint of what he conceived as being close by. Touching the crawling figures etched into the stone, she suddenly realized what they were—the mix of Egyptian and ancient Chinese that her father had described. Pulling back a few feet, in order to see the entire marking, she recognized it from the journal at once: LONG WATER.

Drawing in a deep breath, she was momentarily oblivious to the need for oxygen conservation. Her eyes teared up and she blinked furiously to stem the flow. She had no way to wipe them away. She turned to Sam and mouthed, "This is it. Long Water." It was the culmination of the maps her father had reconstructed throughout his career . . . the very translations that had thrown him into a notoriety he hadn't expected. Her heart pounded against her rib cage. She touched the words again and reveled in the moment.

Sam saw the divers before they saw him. Despite the strong currents, they moved well. He jabbed Danielle repeatedly, gestured toward their assailants and then to a dark place on the shelf. She caught on immediately and knew she needed to conceal herself in a crevice. Sam deflated his buoyancy compensator vest, known as a BC, and sank to the bottom of the river. He settled onto his back with his hand on his regulator, ready to inflate his vest.

The Chinese divers saw Sam's discarded UPV and headed

directly toward it. They were within ten feet of Danielle before they noticed Sam on the floor of the river. A second too late, they reached for spear guns. Sam fully inflated his BC and shot upward with the speed of a champagne cork, grabbing each of them by their regulator hoses as he sped past them. Both men panicked and inhaled water. Kicking wildly, they headed back to the river's surface. Sam's ears popped hard as he surfaced with them. He knew that the pressure change from only twenty feet can cause problems, but he had no other choice.

The two divers coughed and sputtered at the surface, incapacitated. One diver sucked in more water and lost his battle with the river. Ignoring the plight of his partner, the other diver struggled to swim toward Sam.

Sam fired the spear gun automatically, hitting him in the forehead.

The man jerked in surprise and then sank away in the crazed current, a thin trail of blood spreading around him.

30

Connection

Danielle averted her eyes from the carnage above and swam deeper, remembering the details of the excavation site that her father had so carefully described in his journal. Her days as an Olympian were far behind, but she had no problem connecting the smooth strokes that carried her forward. Clicking on her light, she began her descent into the dark water. She kept one hand on the cliff wall to help steady her nerves. Everything her father had written about was still here, just hidden beneath water and time.

Thirty feet down, her light uncovered the ghostly remains of a complete tent, its twisted poles and tattered canvas the only testament to the complex archeological expedition. Starting with this point of reference, she wiggled through the water, scanning every inch of the rock wall.

Near the ruined tent she saw an opening two feet above her

head. She clutched the rocks, and worked her way up to it. The aperture was only the circumference of her arm, but something about it caught and held her attention. The carvings around the hole were more distinct here, familiar somehow. She swam backward from the cliff face and began to shine her light slowly back and forth.

Her light froze. She pushed away from the wall, swimming back several feet to get a better view.

She was looking at four carvings, each one a replica of a side of the obelisk her father had sent her, the Key of Isis. She reached into the pack she had attached to her waist and removed the obelisk from inside a zippered compartment on her BC. This was it, the place her dad described. He must have known he was in the right place but decided to stop. He knew he'd been betrayed, so he gave up the quest just before the final moment. What torture that must have been for him, Danielle thought. He had been at the entrance to the find of a lifetime and he'd known it. But he'd denied it to Huan as well. He'd left it here for Danielle to find all these years later.

She could feel his presence in the water with her. She tried not to think about the fact that William might have already killed him, and instead focused on the deeper meaning behind the carvings before her. The glyphs she studied on the wall were all large depictions of the obelisk she held in her hands, the tip of each pointing to the hole in the middle of the rock. It seemed clear that this was where the Key of Isis was to be inserted but it seemed far too easy. She stuck the obelisk in the hole and twisted it back and forth. Nothing. She fought a wave of frustration, pulled in a deep breath and kept working the obelisk to the left and right. She stopped, removed the small stone and tried to determine if there was too much sediment in the hole. She shined her light into the hole again. It was clear.

"Work!" she screamed to no one but herself. She rammed the stone back in so hard that she bruised her knuckles on the rim of the opening. The pain was intense enough that she thought she might have cracked a bone. She sucked in another long, deep breath and felt the anger subside. She had to figure this out. The obelisk fit perfectly into the stone, it was clearly made for this spot in the rock. She closed her eyes and moved the stone gently back and forth and realized that she could feel parts of the stone moving with it! It fit, it was the Key of Isis and she was just being too stupid to figure out how to use it.

She drew another breath, removed the stone and passed it to Sam, who had just swum up next to her. Perhaps his random twists of the wrist would crack the code. She stared at this back as he worked the stone into the gap once again and felt something itching at the back of her mind. How would her dad solve this? As a scientist, of course. She paddled further back from Sam and stared at the four images of the obelisks carved around the entrance to the small hole. The base of the obelisks were facing out, their tips all pointed toward the hole. She looked at the markings on the carved images one at a time, reading them carefully. She read the final one and started again with the first. They were each displaying a different side of the stone, repeating its markings in order.

That was it! The way the sides of the stone were laid out indicated the way that the real obelisk was to be used. There was something else about the carvings that she couldn't place at first. They were longer than the actual obelisk. There were extra characters in the carvings, one per row that did not appear in the actual obelisk. She patted Sam on the shoulder and took the stone back from him, ignoring his puzzled expression. She looked from the stone in her hands to the ones carved into the stone before her.

The story of Isis was carved into the stone; the first characters of the narrative looked back at her from the black rock in her hand. She looked for the corresponding narrative carved into the rock, and found it on the far right-hand carving. She read the inscription and saw that an extra character had been inserted just behind the first character on the small obelisk she held. She turned the stone in her hand and found the next verse of the narrative, then glanced at the wall and found that the corresponding characters were written on the carving at the bottom of the four. An extra character was inserted behind the second character in this narrative. Her heart began to pound as she read the third panel from the stone in her hand, matched it up with the carving before her and found the extra character, this time behind the third hieroglyphic. The fourth panel of carvings on the stone in her hands matched the carving at the top of those on the wall, but when she read to the fourth symbol, there was not an inserted character. Instead, the character was stuck behind the *fifth* in the line of hieroglyphics. And there was something else, it was not Egyptian, it was Chinese. It was the symbol for *reverse*.

"Could it be that simple?" Danielle asked the dark water before her. She brushed past Sam, noting the concern etched on his face, and gently inserted the obelisk with the symbols for the beginning of the narrative facing the corresponding carving in the wall. She gently turned the stone down and to the right, stopping at a quarter turn when she felt a very slight vibration beneath her fingers. She turned the stone another quarter click to the right and felt another tremor beneath her fingers. She turned it once more, then once again, and stopped. She held her breath and reversed the course of the stone completely, one quarter click at a time until it was back where she had started. Only then did the rush of bubbles engulf her and Sam as an entire section of the cliff face began to rotate inward, drawing the two of them into the dark.

Sam took Danielle by the arm as the entrance to the submerged cave closed behind them. The cave they were in seemed to swallow the light. It was like swimming into an ink well. He could feel the panic in Danielle.

He clicked on his helmet light and forced her to look him in the face. He held up her oxygen gauge; she was down to an eighth of a tank. He motioned for her to slow down and breathe normally. Pointing at his regulator, he showed her that his tank was still half full. She nodded her understanding, but as she gazed about her, every object brought another surge of excitement, causing her to breathe rapidly.

Sam gave the thumbs-up signal. Her father was right; the cave confirmed his speculations.

Emanuel Founder was not a fraud.

Sam aimed his light down the narrow tunnel. Although it was flooded, the walls were perfectly smooth, as if the water were a new arrival.

Danielle swam into the passageway, Sam following. Emanuel may have knocked on the door, but they were the first visitors to this place in three-thousand years. The construction of the cave was so precise that there was no appreciable degradation. The door on the shelf of the river was a brilliant innovation. At the time of its construction, it would have been above the waterline, but the builders had purposely planned for it to withstand water and pressure changes, knowing the river would experience natural flooding.

The building techniques mirrored those used in Egypt. The entrance would have been accessible only by boat or by belaying down the steep cliff walls, as they had just done. And without an accurate map, this miniscule spot on the vast wall would have been all but impossible to locate.

After fifty feet, the tunnel narrowed again. Sam swam ahead of Danielle to scout for any potential danger. He realized within a few feet that he would not be able to turn around. He'd be forced to back his way out. It was better for Danielle to go first so he could keep an eye on her. If she ran out of air, he could detach the hose from his helmet and save her, but the maneuver itself would cost too much time and air. He backed out and motioned for her to take the lead.

As they moved through the cold water, he noticed that Danielle was favoring her right side, especially her arm. He aimed his light on her back and noticed the rough scrape on the fabric left by the cliff wall when she had crashed into it while repelling. She had damaged more than her regulator. The suit was damaged but didn't appear to be leaking.

The murky water in the narrow cave allowed their lights to penetrate only a few feet in front of them. Sam followed closely behind Danielle, keeping one hand on her belt to steady her, the other on the wall. Illuminating the walls next to him, he observed ancient characters unseen for millennia and marveled at a scene of the Egyptian God Thoth performing a ritual Emanuel had described in his journal.

Just ahead the narrow water-filled tunnel curved sharply upward. Within seconds, they entered a chamber above the water line. Not a drop of the river water had reached its confines. Sam pulled a flare from his waterproof bag and ignited it. Then he cautiously turned off his oxygen tank and lifted his helmet. When he'd taken a deep breath of fresh air he realized that the tunnel must connect to the outside. The entire area was riddled with tunnels; that was what had kept the *Vin de Vie* hidden all this time.

He turned to Danielle and helped her remove her helmet.

"We must be close," she said.

The orange glow of the flare lit the walls of the new chamber. They were smooth, except for one prominent inscription—an upside-down urn at the far side of the room. The surface under the inverted urn gleamed in the sputtering light from the flare like heat waves off a desert road.

Closely examining the carving and then the floor of the cave, he fought the feeling of vertigo. The illustration projected an upside down world of urns and dancing figures. Danielle stood beside him and stared with the same bewilderment. The surface of the floor under the carving was not opaque; it shimmered like liquid steel.

"I don't get it," Sam said. "Something's weird about this and I can't put my finger on it."

"Mercury," Danielle said. "It's mercury!"

Sam reached out with his gloved hand and the substance gave way slowly, like molten gelatin. He submerged his hand and withdrew it. Globules of the liquid mercury formed into a perfect ball in the center of his palm. He turned his hand over to let the liquid metal ball fall back to the puddle with a splash.

"Don't let it touch your skin," he said.

"It's astounding when you think about it," Danielle said. "My father theorized that the Hyksos had an advanced understanding of mercury, but this . . ." She stared at the wall and its dancing figures. Picking up her train of thought, she said, "Scientists have been speculating since the 1970s that the tomb of China's first Emperor, Qin Shi Huang, was buried in 210 BC with his own *lake* of mercury. The legend spoke of an enormous replica of the empire built as his tomb, and mercury was used for the oceans instead of water. The legend said that the builders went so far as to recreate the celestial landscape on the ceiling of the tomb in diamonds, and that huge vats of whale oil fueled the torches that would illuminate the emperor's domain forever." She turned back to him and smiled. "Dad believed the builders borrowed the idea from their Hyksos ancestors." The smile faded as she looked past him. "The spilled urn is pointing to where the wine casks are hidden. Somehow, we have to see what's under the mercury."

"I wonder how deep it is," Sam said. He knelt and submerged his arm into the liquid. He felt nothing but the cold weight of the metal against his diving suit. "I can't tell how deep the hole is, but if you're right, we'll have to swim in it."

"I can't ask you to take the risk, but I will. Besides, we . . . we're running out of time. William—"

"Don't think about him right now. One thing at a time." Sam readjusted his helmet, turned on his oxygen and stepped cautiously into the mercury puddle on the floor next to him, slowly submerging himself up to his shoulders. His mask was mere inches from the shimmering surface and he could see a reflection of his unshaven chin. Then his face mask touched the liquid metal and, within seconds, he was enveloped in total darkness. The darkness was the most complete he had experienced; the sensory deprivation chambers he had trained in as a SEAL paled in comparison. He fought to breathe normally. He felt the walls around him and quickly found another opening five feet down. He reached back up for Danielle, gave her a thumbs-up, and felt the pressure around him adjust to her entrance. He moved ahead, guided only by touch.

He could feel Danielle hanging onto his flipper and he began his descent.

A minute passed.

Just when he was convinced the mercury was a clever ruse, he felt the floor of the tube beginning to flatten out.

With Danielle's weight on his fin, he propelled himself forward, always keeping one hand in contact with the floor for assurance there would be a way out. In the utter quiet and pitch darkness, only the solid stone allowed him to fight an intense need to move more quickly. The weight of the metal pressed in from all sides and sapped his body heat. Instinctively, he reached for his oxygen meter, forgetting that he couldn't see it. His pulse quickened with the realization.

With a start, Sam realized he was breathing in rapid gasps, greedily sucking down his oxygen. Unsure of how long he had been distracted, he came to a complete stop, closed his eyes, and tried to shift his focus to the task at hand. He was unsuccessful.

He forced himself to inhale slowly, but something was wrong. He realized he had ignored his own advice. With a dull click, he sucked the last life-giving breath out of his tank.

The closeness of death cleared Sam's mind. There was no way

to swim back the way he had come. He had to get through the tunnel. During his last experience with oxygen deprivation in the Yangtze, he was able to swim to the surface. Not now. He owed it to Danielle to fight. He closed his eyes and felt the reassuring solid stone under his hands and knees, and pulled himself forward. The only hope he had was in believing that the tunnel ended in something other than another water-filled room.

Fighting the urge to suck at his dry tank, he focused on the pounding in his head. He moved his hands to the cadence.

Every movement of his body burned more of the precious air left in his blood. As his heart labored to deliver the last of his oxygen, a familiar wet sensation soaked the back of his head, as if warm liquid seeped into his skull. As the heat spread, red spots appeared out of the blackness.

A sense of deep calm settled over him, and his hands lost feeling. It took no effort to propel himself. The events seemed to be taking place from a great distance now.

His world turned a deep burgundy and only a searing pain in his chest registered. He sensed that he would die soon. Pinpoints of light dotted the burgundy haze and then as suddenly as the light around him had disappeared, the mercury covering his face plate slid away in a clean sheet.

Sam blinked into the blinding light. A shape appeared through the fog of his oxygen-deprived mind and with it a new awareness. He was staring at the business end of Axelsen's pistol.

31

Yangtze River Cave System

Sam stood next to Danielle in the narrow, torch-lit cave and stared in wonder at their surroundings. More impressive than the Chinese troops holding them at gunpoint was the reality of her father's life work spread out in front of them. The cave walls were covered with the same markings as those they had seen on the walls of the first cave, but these were massive. High above them, a shaft of light filtered down, exposing the cave's size. The military men surrounding them had blasted their way in from above. Sam smiled at the elegance of the plan. They had needed he and Danielle to get them close, they possessed the ground piercing technology to find the rest of the site on their own. Hieroglyphs previously seen only in Egypt depicted scenes even Emanuel wouldn't be able to fully explain.

Danielle wept openly. "These scenes were meant only for the eyes of the Hyksos high priests. If my father were here, he would know . . . ." She choked and couldn't continue.

Sam could tell she was taking mental snapshots. They wouldn't do her any good, if he couldn't get her out of their predicament alive. Moving only his eyes, he took note of their enclosure and its occupants. Behind the troops, he saw an altar holding three stone vessels. They were sealed with shimmering mercury. The *Vin de Vie*.

A thin pale man with cruel lips stood behind it, looking at them with a mixture of curiosity and scorn. Sam had seen numerous pictures of him before his mission to North Korea. He was China's infamous Major-General Tsang.

Tsang smiled at them. "This place is far better than I expected, Miss Founder. Your father was right. This *is* China's greatest treasure." He dipped a ladle through the mercury and withdrew the thick red liquid beneath. "To life," he said as he tipped the ladle into his mouth. He kept his eyes closed and ignored the wine and mercury that dripped off his chin. Sam glanced toward Danielle and found her staring open-mouthed at the General.

A sickly sweet smell of rotten flowers permeated the chamber as Tsang slurped the draught. He wiped his mouth on his sleeve, leaving an iridescent stain of quicksilver on the fine velvet. "This site will compound the fame and respect my dam project has already provided."

Standing next to the General, Lin Huan cleared his throat and said, "General, it is not advisable to sample the *Vin De Vie* just yet. There is much testing we need—"

"How . . . how could you do this to someone who would have given you everything?" Danielle screamed.

Huan met Danielle's fury without flinching. "Doctor Founder lied to me," he said. "He would have taken full credit for finding this site and the wine. He would have removed it from China and presented it to his university. Vivian told me everything."

Danielle opened her mouth but found no words. Sam touched her with his elbow.

Huan continued, "You showed me where to point my ground-piercing radar systems. I have looked at these cave systems for years, but ruled them all out. They are too far from the bank of the river. I underestimated the Shang." He polished his monocle on his shirt, smiled at her again. "The mercury-filled tunnel was brilliant, don't you think?"

"My father trusted you," Danielle muttered.

Sam counted the men in the cave and calculated their relative distance. He appeared relaxed, but the opposite was true. In addition to the eight Chinese troops, who all carried automatic weapons, there were Lin Huan, Major-General Tsang, who looked intoxicated, and Jonathan Axelsen. The only sound was of water dripping and gloved hands gripping guns too tightly.

Huan seemed to relish humiliating Danielle. "Your father was a fool, Danielle, but your mother loved me. She taught me to take what is mine."

Huan did not notice the change in General Tsang, but Sam did. He had inadvertently indicated that the wine was his.

"You fool," Danielle said. "My mother and William used you."

"I know that . . . now." Huan's voice trailed off, as he cast a wary glance at the general. "It's of no consequence. Thanks to Major-General Tsang's assistance, we have preserved a vital piece of history for the Chinese people." He pulled out a gold cigarette case and worked at trying to light the cigarette he removed. Again, he glanced at the general to gauge his response.

The general didn't appear to be listening. "Mr. Axelsen," he said, "if you please."

With a half smile, Axelsen drew a long-barreled chrome pistol from a holster hidden under his jacket and pressed it to Huan's head. He winked at Sam as he squeezed the trigger.

Danielle shrieked in horror and buried her face in Sam's shoulder as Lin Huan slumped to the floor.

Smoke trailed from the barrel of Axelsen's pistol as he stepped toward them. "Sorry, Drake. You wouldn't understand, but I had to get back to the palace." His mouth twisted around the words. "Once I'd visited, there was no way I could stay away. Life's just too short, you know?"

Sam wondered why he had made the feeble apology. Was the traitorous bastard really trying to win his forgiveness before murdering him? His motive was irrelevant; he was giving Sam an opening. "We could have helped you," he said. "You didn't have to do . . . this." He nodded at Lin Huan's body.

"And why not, Sam?" Axelsen folded his arms across his chest, the giant pistol tucked under his armpit. "Did you really think I'd return to the States to be taken off active duty on the suggestion of a subordinate? Maybe then be court-martialed?" He grinned humorlessly. "Oh, yes, I know how you and your team muttered behind my back. You thought I was crazy."

Sam understood his motive now: gloating. He wanted to see Sam's fear before he killed him. "You're not crazy," Sam said. "You're just weak and undisciplined. I've known your type my whole life. It was daddy that got you into the CIA, right?" Sam snorted with a fake laugh and allowed a quiver to enter his voice as he said, "Major-General, how long do you think it will take him to turn on *you*?"

Tsang gazed bleary-eyed at Sam. "Mr. Axelsen and I have an understanding. He has already delivered on his end. The question," he said through a hiccup, "is will I deliver on mine. All Mr. Axelsen wants is an open invitation to the Pleasure Palace. A simple enough request, and one I can surely appreciate." He chuckled. "Of course the palace is not mine, but . . . I might build my own in China."

Axelsen had detected the fear in Sam's voice and he wanted more. He was nearly howling as he said, "You wouldn't have been able to save the unit even if you hadn't been injured. I was too far ahead of you."

"I understand more than you think," Sam said as he shifted his weight and rubbed the back of his neck, as though he were relieving his stiff muscles. Hopefully, his onlookers would be distracted as he prepared himself. "I was your target from the beginning. You and William needed me to guide Danielle here. You knew Mike and Chris would just get her killed."

Everyone in the cave was focused on them.

Axelsen took a step toward Sam and leaned against the wall. "If you hadn't kept the troops at bay, it's unlikely I would have been able to identify myself to them. They came so close to killing me I actually pissed my pants during that firefight. Stupid gook bastards. I figured I owed it to you to get you out after that. The brass was so impressed with my bravery they gave me an award for saving your life. You made it possible, Sam. *You* made the story believable. CIA command thinks I died in battle."

"I should have shot you when I had the chance," Sam said quietly, his shoulders slumped. "It shouldn't be long before Admiral Lantana sends in the Marines."

He glanced at the new skylight created by the general's troops, and hoped Axelsen would follow suit. There was no time for calm reflection or long-term planning. His kick caught Axelsen in the groin and bought him a split second. He pinned the pistol under Axelsen's arm and pivoted behind him as the guard closest brought his gun around. Sam slipped his left arm under Axelsen's chin and squeezed, his right handed fumbled for the combat knife at his waist.

In the guard's moment of hesitation, he drew and threw the heavy blade. An arterial spray drained life onto the cave floor.

Before another guard could react, Sam had wrestled Axelsen's pistol away and placed it firmly against the big man's temple.

"Get back!" he yelled. Guards had moved from both sides of the altar.

They eyed him nervously, while casting helpless looks at their compatriot as he gurgled a final time and lay still. They immediately tried to encircle Tsang, but the general simply laughed as he drew his jade sword. With the fleetness of a ballet dancer, he was across the cave, holding the blade across Danielle's neck.

In the chaos she had crept behind a boulder near the altar, lost from the minds of all but the general. She trembled visibly as Tsang caressed her back with his free hand. He locked eyes first with Sam, then with Axelsen. He laughed again and turned to his wide-eyed guards. "We have the codes; The Emperors Breath is operating as planned. Kill them both!" he said. "I'll save the lady for later pleasure."

The guards opened fire, but missed wide right as Sam and Axelsen dropped to the floor as one. Knowing that Axelsen was fighting for his own life, Sam released him and rolled toward better cover. As the guards focused their shots, Sam dove further away, seeking the rock outcrop near the mercury tube he and Danielle had come through.

The guards fired randomly at both sides of his sparse cover, but they were also sending shots at Axelsen's closer cover point. Sam poked his gun around and squeezed off several shots that ricocheted off the altar, acutely aware that Danielle could be caught in the cross-fire if he weren't careful.

Pinning their quarry down with short bursts of fire, the guards inched forward methodically. Using Danielle as a shield, Tsang moved behind the altar that held the wine casks. Ten feet from Sam, two of the guards stopped to reload. Sam rolled to the left of the rock barrier and squeezed off two quick shots, instantly killing one man and wounding the other. Three of Tsang's reserve bodyguards scampered toward his position.

As Sam drew a deep breath and prepared to make a death stand, an explosion from the roof of the cave sent rocks cascading down, crushing one guard and scattering the others. Before the dust had settled, several members of the Chinese Special Forces streamed into the cavern, repelling down thick nylon ropes.

"Hold your fire!" Tsang screamed to his men, pushing Danielle in front of him. Only two of his elite troops were available to react to his command. Men rocketed down ropes to the stone floor, landing with soft thuds. Within seconds, snipers took position at the mouth of the gaping hole and focused laser sights on Tsang and his remaining men.

The general continued to shout his name and rank at the troops who had descended into the cavern, oddly pleased by their presence.

They ignored him, but made no move to harm him. He scrambled for cover behind the altar, and shoved Danielle aside. Danielle could only gawk at the soldiers filling the space around her. Sam saw the blow coming before she did, and screamed a second too late. Danielle moved, but his sword still caught her in the back. Her parry was a stroke of dumb luck; her air tank took the blow and flakes of jade and aluminum cascaded harmlessly to the floor. Tsang turned on her, wobbled a bit, and advanced. To Sam's horror, the guards made no move to stop them. Sam had no clear shot and their encounter would be over before he could intervene. Tsang raised the sword high above his head, a mistake. Danielle used his slow motion swordsmanship to plant her boot firmly into the side of his knee. Shouting in agony, he swung one-handed and tried to finish her off with a single wild attack. Danielle sandwiched the blade between her gloved palms and twisted it, using the general's force against him.

Sputtering with embarrassment over being disarmed by a woman, Tsang reached for one of the fallen guards' pistols. Danielle brought the jade sword around in a wide ark. Tsang saw it coming and jerked his body away from the blow. The sword missed his neck but bit deeply into his upper shoulder. Without waiting for his rejoinder, Danielle turned and sprinted away. She nearly fell over herself when she recognized who she was running toward. It was Deshi, and he looked quite different.

Within seconds, the Special Forces troops had shimmied down the ropes and taken full control. Sam came out from behind his cover and beamed at the two commanding officers. Deshi and Mingli Tsang, both wearing the uniforms of China's Special Forces, stepped forward.

"I've never been so happy to see enemy forces in my entire life," Sam said.

"If you hadn't signaled me with your GPS transmitter, we may have missed the spot," Deshi said without a trace of an accent. "When technology works, it's a thing of beauty. We've got the rest of the so-called elite troops under guard above." He nodded toward the ceiling of the enclosure.

Mingli Tsang turned to face his father.

With a purple face and narrowed eyes, the general could scarcely speak through his anger. "You would turn on *me*? I am your father, yet you would seek to destroy me?"

"You have nowhere to run," Mingli Tsang said, leveling his pistol. "It is you who have turned. The real Chinese army has captured every last one of your traitors. You are finished as a general and as my father. You are done defiling this nation."

"You are wrong, my son." A horrible shudder shook the walls just then and both men seemed to hold their breaths.

"I'm not who you think I am, father."

"What do you mean? I've known you worked for the secret police since the day you started."

Mingli was speechless for a moment. "When I left the hovercraft it was to call in its exact position to a team of strike helicopters. Your toy is a smoking ruin. We've located the North Korean satellites you're relaying off of to facilitate the weather pattern. Kim Jong-un has taken them offline. The storm is already subsiding. You'll not destroy China. But I needed to hear it from your mouth."

His father only smiled as a colossal clap of thunder echoed from above.

"Sir," the voice of a support guard to Mingli crackled from his radio. "The winds are not subsiding, the storm is too big. The dam, the dam will fail!"

"Take his satellites offline at once," Mingli ordered.

"We have," The terrified guard said.

Realization spread across Mingli's face as he started at his father. "The American," he said glancing across the cavern at Axelsen. "You're using American satellites without their knowledge. You would murder millions of our people in the flood and it will appear that the Americans caused it," he said. "You'll ignite a world war we cannot win. To what end, father? To rule a broken nation?"

The general only sneered in response. "The dam is no more than the emperor's toe nail. I shall clip it off and wash it away, and China shall fall with it," he said, wiping at his brow. "I shall rebuild the nation as it was meant to be." The weight of what he was prepared to do seemed to suck the air from the cave. The guards sensed the change in the timber of the encounter and stared at their leader, only moments ago assured of victory, now standing uncertainly before his father.

General Tsang was waving his arms as he said, "The emperor shall live forever! The breath of the emperor can move mountains and lay low the countryside. I *am* the emperor, the descendent of

The Chinese Dam

Qin Shi Huang, the first Emperor of China. You shall fear me or perish." He said the words softly. "I will have the following document signed by the other major-generals. They shall change their personal security codes to the following," he handed a small slip of paper to his son. "Once their access codes are changed, my staff will alert me, and I will allow the breath of the emperor to subside. Fail me and China shall fall."

Sam stared at the men before him, watching as Mingli grasped that his father was more than mad, he was also a genius. With the *Vin De Vie* in his control and the power to destroy the dam, he would become the ruler of China. He had made it this far, perhaps he was right. But he had a horrible glazed look in his eyes, one that far surpassed his usual drug stupor.

Mingli had no answer. Instead, he clicked his com link and barked a command. A moment later the reply from his superiors came in. "We...agree to your terms."

The air was heavy in the cave. No one spoke for several seconds until Mingli looked at his father and said, "This has always been about control? You never cared about this wine."

"Ancient wine? Who could squabble over such trivialities. It was the perfect way to get you out from under Zhu's thumb. You shall be emperor after me, as Kim Jong-un has followed Kim Jong-Il in the North. Soon we will unite North and South Korea and join them to us. Then we will take Japan. But that is for another day," he said checking his small tablet computer.

"This wasn't about me, either. You needed an excuse to deploy the weather weapon on the Yangtze, and Zhu gave it to you. If you destroy the dam you'll topple China. You'd kill *a hundred million people*."

"They're peasants; of course I'll sacrifice them. They are mine," he said. "I'll do with them as I please. We are descended of the first *emperor*. By rights, China and all its people are ours."

Mingli looked at Deshi and nodded. He removed his radio and said, "Send the message to Admiral Lantana. Drake was right."

Deshi pulled Danielle to safety. "I-I thought you were from a f-fishing village," she said, out of breath and trembling.

"I was, before the floods started," he said, in flawless English. "Now I work for the political counterpart to General Tsang in Beijing. I've been monitoring you and Sam since you arrived. I'm here to bring China's worst general to justice, but that may be more complex than we thought." He checked his pistol and moved off carefully toward the Tsangs.

"What does this mean? Is he really in charge of China now?" Danielle asked. "He's been guzzling the *Vin De Vie*, look at his eyes."

Deshi looked at General Tsang carefully. "What will it do?"

"No one knows, but my father had suspected that it was poison. He only wanted to study it, not drink it."

Danielle turned from the glassy-eyed general and screamed, "No!" a second too late.

Sam spun around and narrowly avoided the worst of the blow.

Jonathan Axelsen had tried to stab him in the back. Danielle's warning had saved his life, but Axelsen's small knuckle dagger still tore through his dry suit and into his hip. Momentarily dazed, he was just able to side-step Axelsen's next powerful swing with the vicious-looking blade. Off balance, Sam chopped Axelsen's wrist with the butt of his empty pistol. Axelsen countered with a brutal left fist to Sam's jaw, knocking him to the cavern floor. His thick lips curled into a leering grin as he recovered his dagger and raised it two-handed above his head. "I should have done this a long time ago, pal."

Just as Axelsen began his downward thrust of the knife, he jerked forward and stumbled to his knees.

Danielle had stuck several inches of the jade sword into his back but hadn't managed to penetrate him. He twisted to his right and the tip of the sword broke off, leaving a jagged serrated tip on the ancient blade still in her hands. Axelsen stood back up and screamed in anger and pain, as he faced her. She backed away slowly, the ruined sword shaking in her hands. Axelsen grimaced, and then charged her. She aimed the tip for his chest but at the last second he swung his arm up, knocking the blade harmlessly to the ground.

Then he was on her. He grabbed her in a tight embrace, easily twisting her around so that her back was to him. He licked her from the nape of her neck to her ear and smiled as he placed his right hand under her chin. He yelled, "I want you to see this, Drake!" and spun around, Danielle hanging limply in front of him toward the spot where he had left Sam. There was a moment of stunned silence from him as he realized that Sam was gone.

He relaxed his grip on Danielle for a second, preparing to snap her neck like a felled dove when he saw the flash of green. He had no time to react as the broken jade sword, now only a third as long as it had once been, plunged into his left eye and stopped at the hilt. The tip protruded from the back of his head, just above his collar. It had missed his brain, mostly. He sputtered, tried to talk, couldn't. He released his grip on Danielle and she fell to the floor.

Sam charged him with a lowered shoulder and hit him in the back, propelling him forward into a stumbling, bleeding mass. He nearly regained his balance as he reached for a hidden pistol, then stumbled over a rock outcropping and fell forward. Through his one good eye, he realized what he was falling toward and he seemed to move in slow motion, arms grasping at air as gravity and fate pulled him toward the opening to the mercury tube. He hit the surface with a messy splash and sank as if pulled from below. He scratched back to the surface momentarily to scream but only managed to open and close his dying lips like a silent fish out of water before he sank away amid his own dark blood.

"That's twice," Danielle said.

Sam met her eyes. "I'll accept the gift of my life. We'll discuss whether or not I have earned it later."

Mingli Tsang cocked his pistol and Tsang realized that his own son would shoot him. Mingli's radio crackled again. "The

American admiral was waiting for our call, sir. Lantana and Deshi had alerted him. All he needed was the coordinates of the satellites. He has deactivated them."

General Tsang stared at his son. The wind was already dying out above them. All his planning, all his work, meant nothing.

"I couldn't allow you to rule China. You are poison," Mingli Tsang said.

"China is great because of men like me," Tsang said. "I have done our ancestors great honor by constructing the Three Gorges Dam and I have secured your place in history alongside me. Lower your weapon, boy. All of this was for you, for *us*."

"You caused the 1998 flood. You have the blood of millions on your hands and you expect me to *honor* you? You disgust me and you disgrace our ancestors by pillaging this tomb in the name of your greed."

"This tomb is not sacred. It holds the filthy remains of the savages who would destroy us."

"And what of North Korea? Our ancestors are ashamed . . . *I* am ashamed of your Pleasure Palace. You are worse than the Western emperor Caligula."

Tsang lowered his pistol and brushed a hand across his eyes. The wine was coarsening through his body now and he didn't feel well. He wanted to sit down. "I'm not well," he said. "The *Vin de Vie* . . . it must be p-poisonous. It was a cruel joke. It was meant to *kill* the pharaohs." Swaying, he faced his son one more time, before placing the muzzle of the pistol against his head. His son made no move to stop him.

He closed his eyes and pulled the trigger.

"We're too late," Sam said.

They had been out of the cave less than an hour. Deshi and Mingli Tsang had been in contact with the FBI regarding William McCrystal. The news was not good. The FBI had been monitoring William for months over suspicious overseas calls he had made, but two days ago he had slipped to sea without warning.

"I know where he'll go," Danielle said. Her face was still ashen from the experience in the cave. "Send them to William's father's place in the Keys."

32

Boom

William fought his tears as he stared at a picture of his nephews at Fenway Park. His boat was a fucking prison today. Vivian was acting strangely and so was Emanuel.

It was time. Whether Sam and Danielle brought him the *Vin de Vie* or not, Emanuel had outlived his usefulness.

William scratched at his chin harder than he intended to. Annoyed with himself, he looked at his fingers and saw that he had bloodied them. He went below deck into the tiny bathroom and looked for toilet paper. Vivian had used it all up, again. He would need to pump out the toilet as well. She was so fucking useless. He looked at himself in the mirror and decided that it was really time to deal with Vivian too. He hadn't slept well all week. The thought of killing Emanuel was keeping him up, making him wonder if perhaps there were not another way out. But he knew it was too late for all that now. The meet-up time was hours past. He had let Drake stall him until the end of the week and he was no closer to having the *Vin de Vie,* much less a shot at being treated aboard the *Pura Vida*. They were probably working with the FBI. He had told Vivian what he intended to do and she had gone into hysterics over the idea. He had been forced to smack her across the face with the back of his hand. That had calmed her down.

Still staring in the mirror, he cleared his throat and stuck his hand into his coat pocket. The reassuring rubber grip of the pistol was there. He took a deep breath, pulled the revolver out and checked the cartridges. They were the same six shots that had been in the gun the last ten times he had looked. He realized how pathetic he was being and snapped the gun closed as hard as he could. He opened the door so fast he broke one of the hinges and stormed onto the deck where he had left Emanuel. His heart froze.

He was alone on deck. They were gone. How had he not heard them? He looked up and down the boat frantically, and then trained his eyes out to sea. There was nothing to port; then he checked to starboard and saw it. His fucking dingy was in the water, speeding toward the shore.

"Bitch!" He screamed. He pointed the pistol out to sea and fired two shots, both missed wildly. His hands were shaking. He moved to the far side of the boat and sat down with his legs hanging over the side, his arms balanced on the safety line. He squeezed off three more rounds. One hit the water very close to the dingy and he knew he could make the shot. He held his breath, closed his left eye and aimed carefully down the sight. Then he realized his mistake. The boat was empty!

He opened the cylinder of the pistol and ejected the spent shells into the ocean. He fished in his left pocket for more bullets. As the first round slid into the chamber he thought he heard something scraping on the deck behind him. He felt the boat turn, and glanced up at a fluttering in the sail overhead. He turned his head in time to see the boom of the boat careening toward him. Vivian had untied the line securing it and the wind had grabbed hold of the sail. He ducked but still caught the brunt of the blow in the shoulder and upper back. His pistol skidded across the deck and stopped in front of Emanuel's wheelchair. The pain in his back was horrific but nothing seemed broken. He ignored it, because to his horror, Emanuel was moving. He shouldn't have been able to lift a goddam fork to his mouth, but he was leaning forward in his chair, grasping for the pistol. William rubbed at this shoulder as he stood back up. Vivian was here somewhere too, he realized a moment to late.

He turned as Vivian swung his fire extinguisher. She was too small to put much behind it and he was able to raise his arm to block the blow. Unfortunately, though, he raised the hand with his spare shells in it, and the force of the blow knocked his last five rounds into the water. He nearly went over the side but grabbed the safety line in time. He looked back at the deck. Emanuel had his gun.

He pointed the revolver at William and squeezed the trigger. Nothing happened. A jam? William looked at the gun with a puzzled expression and realized that the one round he had loaded was out of firing sequence. He had no idea when it would discharge, like a game of Russian Roulette. Emanuel pointed the barrel at William again, who was now on his feet and staggering toward him. He managed to pull the trigger two more times in rapid succession before William was on him.

William was hurt but heavy, and he managed to push the gun away from himself. He didn't want to risk wasting the last shot but he knew he could overpower the weakened man so he let Emanuel push his arm down so that he could swing his left fist into the side of Emanuel's chin. It was like punching granite.

Emanuel took blow after blow and seemed unperturbed. His face was bloody but his hold on William's gun seemed unshakable. Vivian must have given him a full dose of the antidote. Stupid bitch.

He leaned in and bit Emanuel's cheek. This got an angry whimper from him and a change in posture. Emanuel released William's right arm and grabbed him by the throat in a feeble attempt to choke him. William then grabbed the gun and brought his right hand back up and squeezed the trigger two more times.

He smiled as the last bullet exploded in the gun. The shot only grazed Emanuel's leg, but the gun was empty. He could easily deal with both of them now. He was face to face with Emanuel, less than an inch separated their eyes. Emanuel was smiling at him. William didn't understand. He had shot the bastard. It was only a matter of time now before the whole thing would be over. Then he felt jab of pain in his neck and a warm sensation spread through his back, down to his ass. It was like lukewarm soup being poured over him. His penis felt numb, then his legs and arms too.

He realized with a jolt of horror what Vivian had just done to him. His arms felt like they were stuck to his body. It took all his might to raise his right hand and feel around at his neck. He found the syringe of neurotoxin but lacked the strength to pull it out. Emanuel was still leaning on him, his weight pushing them both toward the safety line. They somersaulted into the freezing water and splashed like bait fish, then floated to the surface together. William was on his side, staring at Emanuel. A trickle of blood was oozing from his old friend's smiling mouth as he wrapped his arms around a life vest and moved his feet into position between them.

"For Danielle," Emanuel said. He kicked at him until he began to bob under the surface of the water. William tried to scream but he was already under, sinking fast. He could still see Emanuel's shoes above him for several seconds before the dark water blocked them out. That was when he screamed and took a breath.

33

Safety

One hour later, in Nanjing, Sam stood up to greet a smiling Deshi. They were in a military compound, but the threat was gone. Sam could tell by the look on Deshi's face that he had good news. His hands felt sweaty as he reached out to shake with Deshi. "We have word that Dr. Founder and Mrs. Goldfarb are safe," he said.

Sam put his arm around Danielle and pulled her in close. He took a deep breath and said, "We wouldn't be on our way back to the States without you. If you hadn't slipped up a couple times, revealing your impeccable English, I wouldn't have suspected you of being anyone other than a simple fisherman."

Deshi grinned. "Without your insistence that I take your spare GPS receiver, we wouldn't have been able to track your transmitter."

Sam gave him a nod and squeezed Danielle. "I hoped that my suspicions about your accent were on point. I thought that you must be working for the Chinese secret police."

"A good guess. My superior in Beijing has been in touch with the American ambassador. It seems that your safe return has been useful in smoothing over a dispute over alleged space weapons."

Sam, Danielle, and Deshi all smiled now.

Deshi kept a straight face but winked at them and said, "Now, it is my wish that you will find your families in good health. If there is anything I can do to assist you, please let me know."

Sam nodded. "I will."

Forthcoming by Benjamin C. Yablon

Pure Death

Lawrence Lantana arrived right on time. The pretty secretary escorted him back to the office where he was warmly greeted before the door was all the way open.

"Admiral Lantana, thank you for coming."

Lawrence walked slowly into the lavish office. He had been summoned the day before by his friend George Thormopolis, the Under Secretary of the Navy. "Of course, George. What can I do for you?"

"I need to discuss the ongoing salvage operation. You know how much gold went down with that ship, yes?"

Lawrence nodded.

"Hello, Admiral," came a sweet female voice from behind him.

"Christiana?" he said, turning toward the sound.

"It's good to see you," she said. This was odd. Christiana was the deputy station chief of the NSA. She didn't usually have any contact with the Navy.

The Under Secretary cleared his throat and continued, "There are interested parties at the highest levels."

"Understood. What does that have to do with me?"

"We need you to convince him to help us. We need him to review some chatter coming to us from the wreck,"

"Chatter?"

"Yeah, some of the systems of the ship are operational and broadcasting. We think it's a message Mendelbaum left for James."

"Get this through your head, George: it's over. The boat sank. She went critical, exploded, and drifted to one of the deepest, coldest places on the planet. It serves that bastard right."

The Under Secretary remained silent and calm, a fact that made Lawrence want to slug his old friend. "He owes us, Lawrence. You owe us. We supplied the finest team of doctors in the country to treat him. It's a miracle he lived even with their help."

"I'm not dragging Jim back into this. He's making a new life with Abigail. Besides, the wreck is too deep and too hot to salvage. That gold can't be touched for fifty years at least."

"Maybe."

"Maybe? George, what the hell are you talking about? I've seen the report. It's hotter than Three Mile Island down there."

"The vaults were lined with lead. It's likely that some of the material avoided the worst of the contamination. Anyhow, the wreck is in international water. The Kuminyaga Trench can be accessed by anyone with the desire and budget to make the attempt."

"I know all of that. There've been what, six failed expeditions over the last ten months? It's too deep for manned missions, and it's going to take a manned mission to make a proper recovery. Only the Chinese are willing to sacrifice their divers over it. Let them have it. You're not sending in Navy divers, are you? What aren't you telling me? It's the signal you've intercepted."

"I can't give details; it's eyes only."

"And you're telling me that James has clearance?"

Christiana put her hand on Lawrence's arm and said, "The message is for him. Make the call. Please."

"I will. But there's someone I need first."

"Drake?" The under secretary said. "You know he's off limits after what he did to Axelsen's boy."

"Your assistant was way out of line getting his son appointed CIA liaison and you know it. Drake owes me, and we need him."

Five minutes later Lawrence was talking on his phone as he walked back to his car. He allowed the usual pleasantries to flow like water until he was inside his secure Mercedes S class. The car's hands-free signal took over and routed the conversation though a highly classified scrambler, making the next words impossible to intercept.

"I need your help, Sam," Lawrence said.

"I thought I was clear. I'm out. Danielle and I are making a new life."

"You owe me," Lawrence said. He let the statement hang in the air.

"I know," Sam said. "But I sure didn't think you'd be calling it in his quickly."

"It's out of my control. My son…he's making a new life for himself, too. But he's hurt. I don't think he's up to this."

"Up to what?" Sam asked.

"They are going to make him relive a nightmare that only just ended. He doesn't know it yet, but he needs someone like you, someone who can run a SEAL team."

"I'd hoped to have more time with Danielle before my life was at risk again." There was a long pause before Sam said, "I'd hoped not to risk my life again period."

"I know. But you're the best, you proved that in China."

"Better than your son?"

"Different. And in your way, yes, better."

"When?"

"Now. I'll email your plane ticket to you. You leave tonight for D.C. I'll fill you in on the rest then."

Lawrence severed the connection and stared the engine. As he pulled away from the curb he was already dialing Jim's cell phone. He was sent to voice mail on the first ring. That was what he'd expected, but even so he was unprepared for the beep that prompted him to leave a message.

"James," he began. "I mean, Jim. Sorry to bother you. I just had a conversation with Thormopolis. There's something he needs to discuss with you. I know that you want to be left alone with

Abigail and the kids, but this is ah, this is important. He won't give me the details. Only that it involves the wreak of the 'Vida, and some kind of signal that's meant for you. I don't know why, but I get the feeling that it has to do with Sharon. Call me back. Please."

Lawrence hung up and drove in silence toward his lavish, but perpetually empty, Virginia home. Jim and his new family had been to visit only once, the experience proving unbearably awkward for he and Jim. Since then Lawrence had buried himself in work and done his best to keep his distance from his son. Abigail and the kids on the other hand were regular, and most welcome, visitors.

He was in his driveway when Jim called him back. He answered on the first ring.

"I got your message," Jim said. Lawrence could hear Abigail banging around in the kitchen behind him. "Do you want to ah -"

"Just ask him you big baby," Came Abigail's slightly accented, and utterly sweet voice over his son's.

"Would you like to come to dinner tonight?" Jim asked mechanically.

"Um, well, of course. As long as it's not an imposition," Lawrence stuttered.

"Well, actually, Edvard has a test tomorrow and Katarina is fighting a bit of a cold - "

"Give me the phone," Abigail said. There was a moment of rustling and then her voice was firmly on the other end of the line.

"Lawrence, it's Abigail."

"Oh, hi Abigail. Nice to speak to you," Lawrence said.

"It's been too long since we've *all* seen you," she said. "You must come by for dinner tonight. I've pickled some herring,"

"He hates it," Jim yelled from behind her.

"Herring sounds wonderful, thank you for inviting me. I'm close by, shall I come over?"

"Yes, come now," Abigail yelled with excitement. She had been inviting him over every week for the past three months. She was clearly going to be the one that brokered the peace between he and Jim. It seemed to Lawrence that his son's anger was gone, but their ability to relate to one another had left with it.

Lawrence smiled in spite of himself. Jim had always been lucky in love and Abigail was no exception. She was a force of nature. He cleared his throat and said, "I'm in the car now. I'll be there in fifteen minutes."

The drive across Arlington flowed by in a late Autumn haze of muted colors. Lawrence found that he was picking out the slightest details as he passed, the white picket fences, and the neatly trimmed shrubs poised like happy sentinels before the coming winter. He pulled into his son's driveway and marveled at their home. Abigail was not only a famous doctor, she was the heir to a Swedish pharmaceutical fortune. Her share of the family trust kicked out nearly five million Euros a year. There was no need for either of them to work, yet she still did. Jim on the other hand was as lost now as he'd been when Lawrence plucked him out of the Ocean in the horrible walker-suit that had saved his life. It had protected him from most of the radiation, but not all.

Lawrence rang the door bell and turned to look out at the sun setting at the far end of the estate. He really couldn't blame Jim at all for spending his days here, with her, but he needed more. His bid for the Senate long abandoned, his only focus now seemed to be a desire to consume cable news.

"Papa Larry!" Came the howl from within.

"Sharon," he said as he turned, the name catching in his throat.

Jim was standing with the four year old in his huge arms, his mouth slightly agape at his fathers indiscretion.

A second later he put Katarina down and motioned for his father to enter. He didn't say a word as he led him though the domed entryway of the house and back toward the kitchen. The dome had always reminded Lawrence of a mosque, but Abigail and insisted that it be included. Jim looked over his shoulder and broke a faint smile though. "Wanna drink, dad?"

"Dear god yes," Lawrence said, his nerves frayed.

Jim poured them each a glass of twenty one year old scotch and led the way toward the kitchen. Even before he entered, Lawrence knew that Abigail was up to no good. The subtle reek of pickled herring wafted to him, instantly abrogating his hunger. He stopped walking and took a long pull of his scotch.

"I told her you hate the stuff," Jim said as the entered the restaurant-sized kitchen. "But until you tell her yourself she's always going to prepare it. Do us both a favor?"

"I don't know what he's talking about," Lawrence lied as he

embraced Abigail. She was as lean and lithe as the day he'd pulled her out of the water. Her nearly white blonde hair was pulled back into pony tail, showing off the sharp lines of her neck and chin.

"Papa Larry!" Edvard yelled. He'd been playing a video game on his portable handset at the kitchen table. Lawrence was one of the few people for whom he'd voluntarily relinquish the device. Lawrence released Abigail and turned in time to scoop the boy up.

"I hope you're not playing that thing too much," Lawrence said.

"He plays it constantly," Jim said from behind them. "Thanks for getting him the deluxe game pack,"

"My pleasure," Lawrence said over his shoulder. At least Jim was talking to him.

Abigail approached with a platter in her hands and offered Lawrence an opportunity to look closely at the cold gelatinous fish she'd made. The grey chunks were awash in a thick onion and cream sauce. He felt the bile rise in his throat as he lifted one of the tiny forks off the end of the plate, speared the smallest piece he could find and steeled himself. All eyes focused on him as he slowly lifted the herring to his mouth and closed his lips. He didn't chew: the rest of his scotch was used to wash the bite down nearly untasted. The display satisfied Abigail - who lit up with a rosy cheeked smile, and drew a loud guffaw from Jim.

"Delicious," Lawrence wheezed.

"Your dink is empty," Abigail said. "No more of that nasty whisky, I have something special,"

"Whatever you've got, I'll drink," Lawrence said.

She walked to the expansive wet bar next to her wine fridge and removed a bottle of straw colored liquor from a bowl of ice. Lawrence recognized Aquavit, a Scandinavian beverage he'd spent his life avoiding.

"Ah, herring's natural accoutrement," Lawrence said.

"That's right!" Abigail said happily. "This is my family's own recipe. We use cardamom to flavor it and a hint of cumin,"

"Well, pour it up," Jim said. Lawrence noted that he'd refilled his scotch. Jim was looking softer around the middle, as if he'd given up on working out.

Abigail removed three tall thin glasses from the door of her stainless steel freezer and filled them.

They touched glasses and sipped the aromatic liquor. It was far better than Lawrence remembered it. Perhaps because Abigail had given it him. Everything was better when she was a part of it. Lawrence felt a wave of guilt at the love he felt for her, as if he were betraying the memory of Sharon just by being in Abigail's presence.

She sensed his mood and refilled his Aquavit. "I'm so glad that you could come over. The kids have been asking when you'd make another appearance here. They are getting sick of only seeing you for lunch at your golf club,"

"I'm glad to be here," Lawrence said somberly. He turned to Jim. "We need to have a private word about the Under Secretary."

"How about dinner first?" Jim asked.

"Of course," Lawrence said. He watched as Edvard and Katarina both set about devouring open faced herring sandwiches. The four year old looked up at him and smiled though a mouthful of fish and said, "Don't be sad Papa. You don't have to eat the fish if you don't like it,"

The tone of her voice, the cadence with which she spoke, and most of all her eyes – Lawrence felt his knees begin to buckle and sat down quickly. Jim noticed, Abigail pretended not to. This girl, this four year old, was Sharon Lantana reincarnated. She was a clone of the woman he'd tried so hard to save. And more than that. Things had been done to her on the ship that Lawrence relived in his nightmares nearly every night. How could Jim possibly put himself back together living like this? Lawrence raised his hand to his mouth to stifle an imaginary cough, then said, "Jim. We really need to talk. Dinner can wait."

Lawrence's tone bridged no argument from his son. The two men retired to the veranda off the main sitting room. The last light of the sunset was still visible, the lights of the Lincoln Monument twinkling to life on the horizon, unseen by either man. Jim had brought the scotch with him. He poured himself three fingers of brown liquid and set the bottle between them. Lawrence had drank enough. "Jim, the message that is coming from the wreck is making high ranking people nervous. They are insisting that you come in and hear what's being broadcast from the wreck."

"Broadcast?"

"That's what Christiana told me."

"Christiana Facchinetti? What's she got to do with this?" Jim said.

"Apparently she's still in the intelligence business."

"Didn't she elope with Zakar?"

"Yes, she did. I'd have thought that her career would be hamstrung as a result, but she was in the meeting with the Under Secretary this morning. She was the one running the meeting I'd say."

"Tell me about the message," Jim said around a deep pull of his scotch.

"All they told me was that it was some kind of 'chatter,' and that it was eyes only. Your eyes, apparently."

"You're a retired Admiral, they wouldn't give you the details? I thought George was a friend."

"He is, and I think he's uncomfortable with the whole thing. This has to come from higher up. Jim, the reality is that there were *thousands* of important people stored aboard that ship. They were from all over the world, but important Americans want answers."

"You don't think this is about the billion in gold that went down?"

"Why would the US give a dam about that? We can print a billion dollars in an hour if we want to. And that gold is radioactive. It's whatever Mendelbaum is broadcasting from the bottom of the Ocean."

The Chinese Dam

ABOUT THE AUTHOR

Benjamin C. Yablon is an attorney and fiction writer in Denver, Colorado. When he's not writing, he's in the mountains with his family.

Explore the Pure Life series and sign up for exclusive giveaways by visiting PureLifeNovel.com

Join the debate over the future of ethical medicine at facebook.com/PureLifeNovel

Apple Tree
PUBLISHING
Pick from the Apple Tree of Life

Printed in Great Britain
by Amazon